THE
ARCHIVED

DISCARD

THE
ARCHIVED

VICTORIA SCHWAB

HYPERION
New York

First Edition
1 3 5 7 9 10 8 6 4 2
G475-5664-5-12384

Printed in the United States of America

This book is set in Perpetua and Clarendon.

Designed by Tyler Nevins

Library of Congress Cataloging-in-Publication Data
Schwab, Victoria.
The archived/Victoria Schwab.—1st ed.
p. cm.
Summary: "When an otherworldly library called the Archive is compromised
from within, sixteen-year-old Mackenzie Bishop must prevent violent, ghost-like
Histories from escaping into our world"—Provided by publisher.
ISBN 978-1-4231-5731-1 (hardback)—ISBN 1-4231-5731-1
[1. Future life—Fiction. 2. Dead—Fiction. 3. Supernatural—Fiction. 4. Libraries—
Fiction. 5. Family problems—Fiction. 6. Apartment houses—Fiction.] I. Title.
PZ7.S39875Arc   2013
[Fic]—dc23   2012025485

Reinforced binding

Visit www.un-requiredreading.com

To Bob Ledbetter, whose History I'd love to read

And to Shelley McBurney, who leaves a mark
on everything she touches, and everyone she meets

Do not stand at my grave and weep
I am not there; I do not sleep.
—Mary Elizabeth Frye

THE NARROWS remind me of August nights in the South.

They remind me of old rocks and places where the light can't reach.

They remind me of smoke—the stale, settled kind—and of storms and damp earth.

Most of all, Da, they remind me of you.

I step into the corridor and breathe in the heavy air, and I am nine again, and it is summer.

My little brother, Ben, is sprawled inside by the fan, drawing monsters in blue pencil, and I am on the back porch looking up at the stars, all of them haloed by the humid night. You're standing beside me with a cigarette and an accent full of smoke, twirling your battered ring and telling stories about the Archive and the Narrows and the Outer in calm words, with your Louisiana lilt, like we're talking weather, breakfast, nothing.

You unbutton your cuffs and roll your sleeves up to the elbows as you speak, and I notice for the first time how many scars you have. From the three lines carved into your forearm to the dozens of other marks, they cut crude patterns in your skin, like cracks in old leather. I try to remember the last time you wore short sleeves. I can't.

That old rusted key hangs from its cord around your neck the way it always does, and somehow it catches the light, even though the night is pitch-black. You fidget with a slip of paper, roll it and unroll it, eyes scanning the surface as if something should be written there; but it's blank, so you roll it again until it's the size and shape of a cigarette, and tuck it behind your ear. You start drawing lines in the dust on the porch rail as you talk. You could never sit still.

Ben comes to the porch door and asks a question, and I wish I could remember the words. I wish I could remember the sound of his voice. But I can't. I do remember you laughing and running your fingers through the three lines you'd drawn in the dust on the railing, ruining the pattern. Ben wanders back inside and you tell me to close my eyes. You hand me something heavy and smooth, and tell me to listen, to find the thread of memory, to take hold and tell you what I see, but I don't see anything. You tell me to try harder, to focus, to reach inside, but I can't.

Next summer it will be different, and I will hear the hum and I will reach inside and I will see something, and you will be proud and sad and tired at the same time, and the summer after that you will get me a ring just like yours, but newer, and the summer after that you'll be dead and I'll have your key as well as your secrets.

But this summer is simple.

This summer I am nine and you are alive and there is still time. This summer when I tell you I can't see anything, you just shrug and light another cigarette, and go back to telling stories.

Stories about winding halls, and invisible doors, and places where the dead are kept like books on shelves. Each time you finish a story, you make me tell it back to you, as if you're afraid I will forget.

I never do.

ONE

THERE IS NOTHING fresh about this start.

I lean back against the car and stare up at the Coronado, the hotel-turned-apartment building that my mother and father find "so charming." It stares back, wide-eyed, gaunt. I spent the whole drive twisting the ring on my finger, running my thumb over the three lines etched into its surface, as if the silver band were a rosary or a charm. I prayed for someplace simple, uncluttered, and new. And I got this.

I can see the dust from across the street.

"Isn't it divine?" squeals my mother.

"It's . . . old."

So old that the stones have settled, the cracks deep enough to give the whole facade a tired look. A fist-size piece of stone loosens before my eyes and tumbles down the side of the building.

I look up to find a roof dotted with gargoyles. Not at the corners, where you'd expect gargoyles to be, but perching at random intervals like a line of crows. My eyes slide over rippling windows and down six floors to the carved and cracking stone marquee that tops the lobby.

Mom hurries forward, but stops halfway across the road to marvel at the "antiquated" paving stones that give the road so much "character."

"Honey," calls Dad, following. "Don't stand in the street."

There should be four of us. Mom, Dad, Ben, me. But there's not. Da's been dead for four years, but it hasn't even been a year since Ben died. A year of words no one can say because they call up images no one can bear. The silliest things shatter you. A T-shirt discovered behind the washing machine. A toy that rolled under a cabinet in the garage, forgotten until someone drops something and goes to fetch it, and suddenly they're on the concrete floor sobbing into a dusty baseball mitt.

But after a year of tiptoeing through our lives, trying not to set off memories like land mines, my parents decide to quit, but call it change. Call it a fresh start. Call it just what this family needs.

I call it running.

"You coming, Mackenzie?"

I follow my parents across the street, baking in the July sun. Below the marquee is a revolving door, flanked by two regular ones. A few people—mostly older—lounge around the doors, or on a patio to the side.

Before Ben died, Mom had whims. She wanted to be a zookeeper, a lawyer, a chef. But they were *whims*. After he died, they became something more. Instead of just dreaming, she started doing. With a force. Ask her about Ben and she pretends she didn't hear, but ask her about her newest pet project—whatever it happens to be—and she'll talk for hours, giving off enough energy to power the room. But Mom's energy is as fickle as it is bright. She's started switching careers the way Ben switches—*switched*—favorite foods, one week cheese, the next applesauce. . . . In the past year, Mom's gone through seven. I guess I should be thankful she didn't try to switch lives, too, while she was at it. Dad and I could have woken up one day and found only a note in her nearly illegible script. But she's still here.

Another stone crumbles off the side of the building.

Maybe this will keep her busy.

The deserted space on the first floor of the Coronado, tucked behind the patio and below the awnings, is the future home of my mother's biggest whim—she prefers to call this one her "dream endeavor"—Bishop's Coffee Shop. And if you ask her, she'll tell you this is the only reason we're moving, that it has nothing to do with Ben (only she wouldn't say his name).

We step up to the revolving doors, and Dad's hand lands on my shoulder, filling my head with a jumble of static and wavering bass. I cringe and force myself not to pull away. The dead are silent, and objects, when they hold impressions, are quiet until you reach through them. But the touch of the living is loud. Living people haven't been compiled, organized—which means they're a jumble of memory and thought and emotion, all tangled up and held at bay only by the silver band on my finger. The ring helps, but it can't block the noise, just the images.

I try to picture a wall between Dad's hand and my shoulder, like Da taught me, a second barrier, but it doesn't work. The sound is still there, layered tones and statics, like radios tuned wrong, and after an appropriate number of seconds, I take a step forward, beyond his reach. Dad's hand falls away, and the quiet returns. I roll my shoulders.

"What do you think, Mac?" he asks, and I look up at the hulking shape of the Coronado.

I think I'd rather shake my mother until a new idea falls out and leads us somewhere else.

But I know I can't say this, not to Dad. The skin beneath his eyes is nearly blue, and over the last year he's gone from slim to thin. Mom might be able to power a city, but Dad barely stays lit.

"I think . . ." I say, managing a smile, "it will be an adventure."

I am ten, almost eleven, and I wear my house key around my neck just to be like you.

They tell me I have your gray eyes, and your hair—back when it was reddish brown instead of white—but I don't care about those things. Everyone has eyes and hair. I want the things most people don't notice. The ring and the key and the way you have of wearing everything on the inside.

We're driving north so I'll be home for my birthday, even though I would rather stay with you than blow out candles. Ben is sleeping in the backseat, and the whole way home, you tell me stories about these three places.

The Outer, which you don't waste much breath on because it's everything around us, the normal world, the only one most people ever know about.

The Narrows, a nightmarish place, all stained corridors and distant whispers, doors and darkness thick like grime.

And the Archive, a library of the dead, vast and warm, wood and stone and colored glass, and all throughout, a sense of peace.

As you drive and talk, one hand guides the steering wheel, and the other toys with the key around your neck.

"The only things the three places have in common," you say, "are doors. Doors in, and doors out. And doors need keys."

I watch the way you fiddle with yours, running a thumb over the teeth. I try to copy you, and you catch sight of the cord around my neck and ask me what it is. I show you my silly house key on a string, and there's this strange silence that fills the car, like the whole world is holding its breath, and then you smile.

You tell me I can have my birthday present early, even though you know how Mom likes to do things right, and then you pull a small unwrapped box from your pocket. Inside is a silver ring, the three lines that make up the Archive mark carefully etched into the metal, just like yours.

I don't know what it's for, not yet—a blinder, a silencer, a buffer against the world and its memories, against people and their cluttered thoughts—but I'm so excited I promise I will never take it off. And then the car hits a bump and I drop it under the seat. You laugh, but I make you pull off the freeway so I can get it back. I have to wear it on my thumb because it's too big. You tell me I'll grow into it.

We drag our suitcases through the revolving door and into the lobby. Mom chirps with glee, and I wince.

The sprawling foyer is like one of those photos where you have to figure out what's wrong. At first glance it glitters, marble and crown molding and gilt accents. But at second look the marble is coated in dust, the molding is cracked, and the gilt accents are actively shedding gold onto the carpet. Sunlight streams in through the windows, bright despite the aging glass, but the space smells like fabric kept too long behind curtains. This place was once, undeniably, spectacular. What happened?

Two people mill by a front window, seemingly oblivious to the haze of dust they're standing in.

Across the lobby a massive marble staircase leads to the second floor. The cream-colored stone would probably gleam if someone polished it long enough. Wallpaper wraps the sides of the staircase, and from across the room, I see a ripple in the fleur-de-lis pattern there. From here it almost looks like a crack. I doubt anyone would notice, not in a place like this, but I'm supposed to spot these things. I'm hauling my luggage toward the ripple when I hear my name and turn to see my parents vanishing around a corner. I hoist my bags and catch up.

I find them standing in front of a trio of elevators just off the lobby.

The wrought iron cages look like they might safely hold two. But we're already climbing into one of them, three people and four suitcases. I whisper something halfway between a prayer and a curse as I pull the rusted gate closed and press the button for the third floor.

The elevator groans to life. There might be elevator music, too, but it's impossible to hear over the sounds the machine makes simply hoisting us up. We rise through the second floor at a glacial pace, padded in by luggage. Halfway between the second and third floor, the elevator pauses to think, then heaves upward again. It gives a death rattle at the third floor, at which point I pry the jaws open and set us free.

I announce that I'm taking the stairs from now on.

Mom tries to free herself from the barricade of luggage. "It has a certain . . ."

"Charm?" I parrot, but she ignores the jab and manages to get one leg over the suitcases, nearly toppling as her heel snags on a strap.

"It has personality," adds my father, catching her arm.

I turn to take in the hall, and my stomach drops. The walls are lined with doors. Not just the ones you would expect, but a dozen more—unusable, painted and papered over, little more than outlines and ridges.

"Isn't it fascinating?" says my mother. "The extra doors are from way back when it was a hotel, before they began knocking down walls and combining rooms, converting spaces. They left the doors, papered right over them."

"Fascinating," I echo. And eerie. Like a well-lit version of the Narrows.

We reach the apartment at the end, and Dad unlocks the door—an ornate 3F nailed to its front—and throws it open. The apartment has the same scuffed quality as everything else. Lived-in. This place has marks, but none of them are ours. In our old house, even when you took away the furniture and packed up the *stuff*, there were all these marks. The dent in the wall where I threw that book, the stain on the kitchen ceiling from Mom's failed blender experiment, the blue doodles in the corners of rooms where Ben drew. My chest tightens. Ben will never leave a mark on this place.

Mom *oohs* and *ahhs*, and Dad drifts quietly through the rooms, and I'm about to brave the threshold when I feel it.

The scratch of letters. A name being written on the slip of Archive paper in my pocket. I dig the page out—it's roughly the size of a receipt and strangely crisp—as the History's name scrawls itself in careful cursive.

Emma Claring. 7.

"Mac," calls Dad, "you coming?"

I slide back a step into the hall.

"I left my bag in the car," I say. "I'll be right back."

Something flickers across Dad's face, but he's already nodding, already turning away. The door clicks shut, and I sigh and turn to the hall.

I need to find this History.

To do that, I need to get to the Narrows.

And to do that, I need to find a door.

TWO

I'M ELEVEN, AND you are sitting across from me at the table, talking under the sound of dishes in the kitchen. Your clothes are starting to hang on you—shirts, pants, even your ring. I overheard Mom and Dad, and they said that you're dying—not the fast, stone-drop way, there and then gone, but still. I can't stop squinting at you, as if I might see the disease picking you clean, stealing you from me, bite by bite.

You're telling me about the Archive again, something about the way it changes and grows, but I am not really listening. I'm twirling the silver ring on my finger. I need it now. Fractured bits of memory and feeling are starting to get through whenever someone touches me. They're not jarring or violent yet, just kind of messy. I told you that and you told me it would get worse, and you looked sorry when you said it. You said it was genetic, the potential, but it doesn't manifest until the predecessor makes the choice. And you chose me. I hope you weren't sorry. I'm not sorry. I'm only sorry that as I get stronger, you seem to get weaker.

"Are you listening?" you ask, because it's obvious I'm not.

"I don't want you to die," I say, surprising us both, and the whole moment hardens, stops, as your eyes hold mine. And then you soften and shift in your seat, and I think I can hear your bones moving.

"What are you afraid of, Kenzie?" you ask.

You said you passed the job to me and I can't help but wonder if that's why you're getting worse now. Fading faster. "Losing you."

"Nothing's lost. Ever."

I'm pretty sure you're just trying to make me feel better, half expect you to say something like *I'll live on in your heart.* But you would never say that.

"You think I tell you stories just to hear my own voice? I mean what I said. Nothing's lost. That's what the Archive's for."

Wood and stone and colored glass, and all throughout, a sense of peace . . .

"That's where we go when we die? To the Archive?"

"You don't, not exactly, but your History does." And then you start using your "Pay Attention" voice, the one that makes words stick to me and never let go. "You know what a History is?"

"It's the past," I say.

"No, Kenzie. That's history with a little *h.* I mean History with a big *H.* A History is . . ." You pull out a cigarette, roll it between your fingers. "You might think of it as a ghost, but that's not what it is, really. Histories are records."

"Of what?"

"Of us. Of everyone. Imagine a file of your entire life, of every moment, every experience. All of it. Now, instead of a folder or a book, imagine the data is kept in a body."

"What do they look like?"

"However they looked when they died. Well, *before* they died. No fatal wounds or bloated corpses. The Archive wouldn't find that tasteful. And the body's just a shell for the life inside."

"Like a book cover?"

"Yes." You put the cigarette in your mouth, but know better than to light it in the house. "A cover tells you something about a book. A body tells you something about a History."

I bite my lip. "So . . . when you die, a copy of your life gets put in the Archive?"

"Exactly."

I frown.

"What is it, Kenzie?"

"If the Outer is where we live, and the Archive is where our Histories go, what are the Narrows for?"

You smile grimly. "The Narrows are a buffer between the two. Sometimes a History wakes up. Sometimes Histories get out, through the cracks in the Archive, and into those Narrows. And when that happens, it's the Keeper's job to send them back."

"What's a Keeper?"

"It's what I am," you say, pointing to the ring on your hand. "What you'll be," you add, pointing to my own ring.

I can't help but smile. You chose me. "I'm glad I get to be like you."

You squeeze my hand and make a sound somewhere between a cough and a laugh, and say, "Good thing. Because you haven't got a choice."

Doors to the Narrows are everywhere.

Most of them started out as *actual* doors, but the problem is that buildings change—walls go down, walls go up—and these doors, once they're made, don't. What you end up with are cracks, the kind most people wouldn't even notice, slight disturbances where the two worlds—the Narrows and the Outer—run into each other. It's easy when you know what you're looking for.

But even with good eyes, finding a Narrows door can take a while. I had to search my old neighborhood for two days to find the nearest one, which turned out to be halfway down the alley behind the butcher shop.

I think of the ripple in the fleur-de-lis paper in the lobby, and smile.

I head for the nearest stairwell—there are two sets, the south stairs at my end of the hall, and the north stairs at the far end, past the metal cages—when something makes me stop.

A tiny gap, a vertical shadow on the dust-dull yellow wallpaper. I walk over to the spot and square myself to the wall, letting my eyes adjust to the crack that is most definitely there. The sense of victory fades a little. Two doors so close together? Maybe the crack in the lobby was just that—a crack.

This crack, however, is something more. It cuts down the wall between apartments 3D and 3C, in a stretch of space without any ghosted doors, a dingy patch interrupted only by a painting of the sea in an old white frame. I frown and slide the silver ring from my finger and feel the shift, like a screen being removed. Now when I stare at the crack, I see it, right in the center of the seam. A keyhole.

The ring works like a blinder. It shields me—as much as it can—from the living, and blocks my ability to read the impressions they leave on things. But it also blinds me to the Narrows. I can't see the doors, let alone step through them.

I pull Da's key from around my neck, running a thumb over the teeth the way he used to. For luck. Da used to rub the key, cross himself, kiss his fingers and touch them to the wall—any number of things. He used to say he could use a little more luck.

I slide the key into the keyhole and watch as the teeth vanish into the wall. First comes the whisper of metal against metal. Then the Narrows door surfaces, floating like a body up through water until it presses against the yellow paper. Last, a single strand of crisp light draws itself around the frame, signaling that the door is ready.

If someone came down the hall right now, they wouldn't see the door. But they would hear the click of the lock as I turned Da's rusted key, and then they would see me step straight through the yellow paper into nothing.

There's no sky in the Narrows, but it always feels like night, smells like night. Night in a city after rain. On top of that there's a breeze, faint but steady, carrying stale air through the halls. Like you're in an air shaft.

I knew what the Narrows looked like long before I saw them. I had this image in my head, drawn by Da year after year. Close your eyes and picture this: a dark alley, just wide enough for you to spread your arms and skim the rough walls on either side with your fingers. You look up and see . . . nothing, just the walls running up and up and up into black. The only light comes from the doors that line the walls, their outlines giving off a faint glow, their keyholes letting in beams of light that show like threads in the dusty air. It is enough light to see by, but not enough to see well.

Fear floats up my throat, a primal thing, a physical twinge as I step through, close the door behind me, and hear the voices. Not true voices, really, but murmurs and whispers and words stretched thin by distance. They could be halls, or whole territories, away. Sounds travel here in the Narrows, coil through the corridors, bounce off walls, find you from miles away, ghostlike and diffused. They can lead you astray.

The corridors stretch out like a web or a subway, branching, crossing, the walls interrupted only by those doors. City blocks' worth of doors mere feet apart, space compressed. Most of them are locked. All of them are marked.

Coded. Every Keeper has a system, a way to tell a good door from a bad one; I cannot count the number of X's and slashes and circles and dots scribbled against each door and then rubbed away. I pull a thin piece of chalk from my pocket—it's funny, the things you learn to keep on you at all times—and use it to draw a quick Roman numeral I on the door I just came through, right above the keyhole (the doors here have no handles, can't even be tried without a key). The number is bright and white over the dozens of old, half-ruined marks.

I turn to consider the hall and the multitude of doors lining it. Most of them are locked—inactive, Da called them—doors that lead back into the Outer, to different rooms in different houses, disabled because they go places where no Keeper is currently stationed. But the Narrows is a buffer zone, a middle ground, studded with ways out. Some doors lead to and from the Archive. Others lead to Returns, which isn't its own world, but it might as well be. A place where even Keepers aren't allowed to go. And right now, with a History on my list, that's the door I need to find.

I test the door to the right of Door I, and to my surprise it's unlocked, and opens onto the Coronado's lobby. So it wasn't just a ripple in the wallpaper after all. Good to know. An old woman ambles past, oblivious to the portal, and I tug the door shut again and draw a II above the keyhole.

I take a step back to consider the numbered doors, set side by side—my ways out—and then continue down the hall, testing every lock. None of the other doors budge, and I mark each one with an X. There's this sound, a fraction louder than the others, a *thud thud thud* like muffled steps, but only a fool hunts down a History before finding a place to send him, so I quicken my pace, rounding a corner and testing two more doors before one finally gives.

The lock turns and the door opens, this time into a room made of light, blinding and edgeless. I draw back and close the door, blinking away little white dots as I mark its surface with a circle and quickly shade it in. *Returns.* I turn to the next door over and don't even bother to test the lock before I draw a circle, this one hollow. *The Archive.* The nice thing about the Archive doors is that they're always to the right of Returns, so if you can find one, you've found the other.

And now it's time to find Emma.

I flex my hands and bring my fingers to the wall, the silver ring safely in my pocket. Histories and humans alike have to touch a surface to leave an impression, which is why the floors here are made of the same concrete as the walls. So I can read the entire hallway with a touch. If Emma set a foot here, I'll see it.

The surface of the wall hums beneath my hands. I close my eyes and press down. Da used to say there was a thread in the wall, and you had to reach, reach right through the wall until you catch hold of that thread and not let go. The humming spreads up my fingers, numbing them as I focus. I squeeze my eyes shut harder and reach, and feel the thread tickling my palms. I catch hold, and my hands go numb. Behind my eyes the darkness shifts, flickers, and then the Narrows take shape again, a smudged version of the present, distorted. I see myself standing here, touching the wall, and guide the memory away.

It plays like a skipping film reel, winding back from present to past, flickering on the insides of my eyelids. The name showed on my list an hour ago, when Emma Claring's escape was registered, so I shouldn't have to go back far. When I twist the memories back two hours and find no sign of her, I pull away from the wall and open my eyes. The past of the Narrows vanishes, replaced by an only slightly brighter but definitely clearer present. I head down the hall to the next branching corridor and try again: closing my eyes, reaching, catching hold, winding time forward and back, sweeping the last hour for signs of—

A History flickers in the frame, her small form winding down the hall to a corner just ahead, then turning left. I blink and let go of the wall, the Narrows sharpening as I follow, turn the corner, and find . . . a dead end. More accurately, a territory break, a plane of wall marked by a glowing keyhole. Keepers have access only to their own territories, so the speck of light serves as nothing more than a stop sign. But it does keep the Histories from getting too far away; and sitting on the floor right in front of the break is a girl.

Emma Claring sits in the hall, her arms wrapped tightly around her knees. She's not wearing any shoes, only grass-stained shorts and a T-shirt; and she's so small that the corridor seems almost cavernous around her.

"Wake up, wake up, wake up."

She rocks back and forth as she says it, the beat of her body against the wall making the *thud thud thud* I heard earlier. She squeezes her eyes shut, then opens them wide, panic edging into her voice when the Narrows don't disappear.

17

She's obviously slipping.

"Wake up," the girl pleads again.

"Emma," I say, and she startles.

Two terrified eyes swivel toward me in the dark. The pupils are spreading, the black chewing away the color around them. She whimpers but doesn't recognize me yet. That's good. When Histories slip far enough, they start to see other people when they look at you. They see whomever it is they want or need or hate or love or remember, and it makes the confusion worse. Makes them fall faster into madness.

I take a slow step forward. She buries her face in her arms and continues whispering.

I kneel in front of her. "I'm here to help you," I say.

Emma Claring doesn't look up. "Why can't I wake up?" she whispers. Her voice hitches.

"Some dreams," I say, "are harder to shake."

Her rocking slows, and her head rolls side to side against her arms.

"But do you know what's great about dreams?" I mimic the tone my mother used to use with me, with Ben. Soothing, patient. "Once you know you're in a dream, you can control it. You can change it. You can find a way out."

Emma looks up at me over her crossed arms, eyes shining and wide.

"Do you want me to show you how?" I ask.

She nods.

"I want you to close your eyes"—she does—"and imagine a door." I look around at this stretch of hall, every door unmarked, and wish I'd taken the time to find another Returns door nearby. "Now, on the door, I want you to imagine a white circle, filled in.

And behind the door, I want you to imagine a room filled with light. Nothing but light. Can you see it?"

The girl nods.

"Okay. Open your eyes." I push myself up. "Let's go find your door."

"But there are so many," she whispers.

I smile. "It will be an adventure."

She reaches out and takes my hand. I stiffen on instinct, even though I know her touch is simply that, a touch, so unlike the wave of thought and feeling that comes with grazing a living person's skin. She may be full of memories, but I can't see them. Only the Librarians in the Archive know how to read the dead.

Emma looks up at me, and I give her hand a small squeeze and lead her back around the corner and down the hall, trying to retrace my steps. As we weave through the Narrows, I wonder what made her wake up. The vast majority of names on my list are children and teens, restless but not necessarily bad—just those who died before they could fully live. What kind of kid was she? What did she die of? And then I hear Da's voice, warning about curiosity. I know there's a reason Keepers aren't taught to read Histories. To us, their pasts are irrelevant.

I feel Emma's hand twist nervously in mine.

"It's okay," I say quietly as we reach another hall of unmarked doors. "We'll find it." I hope. I haven't exactly had a wealth of time to learn the layout of this place, but just as I'm starting to fidget too, we turn onto another corridor, and there it is.

Emma pulls free and runs up to the door, stretching her small fingers over the chalk circle. They come away white as I get the key in the lock and turn, and the Returns door opens, showering us both in brilliant light. Emma gasps.

For a moment, there is nothing but light. Like I promised.

"See?" I say, pressing my hand against her back and guiding her forward, over the threshold and into Returns.

Emma is just turning back to see why I haven't followed her when I close my eyes and pull the door firmly shut between us. There's no crying, no pounding on the door; only a deathly quiet from the other side. I stand there for several moments with my key in the lock, something like guilt fluttering behind my ribs. It fades as fast. I remind myself that Returning is merciful. Returning puts the Histories back to sleep, ends the nightmare of their ghostly waking. Still, I hate the fear that laces the younger eyes when I lock them in.

I sometimes wonder what happens in Returns, how the Histories go back to the lifeless bodies on the Archive shelves. Once, with this boy, I stayed to see, waited in the doorway of the infinite white (I knew better than to step inside). But nothing happened, not until I left. I know because I finally closed the door, only for a second, a beat, however long it takes to lock and then unlock, and when I opened it again, the boy was gone.

I once asked the Librarians how the Histories got out. Patrick said something about doors opening and closing. Lisa said the Archive was a vast machine, and all machines had glitches, gaps. Roland said he had no idea.

I suppose it doesn't matter *how* they get out. All that matters is they do. And when they do, they must be found. They must go back. Case open, case closed.

I push off the door and dig the slip of Archive paper from my pocket, checking to make sure Emma's name is gone. It is. All that's left of her is a hand-shaped smudge in the white chalk.

I redraw the circle and turn toward home.

THREE

"**GET WHAT YOU WANTED** from the car?" asks Dad as I walk in.

He spares me the need to lie by flashing the car keys, which I neglected to take. Never mind that, judging by the low light through the window and the fact that every inch of the room behind him is covered with boxes, I was gone way too long. I quietly curse the Narrows and the Archive. I've tried wearing a watch, but it's useless. Doesn't matter how it's made—the moment I leave the Outer, it stops working.

So now I get to pick: truth or lie.

The first trick to lying is to tell the truth as often as possible. If you start lying about everything, big and small, it becomes impossible to keep things straight, and you'll get caught. Once suspicion is planted it becomes exponentially harder to sell the next lie.

I don't have a clean record with my parents when it comes to lying, from sneaking out to the occasional inexplicable bruise—some Histories don't want to be Returned—so I have to tread carefully, and since Dad paved the way for truth, I roll with it. Besides, sometimes a parent appreciates a little honesty, confidentiality. It makes them feel like the favorite.

"This whole thing," I say, slumping against the doorway, "it's a lot of change. I just needed some space."

"Plenty of that here."

"I know," I say. "Big building."

"Did you see all seven floors?"

"Only got to five." The lie is effortless, delivered with an ease that would make Da proud.

I can hear Mom several rooms away, the sounds of unpacking overlapped with radio music. Mom hates quiet, fills every space with as much noise and movement as possible.

"See anything good?" asks Dad.

"Dust." I shrug. "Maybe a ghost or two."

He offers a conspiratorial smile and steps aside to let me pass.

My chest tightens at the sight of the boxes exploding across every spare inch of the room. About half of them just say STUFF. If Mom was feeling ambitious, she scribbled a small list of items beneath the word, but seeing as her handwriting is virtually illegible, we won't know what's in each box until we actually open it. Like Christmas. Except we already own everything.

Dad's about to hand me a pair of scissors when the phone rings. I didn't know we had a phone yet. Dad and I scramble to find it among the packing materials, when Mom shouts, "Kitchen counter by the fridge," and sure enough, there it is.

"Hello?" I answer, breathless.

"You disappoint me," says a girl.

"Huh?" Everything is too strange too fast, and I can't place the voice.

"You've been in your new residence for hours, and you've already forgotten me."

Lyndsey. I loosen.

"How do you even know this number?" I ask. "*I* don't know this number."

"I'm magical," she says. "And if you'd just get a cell . . ."

"I have a cell."

"When's the last time you charged it?"

I try to think.

"Mackenzie Bishop, if you have to think about it, it's been too long."

I want to deliver a comeback, but I can't. I've never needed to charge the phone. Lyndsey is—was—my next door neighbor for ten years. Was—is—my best friend.

"Yeah, yeah," I say, wading through the boxes and down a short hall. Lyndsey tells me to hold and starts talking to someone else, covering the phone with her hand so all I hear are vowels.

At the end of the hall there's a door with a Post-it note stuck to it. There's a letter on it that vaguely resembles an *M*, so I'm going to assume this is my room. I nudge the door open with my foot and head inside to find more boxes, an unassembled bed, and a mattress.

Lyndsey laughs at something someone says, and even sixty miles away, through a phone and her muffled hand, the sound is threaded with light. Lyndsey Newman is made of light. You see it in her blond curls, her sun-kissed skin, and the band of freckles across her cheeks. You feel it when you're near her. She possesses this unconditional loyalty and the kind of cheer you start to suspect no longer exists in the world until you talk to her. And she never asks the wrong questions, the ones I can't answer. Never makes me lie.

"You there?" she asks.

"Yeah, I'm here," I say, nudging a box out of the way so I can reach the bed. The frame leans against the wall, the mattress and box spring stacked on the floor.

"Has your mom gotten bored yet?" Lyndsey asks.

"Sadly, not yet," I say, collapsing onto the bare mattress.

Ben was madly in love with Lyndsey, or as in love as a little boy can get. And she adored him. She's the kind of only child who dreams of siblings, so we just agreed to share. When Ben died, Lyndsey only got brighter, fiercer. An almost defiant kind of optimism. But when my parents told me we were moving, all I could think was, *What about Lynds? How can she lose us both?* The day I told her about the move, I saw her strength finally waver. Something slipped inside her, and she faltered. But moments later, she was back. A nine-out-of-ten smile— but still, wider than what anyone in my house had been able to muster.

"You should convince her to open up an ice cream parlor in some awesome beachside town. . . ." I slide my ring to the edge of my finger, then roll it back over my knuckle as Lynds adds, "Oh, or in, like, Russia. Get out, see the world at least."

Lyndsey has a point. My parents may be running, but I think they're scared of running so far they can't look back and see what they've left. We're only an hour from our old home. Only an hour from our old lives.

"Agreed," I say. "So when are you going to come crash in the splendor that is the Coronado?"

"Is it incredible? Tell me it's incredible."

"It's . . . old."

"Is it haunted?"

Depends on the definition of haunted, really. *Ghost* is just a term used by people who don't know about Histories.

"You're taking an awfully long time to answer that, Mac."

"Can't confirm ghosts yet," I say, "but give me time."

I can hear her mother in the background. "Come on, Lyndsey. Mackenzie might have the luxury of slacking, but you don't."

Ouch. *Slacking.* What would it feel like to slack? Not that I can argue my case. The Archive might take issue with my exposing them just to prove that I'm a productive teen.

"Ack, sorry," says Lyndsey. "I need to go to practice."

"Which one?" I tease.

"Soccer."

"Of course."

"Talk soon, okay?" she says.

"Yeah."

The phone goes dead.

I sit up and scan the boxes piled around the bed. They each have an *M* somewhere on the side. I've seen *M*'s, and *A*'s (my mother's name is Allison) and *P*'s (my father's name is Peter) around the living room, but no *B*'s. A sick feeling twists my stomach.

"Mom!" I call out, pushing up from the bed and heading back down the hall.

Dad is hiding out in a corner of the living room, a box cutter in one hand and a book in the other. He seems more interested in the book.

"What's wrong, Mac?" he asks without looking up. But Dad didn't do this. I know he didn't. He might be running, too, but he's not leading the pack.

"Mom!" I call again. I find her in her bedroom, blasting some talk show on the radio as she unpacks.

"What is it, love?" she asks, tossing hangers onto the bed.

When I speak, the words come out quiet, as if I don't want to ask. As if I don't want to know.

"Where are Ben's boxes?"

There is a very, very long pause. "Mackenzie," she says slowly. "This is about fresh starts—"

"Where are they?"

"A few are in storage. The rest . . ."

"You didn't."

"Colleen said that sometimes change requires drastic—"

"You're going to blame your therapist for throwing out Ben's

25

stuff? Seriously?" My voice must have gone up, because Dad appears behind me in the doorway. Mom's expression collapses, and he goes to her, and suddenly I'm the bad guy for wanting to hold on to something. Something I can read.

"Tell me you kept some of it," I say through gritted teeth.

Mom nods, her face still buried in Dad's collar. "A small box. Just a few things. They're in your room."

I'm already in the hall. I slam my door behind me and push boxes out of the way until I find it. Shoved in a corner. A small *B* on one side. It's little bigger than a shoe box.

I slice the clear packing tape with Da's key, and turn the box over on the bed, spreading all that's left of Ben across the mattress. My eyes burn. It's not that Mom didn't keep anything, it's that she kept the wrong things. We leave memories on objects we love and cherish, things we use and wear down.

If Mom had kept his favorite shirt—the one with the *X* over the heart—or any of his blue pencils—even a stub—or the mile patch he won in track, the one he kept in his pocket because he was too proud to leave it at home, but not proud enough to put it on his backpack . . . but the things scattered on my bed aren't really his. Photos she framed for him, graded tests, a hat he wore once, a small spelling trophy, a teddy bear he hated, and a cup he made in an art class when he was only five or six.

I tug off my ring and reach for the first item.

Maybe there's something.

There has to be something.

Something.

Anything.

• • •

"It's not a party trick, Kenzie," you snap.

I drop the bauble and it rolls across the table. You are teaching me how to read—things, not books—and I must have made a joke, given the act a dramatic flair.

"There's only one reason Keepers have the ability to read things," you say sternly. "It makes us better hunters. It helps us track down Histories."

"It's blank anyway," I mutter.

"Of course it is," you say, retrieving the trinket and turning it over between your fingers. "It's a paperweight. And you should have known the moment you touched it."

I could. It had the telltale hollow quiet. It didn't hum against my fingers. You hand me back my ring, and I slip it on.

"Not everything holds memories," you say. "Not every memory's worth holding. Flat surfaces—walls, floors, tables, that kind of thing—they're like canvases, great at taking in images. The smaller the object, the harder it is for it to hold an impression. But," you add, holding up the paperweight so I can see the world distorted in the glass, "if there is a memory, you should be able to tell with a brush of your hand. That's all the time you'll have. If a History makes it into the Outer—"

"How would they do that?" I ask.

"Kill a Keeper? Steal a key? Both." You cough, a racking, wet sound. "It's not easy." You cough again, and I want to do something to help; but the one time I offered you water, you growled that water wouldn't fix a damn thing unless I meant to drown you with it. So now we pretend the cough isn't there, punctuating your lectures.

"But," you say, recovering, "if a History does get out, you have to track them down, and fast. Reading surfaces has to be second nature. This gift is not a game, Kenzie. It's not a magic trick. We read the past for one reason, and one alone. To hunt."

I know what my gift is for, but it doesn't stop me from sifting through every framed photo, every random slip of paper, every piece of sentimental junk Mom chose, hoping for even a whisper, a hint of a memory of Ben. And it doesn't matter anyway because they're all useless. By the time I get to the stupid art camp cup, I'm desperate. I pick it up, and my heart flutters when I feel the subtle hum against my fingertips, like a promise; but when I close my eyes—even when I reach past the hum—there's nothing but pattern and light, blurred beyond readability.

I want to pitch the cup as hard as I can against the wall, add another scratch. I'm actually about to throw it when a piece of black plastic catches my eye, and I realize I've missed something. I let the cup fall back on the bed and retrieve a pair of battered glasses pinned beneath the trophy and the bear.

My heart skips. The glasses are black, thick-rimmed, just frames, no lenses, and they're the only thing here that's *really* his. Ben used to put them on when he wanted to be taken seriously. He'd make us call him Professor Bishop, even though that was Dad's name, and Dad never wore glasses. I try to picture Ben wearing them. Try to remember the exact color of his eyes behind the frames, the way he smiled just before he put them on.

And I can't.

My chest aches as I wrap my fingers around the silly black frames. And then, just as I'm about to set the glasses aside, I feel it, faint and far away and yet right there in my palm. A soft hum, like a bell trailing off. The tone is feather-light, but it's there, and I close my eyes, take a slow, steadying breath, and reach for the thread of memory. It's too thin and it keeps slipping through my fingers, but finally I catch it. The dark shifts behind my eyes and lightens into gray, and the gray twists from a flat shade into shapes, and from shapes into an image.

There's not even enough memory to make a full scene, only a kind of jagged picture, the details all smeared away. But it doesn't matter, because Ben is there—well, a Ben-like shape—standing in front of a Dad-like shape with the glasses perched on his nose and his chin thrust out as he looks up and tries not to smile because he thinks that only frowns are taken seriously, and there's just enough time for the smudged line of his mouth to waver and crack into a grin before the memory falters and dissolves back into gray, and gray darkens to black.

My heart hammers in my ears as I clutch the glasses. I don't have to rewind, guide the memory back to the start, because there's only one sad set of images looping inside these plastic frames; and sure enough, a moment later the darkness wobbles into gray, and it starts again. I let the stilted memory of Ben loop five times—each time hoping it will sharpen, hoping it will grow into a scene instead of a few smudged moments—before I finally force myself to let go, force myself to blink, and it's gone and I'm back in a box-filled bedroom, cradling my dead brother's glasses.

My hands are shaking, and I can't tell if it's from anger or sadness or fear. Fear that I'm losing him, bit by bit. Not just his face—that started to fade right away—but the marks he made on the world.

I set the glasses by my bed and return the rest of Ben's things to their box. I'm about to put my ring back on when a thought stops me. *Marks.* Our last house was new when we moved in. Every scuff was ours, every nick was ours, and all of them had stories.

Now, as I look around at a room filled not only with boxes but plenty of its own marks, I want to know the stories behind them. Or rather, a part of me wants to know those stories. The other part of me thinks that's the worst idea in the world, but I don't listen to that part. Ignorance may be bliss, but only if it outweighs curiosity. *Curiosity is a gateway drug to sympathy,* Da's warning echoes in my head, and I know, I know; but there are no Histories here to feel sympathy *for*. Which is exactly why the Archive wouldn't approve. They don't approve of any form of recreational reading.

But it's *my* talent, and it's not like a little light goes off every time I use it. Besides, I've already broken the rule once tonight by reading Ben's things, so I might as well group my infractions. I clear a space on the floor, which gives off a low thrum when my fingertips press against the boards. Here in the Outer, the floors hold the best impressions.

I reach, and my hands begin to tingle. The numbness slides up my wrists as the line between the wall and my skin seems to dissolve. Behind my closed eyes, the room takes shape again, the same and yet different. For one thing, I see myself standing in it, just like I was a few moments ago, looking down at Ben's box. The color's been bleached out, leaving a faded landscape of memory, and the whole picture is faint, like a print in sand, recent but already fading.

I get my footing in the moment before I begin to roll the memory backward.

It plays like a film in reverse.

Time spins away and the room fills up with shadows, there and gone and there and gone, so fast they overlap. Movers. Boxes disappear until the space is bare. In a matter of moments, the scene goes dark. Empty. But not ended. Vacant. I can feel the older memories beyond the dark. I rewind faster, searching for more people, more stories. There's nothing, nothing, and then the memories flicker up again.

Broad surfaces hold on to every impression, but there are two kinds—those burned in by emotion and those worn in by repetition—and they register differently. The first is bold, bright, defined. This room is full of the second kind—dull, long periods of habit worn into the surfaces, years pressed into a moment more like a photo than a film. Most of what I see are faded snapshots: a dark wooden desk and a wall of books, a man walking like a pendulum back and forth between the two; a woman stretched out on a couch; an older couple. The room flares into clarity during a fight, but by the time the woman has slammed the door, the scene fades back into shadow, and then dark again.

A heavy, lasting dark.

And yet, I can feel something past it.

Something bright, vivid, promising.

The numbness spreads up my arms and through my chest as I press my hands flush against the floorboards, reaching through the span of black until a dull ache forms behind my eyes and the darkness finally gives way to light and shape and memory. I've pushed too hard, rewound too far. The scenes skip back too fast, a blur, spiraling out of my control so that I have to drag time until it slows, lean into it until it shudders to a stop around me.

When it does, I'm kneeling in a room that is my room and isn't.

I'm about to continue backward, when something stops me. On the floor, a few feet in front of my hands, is a drop of something blackish, and a spray of broken glass. I look up.

At first glance it's a pretty room, old-fashioned, delicate, white furniture with painted flowers . . . but the covers on the bed are askew, the contents of the dresser shelf—books and baubles—are mostly toppled.

I search for a date, the way Da taught me—bread crumbs, bookmarks, in case I ever need to come back to this moment—and find a small calendar propped on the table, the word MARCH legible, but no year. I scan for other temporal markers: a blue dress, bright for the faded memory, draped over a small corner chair. A black book on the side table.

A sinking feeling spreads through me as I roll time forward, and a young man stumbles in. The same slick and blackish stuff is splashed across his shirt, painted up his arms to the elbows. It drips from his fingers, and even in the faded world of the memory, I know it's blood.

I can tell by the way he looks down at his skin, as if he wants to crawl out of it.

He sways and collapses to his knees right beside me, and even though he can't touch me, even though I'm not here, I can't help but shuffle back, careful to keep my hands on the floor, as he wraps his stained arms around his shirt. He can't be much older than I am, late teens, dark hair combed back, strands escaping into his eyes as he rocks back and forth. His lips move, but voices rarely stick to memories, and all I hear is a *hushushush* sound like static.

"Mackenzie," calls my mother. The sound of her voice is distorted, vague and bent by the veil of memory.

The man stops rocking and gets to his feet. His hands return to his sides, and my gut twists. He's covered in blood, but it's not his. There are no cuts on his arms or his chest. One hand looks sliced up, but not enough to bleed this much.

So whose blood is it? And whose *room* is it? There's that dress, and I doubt that the furniture, dappled with tiny flowers, belongs to him, but—

"Mackenzie," my mother calls again, closer, followed by the sound of a doorknob turning. I curse, open my eyes, and jerk my hands up from the floor, the memory vanishing, replaced by a room full of boxes and a dull headache. I'm just getting to my feet when Mom comes barging in. Before I can get the silver band out of my pocket and around my finger, she wraps me in a hug.

I gasp, and suddenly it's not just noise but *cold cavernous cold hollowed out too bright be bright screaming into pillow until I can't breathe be bright smallest bedroom packing boxes with B crossed out it still shows couldn't save him should have been there should have* before I can shove her tangled stream of consciousness out of my head. I try to force a wall between us, a shaky mental version of the ring's barrier. It is fragile as glass. Pushing back worsens the headache, but at least it blocks out my mother's cluttered thoughts.

I'm left feeling nauseous as I pull away from her hug and maneuver my ring back on to my finger, and the last of the noise drops out.

"Mackenzie. I'm sorry," she says, and it takes a moment for me to orient myself in the present, to realize that she isn't apologizing for that hug, that she doesn't know *why* I hate being touched. To remember that the boy I just saw covered in blood isn't here but years in the past, and that I'm safe and still furious with Mom for throwing away Ben's things. I want to stay furious, but the anger is dulling.

"It's okay," I say. "I understand." Even though it's not okay and I don't understand, and Mom should be able to see that. But she can't.

She sighs softly and reaches out to tuck a stray lock of hair behind my ear, and I let her, doing my best not to tense beneath her touch.

"Dinner's ready," she says. As if everything is normal. As if we're home instead of in a cardboard fortress in an old hotel room in the city, trying to hide from my brother's memories. "Come set the table?"

Before I can ask if she even knows where the table is, she guides me into the living room, where she and Dad have somehow cleared a space between the boxes. They've erected our dining table and arranged five cartons of Chinese food in a kind of bouquet in the center.

The table is the only piece of furniture assembled, which makes us look like we're dining on an island made of packing material. We eat off dishes dug out of a box with a surprisingly informative label: KITCHEN—FRAGILE. Mom coos about the Coronado, and Dad nods and offers canned monosyllables of support; and I stare down at my food and see blurred Ben-like shapes whenever I close my eyes, so I wage a staring contest with the vegetables.

After dinner I put Ben's box in the back of my closet, along with two labeled DA. I packed those myself, offered to make space for them, mostly because I was worried Mom would finally get rid of his things if I didn't find room. I never thought she'd get rid of Ben's. I keep out the silly blue bear, which I set beside the bed, and balance Ben's black glasses on its button nose.

I try to unpack, but my eyes keep drifting back to the center of the room, to the floor where the bloodstained boy collapsed. When I pushed the boxes aside, I could almost make out a few dark stains on the wood, and now it's all I can see each time I look at the floor. But who knows if the stains were drops of his blood. Not *his* blood,

I remember. *Someone's*. I want to read the memory again—well, part of me wants to; the other part isn't so eager, at least not on my first night in this room—but Mom keeps finding excuses to come in, half the time not even knocking, and if I'm going to read this, I'd like to avoid another interruption when I do it. It'll have to wait until morning.

I dig up sheets and make my bed, squirming at the thought of sleeping in here with whatever happened, even though I know it was years and years and years ago. I tell myself it's silly to be scared, but I still can't sleep.

My mind swims between Ben's blurred shape and the blood-stained floor, twisting the two memories until Ben is the one surrounded by broken glass, looking down at his red-drenched self. I sit up. My eyes go to the window, expecting to see my yard, and just beyond it the brick side of Lyndsey's house, but I see a city, and in that moment I wish I were home. I wish I could lean out my window and see Lyndsey lounging on her roof, watching stars. Late at night was the only time she let herself be lazy, and I could tell she felt rebellious for stealing even a few minutes. I used to sneak home from the Narrows—three streets over and two up behind the butcher shop—and climb up beside her, and she never asked me where I'd been. She'd stare up at the stars and start talking, pick up midsentence as if I'd been there with her the whole time. As if everything were perfectly normal.

Normal.

A confession: sometimes I dream of being normal. I dream about this girl who looks like me and talks like me, but isn't me. I know she's not, because she has this open smile and she laughs too easily, like Lynds. She doesn't have to wear a silver ring or a rusted key. She doesn't read the past or hunt the restless dead. I dream of her doing mundane things. She sifts through a locker in a crowded school. She lounges poolside, surrounded by girls who swim and talk to her while she flips through silly magazines. She sits engulfed in pillows and watches a movie, a friend tossing up pieces of popcorn for her to catch in her mouth. She misses almost every time.

She throws a party.

She goes to a dance.

She kisses a boy.

And she's so . . . happy.

M. That's what I call her, this normal, nonexistent me.

It's not that I've never done those things, kissed or danced or just "hung out." I have. But it was put-on, a character, a lie. I am so good at it—lying—but I can't lie to myself. I can pretend to be M; I can wear her like a mask. But I can't *be* her. I'll never be her.

M wouldn't see blood-covered boys in her bedroom.

M wouldn't spend her time scouring her dead brother's toys for a glimpse of his life.

The truth is, I know why Ben's favorite shirt wasn't in the box, or his mile patch, or most of his pencils. He had those things with him the day he died. Had the shirt on his back and the patch in his pocket and the pencils in his bag, just like any normal day. Because it was a normal day, right up until the point a car ran a red light two blocks from Ben's school just as he was stepping from the curb.

And then drove away.

What do you do when there *is* someone to blame, but you know you'll never find them? How do you close the case the way the cops do? How do you move on?

Apparently you don't move on; you just move away.

I just want to see him. Not a Ben-like shape, but the real thing. Just for a moment. A glimpse. The more I miss him, the more he seems to fade. He feels so far away, and holding on to empty tokens—or half-ruined ones—won't bring him any closer. But I know what will.

I'm up, on my feet and swapping pajamas for black pants and a long-sleeved T-shirt, donning my usual uniform. My Archive paper sits on the side table, unfolded and blank. I pocket it. I don't care if there are no names. I'm not going to the Narrows. I'm going through them.

To the Archive.

FOUR

BEYOND THE BEDROOM, the apartment is still, but as
I slip into the hall I see a faint line of light along the bottom of
my parents' door. I hold my breath. Hopefully Dad just fell asleep
with his reading light on. The house key hangs like a prize on a hook
by the front door. These floors are so much older than the ones in
our last house that with every step I expect to be exposed, but I
somehow make it to the key without a creak, and slide it from the
hook. All that's left is the door. The trick is to let go of the handle
by degrees. I get through, ease 3F shut, and turn to face the third-
floor hall.

And stop.

I'm not alone.

Halfway down the corridor a boy my age is leaning against the
faded wallpaper, right beside the painting of the sea. He's staring up
at the ceiling, or past it, the thin black wire from his headphones
tracing a line over his jaw, down his throat. I can hear the whisper of
music from here. I take a soundless step, but still he rolls his head,
lazily, to look at me. And he smiles. Smiles like he's caught me cheat-
ing, caught me sneaking out.

Which, in all fairness, he has.

His smile reminds me of the paintings here. I don't think any of
them are hung straight. One side of his mouth tilts up like that, like
it's not set level. He has several inches of spiked black hair, and I'm
pretty sure he's wearing eyeliner.

He closes his eyes and leans his head back against the wall as if to say, *I never saw you*. But that smile stays, and his conspiratorial silence doesn't change the fact that he's standing between me and my brother, his back where the Narrows door should be, the keyhole roughly in the triangle of space between the crook of his arm and his shirt.

And for the first time I'm thankful the Coronado is so old, because I need that second door. I do my best to play the part of a normal girl sneaking out. The pants and long sleeves in the middle of summer complicate the image, but there's nothing to be done about that now, and I keep my chin up as I wander down the hall toward the north stairs (turning back toward the south ones would only be suspicious).

The boy's eyes stay closed, but his smile quirks as I pass by. Odd, I think, vanishing into the stairwell. The stairs run from the top floor down to the second, where they spill me out onto the landing of the grand staircase, which forms a cascade into the lobby. A ribbon of burgundy fabric runs over the marble steps like a tongue, and when I make my way down, the carpet emits small plumes of dust.

Most of the lights have been turned off, and in the strange semi-darkness, the sprawling room at the base of the stairs is draped in shadows. A sign on the far wall whispers CAFÉ in faded cursive. I frown and turn my attention back to the side of the staircase where I first saw the crack. Now the papered wall is hidden in the heavy dark between two lights. I step into the darkness with it, running my fingers over the fleur-de-lis pattern until I find it. The ripple. I pocket my ring and pull Da's key from around my neck, using my other hand to trace down the crack until I feel the groove of the key-hole. I slot the key and turn, and a moment after the metallic click, a thread of light traces the outline of the door against the stairs.

The Narrows sigh around me as I enter, humid breath and words so far away they've bled to sounds and then to hardly anything. I start down the hall, key in hand, until I find the doors I marked before, the filled white circle that designates Returns, and to its right, the hollow one that leads to the Archive.

I pause, straighten, and step through.

The day I become a Keeper, you hold my hand.

You *never* hold my hand. You avoid touch the way I'm quickly learning to, but the day you take me to the Archive, you wrap your weathered fingers around mine as you lead me through the door. We're not wearing our rings, and I expect to feel it, the tangle of memories and thoughts and emotions coming through your skin, but I feel nothing but your grip. I wonder if it's because you're dying, or because you're so good at blocking the world out, a concept I can't seem to learn. Whatever the reason, I feel nothing but your grip, and I'm thankful for it.

We step into a front room, a large, circular space made of dark wood and pale stone. An antechamber, you call it. There is no visible source of light, and yet the space is brightly lit. The door we came through appears larger on this side than it did in the Narrows, and older, worn.

There is a stone lintel above the Archive door that reads SERVAMUS MEMORIAM. A phrase I do not know yet. Three vertical lines, the mark of the Archive, separate the words, and a set of Roman numerals runs beneath. Across the room a woman sits behind a large desk, writing briskly in a ledger, a QUIET PLEASE sign propped at the edge of her table. She sees us and sets her pen down fast enough to suggest that we're expected.

My hands are shaking, but you tighten your grip.

"You're gold, Kenzie," you whisper as the woman gestures over her shoulder at a massive pair of doors behind her, flung open and back like wings. Through them I can see the heart of the Archive, the atrium, a sprawling chamber marked by rows and rows and rows of shelves. The woman does not stand, does not go with us, but watches us pass with a nod and a whispered, cordial "Antony."

You lead me through.

There are no windows because there is no outside, and yet above the shelves hangs a vaulted ceiling of glass and light. The place is vast and made of wood and marble, long tables running down the center like a double spine, with shelves branching off to both sides like ribs. The partitions make the cavernous space seem smaller, cozier. Or at least fathomable.

The Archive is everything you told me it would be: *a patchwork . . . wood and stone and colored glass, and all throughout, a sense of peace.*

But you left something out.

It is beautiful.

So beautiful that, for a moment, I forget the walls are filled with bodies. That the stacks and the cabinets that compose the walls, while lovely, hold Histories. On each drawer an ornate brass cardholder displays a placard with a neatly printed name, a set of dates. It's so easy to forget this.

"Amazing," I say, too loud. The words echo, and I wince, remembering the sign on the Librarian's desk.

"It is," a new voice replies softly, and I turn to find a man perched on the edge of a table, hands in pockets. He's an odd sight, built like a stick figure, with a young face but old gray eyes and dark hair that sweeps across his forehead. His clothes are normal enough—a sweater and slacks—but his dark pants run right into a pair of bright red Chucks, which makes me smile. And yet there's a sharpness to his eyes, a coiled aspect to his stance. Even if I passed him on the street instead of here in the Archive, I'd know right away that he was a Librarian.

"Roland," you say with a nod.

"Antony," he replies, sliding off from the table. "Is this your choice?"

The Librarian is talking about *me*. Your hand vanishes from mine, and you take a step back, presenting me to him. "She is."

Roland arches a brow. But then he smiles. It's a playful smile, a warm one.

"This should be fun." He gestures to the first of the ten wings branching off the atrium. "If you'll follow me . . ." And with that, he walks away. You walk away. I pause. I want to linger here. Soak up the strange sense of quiet. But I cannot stay.

I am not a Keeper yet.

There is a moment, as I pass into the circular antechamber of the Archive and my eyes settle on the Librarian seated behind the desk—a man I've never seen before—when I feel lost. A strange fear takes hold, simple and deep, that my family moved too far away, that I've crossed some invisible boundary and stepped into another branch of the Archive. Roland assured me it wouldn't happen, that each branch is responsible for hundreds of miles of city, suburb, country, but still the panic washes through me.

I look over my shoulder at the lintel above the door, the familiar SERVAMUS MEMORIAM etched there. According to two semesters of Latin (my father's idea), it means "We Protect the Past." Roman numerals run beneath the inscription, so small and so many that they seem more like a pattern than a number. I asked once, and was told that that was the branch number. I still cannot read it, but I've memorized the pattern, and it hasn't changed. My muscles begin to uncoil.

"Miss Bishop."

The voice is calm, quiet, and familiar. I turn back toward the desk to see Roland coming through the set of doors behind it, tall and slim as ever—he hasn't aged a day—with his gray eyes and his easy grin and his red Chucks. I let out a breath of relief.

"You can go now, Elliot," he says to the man seated behind the desk, who stands with a nod and vanishes back through the doors.

Roland takes a seat and kicks his shoes up onto the desk. He digs in the drawers and comes up with a magazine. Last month's issue of some lifestyle guide I brought him. Mom subscribed to them for a while, and Roland insists on staying as much in the loop as possible when it comes to the Outer. I know for a fact he spends most of his time skimming new Histories, watching the world through their lives. I wonder if boredom prompts him to it, or if it's more. Roland's eyes are tinged with something between pain and longing.

He misses it, I think; the Outer. He's not supposed to. Librarians commit to the Archive in every way, leaving the Outer behind for their term, however long they choose to stay, and he's told me himself that being promoted is an honor, to have all that time and knowledge at your fingertips, to protect the past—SERVAMUS MEMORIAM and

43

all—but if he misses sunrises, or oceans, or fresh air, who can blame him? It's a lot to give up for a fancy title, a suspended life cycle, and an endless supply of reading material.

He holds the magazine toward me. "You look pale."

"Keep it," I say, still a little shaken. "And I'm fine. . . ." Roland knows how scared I am of losing this branch—some days I think the constancy of coming here is all that's keeping me sane—but it's a weakness, and I know it. "Just thought for a moment I'd gone too far."

"Ah, you mean Elliot? He's on loan," says Roland, digging a small radio from a drawer and setting it beside the QUIET PLEASE sign. Classical music whispers out, and I wonder if he plays it just to annoy Lisa, who takes the signs as literally as possible. "A transfer. Wanted a change of scenery. So, what brings you to the Archive tonight?"

I want to see Ben. I want to talk to him. I need to be closer. I'm losing my mind.

"Couldn't sleep," I say with a shrug.

"You found your way here fast enough."

"My new place has *two* doors. Right in the building."

"Only two?" he teases. "So, are you settling in?"

I trace my fingers over the ancient ledger that sits on the table. "It's got . . . character."

"Come now, the Coronado's not so bad."

It creeps me out. Something horrible happened in my bedroom. These are weak thoughts. I do not share them.

"Miss Bishop?" he prompts.

I hate the formality when it comes from the other Librarians, but for some reason I don't mind it from Roland. Perhaps because he seems on the verge of winking when he speaks.

"No, it's not so bad," I say at last with a smile. "Just old."

"Nothing wrong with old."

"You'd know," I say. It's a running line. Roland refuses to tell me how long he's been here. He can't be that old, or at least he doesn't look it—one of the perks is that, as long as they serve, they don't age—but whenever I ask him about his life *before* the Archive, his years hunting Histories, he twists the topic, or glides right over it. As for his years as Librarian, he's equally vague. I've heard Librarians work for ten or fifteen years before retiring—just because the age doesn't show doesn't mean they don't feel older—but with Roland, I can't tell. I remember his mentioning a Moscow branch, and once, absently, Scotland.

The music floats around us.

He returns his shoes to the floor and begins to straighten up the desk. "What else can I do for you?"

Ben. I can't dance around it, and I can't lie. I need his help. Only Librarians can navigate the stacks. "Actually . . . I was hoping—"

"Don't ask me for that."

"You don't even know what I was going to—"

"The pause and the guilty look give you away."

"But I—"

"Mackenzie."

The use of my first name makes me flinch.

"Roland. Please."

His eyes settle on mine, but he says nothing.

"I can't find it on my own," I press, trying to keep my voice level.

"You shouldn't find it at all."

"I haven't asked you in weeks," I say. *Because I've been asking Lisa instead.*

Another long moment, and then finally Roland closes his eyes in a slow, surrendering blink. His fingers drift to a notepad the same size and shape as my Archive paper, and he scribbles something on it. Half a minute later, Elliot reappears, his own pad of paper at his side. He gives Roland a questioning look.

"Sorry to call you back," says Roland. "I won't be gone long."

Elliot nods and silently takes a seat. The front desk is never left unattended. I follow Roland through the doors and into the atrium. It's dotted with Librarians, and I recognize Lisa across the way, her black bob disappearing down a side hall toward older stacks. But otherwise I do not look up at the arching ceiling and its colored glass, do not marvel at the quiet beauty, do not linger, in case any pause in my step makes Roland change his mind. I focus on the stacks as he leads me to Ben.

I've tried to memorize the route—to remember which of the ten wings we go down, to note which set of stairs we take, to count the lefts and rights we make through the halls—but I can never hold the pattern in my head, and even when I think I have, it doesn't work out the next time. I don't know if it's me, or if the route changes. Maybe they reorder the shelves. I think of how I used to arrange movies: one day best to worst, the next by color, the next title . . . Everyone in these stacks died in the branch's jurisdiction, but beyond that, there doesn't seem to be a consistent method of filing. In the end, only Librarians can navigate these stacks.

Today Roland leads me through the atrium, then down the sixth wing, through several smaller corridors, across a courtyard, and up a short set of wooden steps before finally coming to a stop in a spacious reading room. A red rug covers most of the floor, and chairs are tucked into corners; but it is, for the most part, a grid of drawers.

Each drawer's face is roughly the size of a coffin's end.

Roland brings his hand gently against one. Above his fingers I can see the white placard in its copper holder. Below the copper holder is a keyhole.

And then Roland turns away.

"Thank you," I whisper as he passes.

"Your key won't work," he says.

"I know."

"It's not him," he adds softly. "Not really."

"I know," I say, already stepping up to the drawer. My fingers hover over the name.

BISHOP, BENJAMIN GEORGE
2003–2013

FIVE

I TRACE MY FINGERS over the dates, and it is last year again and I'm sitting in one of those hospital chairs that look like they might actually be comfortable but they're not because there's nothing comfortable about hospitals. Da has been gone three years. I am fifteen now, and Ben is ten, and he's dead.

The cops are talking to Dad and the doctor is telling Mom that Ben died on impact, and that word—*impact*—makes me turn and retch into one of the hospital's gray bins.

The doctor tries to say there wasn't time to feel it, but that's not true. Mom feels it. Dad feels it. I feel it. I feel like my skeleton is being ripped through my skin, and I wrap my arms around my ribs to hold it in. I walked with him, all the way to the corner of Lincoln and Smith like always, and he drew a stick-figure Ben on my hand like always and I drew a stick-figure Mac on his like always and he told me it didn't even look like a human being and I told him it wasn't and he told me I was weird and I told him he was late for school.

I can see the black scribble on the back of his hand through the white sheet. The sheet doesn't rise and fall, not one small bit, and I can't take my eyes off it as Mom and Dad and the doctors talk and there is crying and words and I have neither because I'm focusing on the fact that I will see him again. I twist my ring, a spot of silver above black fingerless knit gloves that run to my elbows because I cannot cannot cannot look at the stick-figure Ben on the back of my

48

hand. I twist the ring and run my thumb over the grooves and tell myself that it's okay. It's not okay, of course.

Ben is ten and he's dead. But he's not gone. Not for me.

Hours later, after we get home from the hospital, three weak instead of four strong, I climb out my window and run down dark streets to the Narrows door in the alley behind the butcher's.

Lisa is on duty at the desk in the Archive, and I ask her to take me to Ben. When she tries to tell me that it's not possible, I order her to show me the way; and when she still says no, I take off running. I run for hours through the corridors and rooms and courtyards of the Archive, even though I have no idea where I'm going. I run as if I'll just know where Ben is, the way the Librarians know where things are, but I don't. I run past stacks and columns and rows and walls of names and dates in small black ink.

I run forever.

I run until Roland grabs my arm and shoves me into a side room, and there on the far wall halfway up, I see his name. Roland lets go of me long enough to turn and close the door, and that's when I see the keyhole beneath Ben's dates. It's not even the same size or shape as my key, but I still rip the cord from my throat and force the key in. It doesn't turn. Of course it doesn't turn. I try again and again.

I bang on the cabinet to wake my brother up, the metallic sound shattering the precious quiet, and then Roland is there, pulling me away, pinning my arms back against my body with one hand, muffling my shouts with the other.

I have not cried at all, not once.

Now I sink down to the floor in front of Ben's cabinet—Roland's arms still wrapped around me—and sob.

. . .

I sit on the red rug with my back to Ben's shelf, tugging my sleeves over my hands as I tell my brother about the new apartment, about Mom's latest project and Dad's new job at the university. Sometimes when I run out of things to tell Ben, I recite the stories Da told me. This is how I pass the night, time blurring at the edges.

Sometime later, I feel the familiar scratch against my thigh, and dig the list from my pocket. The careful cursive announces:

Thomas Rowell. 12.

I pocket the list and sink back against the shelves. A few minutes later I hear the soft tread of footsteps, and look up.

"Shouldn't you be at the desk?" I ask.

"Patrick's shift now," says Roland, nudging me with a red Chuck. "You can't stay here forever." He slides down the wall beside me. "Go do your job. Find that History."

"It's my second one today."

"It's an old building, the Coronado. You know what that means."

"I know, I know. More Histories. Lucky me."

"You'll never make Crew talking to a shelf."

Crew. The next step above Keeper. Crew hunt in pairs, tracking down and returning the Keeper-Killers, the Histories who manage to get out through the Narrows and into the real world. Some people stay Keepers their whole lives, but most shoot for Crew. The only thing higher than Crew is the Archive itself—the Librarian post— though it's hard to imagine why someone would give up the thrill of the chase, the game, the fight, to catalog the dead and watch lives through other people's eyes. Even harder to imagine is that every Librarian was a fighter first; but somewhere under his sleeves, Roland bears marks of Crew just like Da did. Keepers have the marks, too, the three lines, but carved into our rings. Crew marks are carved into skin.

"Who says I want to make Crew?" I challenge, but there's not much fight behind it.

Da worked Crew until Ben was born. And then he went back to being a Keeper. I never met his Crew partner, and he never talked about her, but I found a photo of them after he died. The two of them shoulder to shoulder except for a sliver of space, both wearing smiles that don't quite reach their eyes. They say Crew partners are bonded by blood and life and death. I wonder if she forgave him for leaving.

"Da gave it up," I say, even though Roland must already know.

"Do you know why?" he asks.

"Said he wanted a life. . . ." Keepers who don't go Crew split into two camps when it comes to jobs: those who enter professions benefited by an understanding of objects' pasts, and those who want to get as far away from pasts as possible. Da must have had a hard time letting go, because he became a private detective. They used to joke in his office, so I heard, that he had sold his hands to the devil, that he could solve a crime just by touching things. "But what he meant was, he wanted to stay alive. Long enough to groom me, anyway."

"He told you that?" asks Roland.

"Isn't it my job," I say, "to know without being told?"

Roland doesn't answer. He is twisting around to look at Ben's name and date. He reaches up and runs a finger over the placard with its clean black print—letters and numbers that should be worn to nothing now, considering how often I touch them.

"It's strange," says Roland, "that you always come to see Ben, but never Antony."

I frown at the use of Da's real name. "Could I see him if I wanted to?"

"Of course not," says Roland in his official Librarian tone before sliding back into his usual warmth. "But you can't see Ben, either, and it never stops you from trying."

I close my eyes, searching for the right words. "Da is etched so clearly in my memory, I don't think I could forget anything about him even if I tried. But with Ben, it's only been a year and I'm already forgetting things. I keep forgetting things, and it terrifies me."

Roland nods but doesn't answer, sympathetic but resolute. He can't help me. He *won't*. I've come to Ben's shelf two dozen times in the year since he died, and Roland has never given in and opened it. Never let me see my brother.

"Where is Da's shelf, anyway?" I ask, changing the subject before the tightness in my chest grows worse.

"All members of the Archive are kept in Special Collections."

"Where is that?"

Roland arches an eyebrow, but nothing more.

"Why are they kept separately?"

He shrugs. "I don't make the rules, Miss Bishop."

He gets to his feet and offers me his hand. I hesitate.

"It's okay, Mackenzie," he says, taking my hand; and I feel nothing. Librarians are pros at walling off thoughts, blocking out touch. Mom touches me and I can't keep her out, but Roland touches me and I feel blind, deaf, normal.

We start walking.

"Wait," I say, turning back to Ben's shelf. Roland waits as I pull the key from around my neck and slip it into the hole beneath my brother's card. It doesn't turn. It never turns.

But I never stop trying.

• • •

52

I'm not supposed to be here. I can see it in their eyes.

And yet here I am, standing before a table in a large chamber off the atrium's second wing. The room is marble-floored and cold, and there are no bodies lining the walls, only ledgers, and the two people on the other side of the table speak a little louder, unafraid to wake the dead. Roland takes his seat beside them.

"Antony Bishop," says the man on the end. He has a beard and small, sharp eyes that scan a paper on the table. "You are here to name your . . ." He looks up, and the words trail off. "Mr. Bishop, you do realize there is an age requirement. Your granddaughter is not eligible for another"—he consults a folder, coughs—"four years."

"She's up for the trial," you say.

"She'll never pass," says the woman.

"I'm stronger than I look," I say.

The first man sighs, rubs his beard. "What are you doing, Antony?"

"She is my only choice," answers Da.

"Nonsense. You can name Peter. Your son. And if, in time, Mackenzie is willing and able, she will be considered—"

"My son is not fit."

"Maybe you don't do him justice—"

"He's bright, but he's got no violence in him, and he wears his lies. He's not fit."

"Meredith, Allen," says Roland, steepling his fingers. "Let's give her a chance."

The bearded man, Allen, straightens. "Absolutely not."

My eyes flick to Da, craving a sign, a nod of encouragement, but he stares straight ahead.

"I can do it," I say. "I'm not the only choice. I'm the best."

Allen's frown deepens. "I beg your pardon?"

"Go home, little girl," says Meredith with a dismissive wave.

You warned me they would resist. You spent weeks teaching me how to hold my ground.

I stand taller. "Not until I've had my trial."

Meredith makes a strangled sound of dismay, but Allen cuts in with, *"You're. Not. Eligible."*

"Make an exception," I say. Roland's mouth quirks up.

It bolsters me. "Give me a chance."

"You think this is a sport? A club?" snaps Meredith, and then her eyes dart to you. "What could you possibly be thinking, bringing a child into this—"

"I think it's a job," I cut in, careful to keep my voice even. "And I'm ready for it. Maybe you think you're protecting me, or maybe you think I'm not strong enough—but you're wrong."

"You are an unfit candidate. And that is the end of it."

"It would be, Meredith," says Roland calmly, "if you were the only person on this panel."

"I really can't condone this. . . ." says Allen.

I'm losing them, and I can't let that happen. If I lose them, I lose you. "I think I'm ready, and you think I'm not. Let's find out who's right."

"Your composure is impressive." Roland stands up. "But you are aware that not all Histories can be won with words." He rounds the table. "Some are troublesome." He rolls up his sleeves. "Some are violent."

The other two Librarians are still trying to get a word in,

but I don't hear them. My focus is on Roland. Da told me to be ready for anything, and it's a good thing he did, because between one moment and the next, Roland's posture shifts. It's subtle—his shoulders loosen, knees unlock, hands curl toward fists—but I see the change a fraction before he attacks. I dodge the first punch, but he's fast, faster even than Da, and before I can strike back, a red Chuck connects with my chest, sending me to the floor. I roll back and over into a crouch, but by the time I look up, he's gone.

I hear him the instant before his arm wraps around my throat, and manage to get one hand between us so I don't choke. He pulls back and up, my feet leaving the ground, but the table is there and I get my foot on top and use it as leverage, pushing up and off, twisting free of his arm as I flip over his head and land behind him. He turns and I kick, aiming for his chest; but he's too tall and my foot connects with his stomach, where he catches it. I brace myself, but he doesn't strike back.

He laughs and lets go of my shoe, sagging against the desk. The other two Librarians sit behind him looking shocked, though I can't tell if they're more surprised by the fight or Roland's good humor.

"Mackenzie," he says, smoothing his sleeves. "Do you want this job?"

"She does not truly know what this job *is*," says Meredith. "So she has a mouth on her and she can dodge a punch. She is a child. And this is a joke—"

Roland holds up a hand, and Meredith goes quiet. Roland's eyes do not leave mine. They are warm. Encouraging. "Do you want this?" he asks again.

I do want it. I want you to stay. Time and disease are taking you from me. You've told me, made it clear, this is the only way I can keep you close. I will not lose that.

"I do," I answer evenly.

Roland straightens. "Then I approve the naming."

Meredith makes a stifled sound of dismay.

"She held composure against *you*, Meredith, and that is something," says Roland, and finally his smile breaks through. "And as for her fighting, I'm in the best position to judge, and I say she has merit." He looks past me, to you. "You've raised quite a girl, Antony." He glances over at Allen. "What do you say?"

The bearded Librarian raps his fingers on the table, eyes unfocused.

"You can't actually be considering . . ." mutters Meredith.

"If we do this, and she proves herself unfit in any way," says Allen, "she will forfeit the position."

"And if she proves unfit," adds Meredith, "you, Roland, will remove her yourself."

Roland smiles at the challenge.

I step forward. "I understand," I say, as loud as I dare.

Allen stands slowly. "Then I approve the naming."

Meredith glowers for a moment before standing too. "I am overruled, and as such, I must approve the naming."

Only then does your hand come to rest against my shoulder. I can feel your pride in your fingertips. I smile.

I will show them all.

For you.

SIX

I YAWN AS ROLAND leads me back through the Archive. I've been here for hours, and I can tell I'm running out of night. My bones ache from sitting on the floor, but it was worth it for a little time with Ben.

Not Ben, I know. Ben's *shelf*.

I roll my shoulders, stiff from leaning so long against the stacks, as we wind back through the corridors and into the atrium. Several Librarians dot the space, busy with ledgers and notepads and even, here and there, open drawers. I wonder if they ever sleep. I look up at the arched stained glass, darker now, as if there were a night beyond. I take a deep breath and am starting to feel better, calmer, when we reach the front desk.

A man with gray hair, black glasses, and a stern mouth behind a goatee is waiting for us. Roland's music has been shut off.

"Patrick," I say. Not my favorite Librarian. He's been here nearly as long as I have, and we rarely see eye to eye.

The moment he catches sight of me, his mouth turns down.

"Miss Bishop," he scolds. He's Southern, but he's tried to obliterate his drawl by being curt, cutting his consonants sharp. "We try to discourage such recurrent disobedience."

Roland rolls his eyes and claps Patrick on the shoulder.

"She's not doing any harm."

Patrick glares at Roland. "She not doing any good, either. I should report her to Agatha." His gaze swivels to me. "Hear that? I should report you."

I don't know who this Agatha is, but I'm fairly certain I don't want to know.

"Restrictions exist for a reason, Miss Bishop. There are no visiting hours. Keepers do not attend to the Histories here. You are not to enter the stacks without *good* reason. Are we clear?"

"Of course."

"Does that mean you will cease this futile and rather tiresome pursuit?"

"Of course not."

A cough of a laugh escapes from Roland, along with a wink. Patrick sighs and rubs his eyes, and I can't help but feel a bit victorious. But when he reaches for his notepad, my spirits sink. The last thing I need is a demerit on my record. Roland sees the gesture, too, and brings his hand down lightly on Patrick's arm.

"On the topic of attending to Histories," he offers, "don't you have one to catch, Miss Bishop?"

I know a way out when I see it.

"Indeed," I say, turning toward the door. I can hear the two men talking in low, tense voices, but I know better than to look back.

I find and return twelve-year-old Thomas Rowell, fresh enough out that he goes without many questions, let alone a fight. Truth be told, I think he is just happy to find someone in the dark halls, as opposed to some*thing*. I spend what's left of the night testing every door in my territory. By the time I finish, the halls—and several spots on the floor—are scribbled over with chalk. Mostly X's, but here and there a circle. I work my way back to my two numbered doors, and discover a third, across from them, that opens with my key.

Door I leads to the third floor and the painting by the sea. Door II leads to the side of the stairs in the Coronado lobby.

But Door III? It opens only to black. To nothing. So why is it unlocked at all? Curiosity pulls me over the threshold, and I step through into the dark and close the door behind me. The space is quiet and cramped and smells of dust so thick, I taste it when I breathe in. I can reach out and touch walls to my left and right, and my fingers encounter a forest of wooden poles leaning against them. A closet?

As I slide my ring back on and resume my awkward groping in the dark, I feel the scratch of a new name on the list in my pocket. Again? Fatigue is starting to eat into my muscles, drag at my thoughts. The History will have to wait. When I step forward, my shin collides with something hard. I close my eyes to cut off the rising claustrophobia; finally, my hands find the door a few feet in front of me. I sigh with relief and turn the metal handle sharply.

Locked.

I could go back into the Narrows through the door behind me and take a different route, but a question persists: Where *am* I? I listen closely, but no sound reaches me. Between the dust in this closet and the total lack of anything resembling noise from the opposite side, I think I must be somewhere abandoned.

Da always said there were two ways to get through any locked door: by key or by force. And I don't have a key, so . . . I lean back and lift my boot, resting the sole against the wood of the door. Then I slide my shoe left until it butts up against the metal frame of the handle. I withdraw my foot several times, testing to make sure I have a clear shot before I take a breath and kick.

Wood cracks loudly, and the door moves; but it takes a second strike before it swings open, spilling several brooms and a bucket out onto a stone floor. I step over the mess to survey the room and find a sea of sheets. Sheets covering counters and windows and sections of floor, dirty stone peering out from the edges of the fabric. A switch is set into the wall several feet away, and I wade through the sheets until I get near enough to flip the lights.

A dull buzzing fills the space. The light is faint and glaring at the same time, and I cringe and switch it back off. Daylight presses in with a muted glow against the sheets over the windows—it's later than I thought—and I cross the large space and pull a make-shift curtain down, showering dust and morning light on everything. Beyond the windows is a patio, a set of suspiciously familiar awnings overhead—

"I see you've found it!"

I spin to find my parents ducking under a sheet into the room.

"Found what?"

Mom gestures to the space, its dust and sheets and counters and broken broom closet, as if showing me a castle, a kingdom.

"Bishop's Coffee Shop."

For a moment, I am genuinely speechless.

"The café sign in the lobby didn't give it away?" asks Dad.

Maybe if I'd come through the lobby. I am still dazed by the fact that I've stepped out of the Narrows and into my mother's newest pet project, but years of lying have taught me to never look as lost as I feel, so I smile and roll with it.

"Yeah, I had a hunch," I say, rolling up the window sheet. "I woke up early, so I thought I'd take a look."

It's a weak lie, but Mom isn't even listening. She's flitting around the space, holding her breath like a kid about to blow out birthday candles as she pulls down sheets. Dad is still looking at me rather intently, eyes panning over my dark clothes and long sleeves, all the pieces that don't line up.

"So," I say brightly, because I've learned if I can talk louder than he can think, he tends to lose his train of thought, "you think there's a coffee machine under one of these sheets?"

He brightens. My father needs coffee like other men need food, water, shelter. Between the three classes he's set to teach in the history department and the ongoing series of essays he's composing, caffeine ranks way up there on his priority list. I think that's all it took for Mom to get him to support her dream of owning a café: an invitation from the local university and the guarantee of continuous coffee. Brew it, and they will come.

I try to stifle a yawn.

"You look tired," he says.

"So do you," I shoot back, pulling the covers off a piece of equipment that might have once been a grinder. "Hey, look."

"Mackenzie . . ." he presses, but I flip the switch and the machinery does in fact grind to life, drowning him out with a horrible sound like it's eating its own parts, chewing up metal nuts and bolts and gobbling down air. Dad winces, and I turn it off, sounds of mechanic agony echoing through the room, along with a smell like burning toast.

I can't help glancing back at the cleaning closet, and Mom must have followed my gaze, because she heads straight for it.

"I wonder what happened here," she says, swinging the door on its broken hinges.

I shrug and head over to an oven, or something like it, and pry the door open. The inside is stale and scorched.

"I was thinking that we should bake some muffins," says Mom.

"'Welcome' muffins!" She doesn't say it like *welcome* but rather like *Welcome!* "You know, to let everyone know that we're here. What do you think, Mac?"

In response, I nudge the oven door, and it swings shut with a bang. Something dislodges and lands with a *tinktinktinktink* across the stone before rolling up against her shoe.

Her smile doesn't even falter. It turns my stomach, her sickly-sweet-everything's-better-than-fine pep. I've seen the inside of her mind, and this is all a stupid act. I lost Ben. I shouldn't have to lose her, too. I want to shake her. I want to say . . . But I don't know what to say. I don't know how to get through to her, how to make her see that she's making it worse.

So I tell the truth. "I think it's falling apart."

She misses my meaning. Or steps around it. "Well then," she says cheerfully, stooping to fetch the metal bolt, "we'll just use the apartment oven until we get this one in shape."

With that she turns on her heel and bobs away. I look around, hoping to find Dad, and with him some measure of sympathy or at least commiseration, but he's on the patio, staring up at the awnings.

"Chop chop, Mackenzie," Mom calls through the door. "You know what they say—"

"I'm pretty sure no one says it but you—"

"Up with the sun and just as bright."

I look out the window at the light and cringe, and follow.

We spend the rest of the morning in the apartment baking *Welcome!* muffins. Or rather, Dad ducks out to run some errands, and Mom makes muffins while I do my best to look busy. I could really use a few hours of sleep and a shower, but every time I make a move to leave, Mom thinks up something for me to do. While she's distracted pulling a fresh batch from the oven, I dig the Archive list from my pocket. But when I unfold it, it's blank.

Relief washes over me before I remember that there should be a name on it. I could swear I felt the scrawl of a new History being added when I was stuck in the café closet. I must have imagined it. Mom sets the tray of muffins on the counter as I refold the paper and tuck it away. She drapes a cloth over them, and out of nowhere I remember Ben standing on his toes to peek beneath the towel and steal a pinch even though it was always too hot and he burned his fingers. It's like being punched in the chest, and I squeeze my eyes shut until the pain passes.

I beg off baking duty for five minutes just to change clothes—mine smell like Narrows air and Archive stacks and café dust. I pull on jeans and a clean shirt, but my hair refuses to work with me, and I finally dig a yellow bandana out of a suitcase and fashion a head-band, trying to hide the mess as best I can. I'm tucking Da's key beneath my collar when I catch sight of the dark spots on my floor and remember the bloodstained boy.

I kneel down, trying to tune out the clatter of baking trays beyond the door as I slide off my ring and bring my fingertips to the floorboards. The wood hums against my hands as I close my eyes and reach, and—

"Mackenzie!" Mom calls out.

I sigh and blink, pushing up from the floor. I straighten just as Mom knocks briskly on the door. "Have I lost you?"

"I'm coming," I say, shoving the ring back on as her footsteps fade. I cast one last glance at the floor before I leave. In the kitchen, the muffins are already wrapped in blossoms of cellophane. Mom is filling a basket, chattering about the residents, and that's when I get an idea.

Da was a Keeper, but he was a detective too, and he used to say you could learn as much by asking people as by reading walls. You get different answers. My room has a story to tell, and as soon as I can get an ounce of privacy, I'll read it; but in the meantime, what better way to learn about the Coronado than to ask the people in it?

"Hey, Mom," I say, pushing up my sleeves, "I'm sure you've got a ton of work to do. Why don't you let me deliver those?"

She pauses and looks up. "Really? Would you?" She says it like she's surprised I'm capable of being nice. Yes, things have been rocky between us, and I'm offering to help because it helps me—but still.

She tucks the last muffin into a basket and nudges it my way.

"Sure thing," I say, managing a smile, and her resulting one is so genuine that I almost feel bad. Right up until she wraps me in a hug and the high-pitched strings and slamming doors and crackling paper static of her life scratches against my bones. Then I just feel sick.

"Thank you," she says, tightening her grip. "That's so sweet." I can barely hear the words through the grating noise in my head.

"It's . . . really . . . nothing," I say, trying to picture a wall between us, and failing. "Mom," I say at last, "I can't breathe." And then she laughs and lets go, and I'm left dizzy but free.

"All right, get going," she says, turning back to her work. I've never been so happy to oblige.

I start down the hall and peel the cellophane away from a muffin, hoping Mom hasn't counted them out as I eat breakfast. The basket swings back and forth from the crook of my arm, each muffin individually wrapped and tagged. BISHOP'S, the tag announces in careful script. A basket of conversation starters.

I focus on the task at hand. The Coronado has seven floors—one lobby and six levels of housing—with six apartments to a floor, A through F. That many rooms, odds are someone knows something.

And maybe someone does, but nobody seems to be home. There's the flaw in both my mother's plans and in mine. Late morning on a weekday, and what do you get? A lot of locked doors. I slip out of 3F and head down the hall. 3E and 3D are both quiet, 3C is vacant (according to a small slip of paper stuck to the door), and though I can hear the muffled sounds of life in 3B, nobody answers. After several aggressive knocks on 3A, I'm getting frustrated. I drop muffins on each doorstep and move on.

One floor up, it's more of the same. I leave the baked goods at 4A, B, and C. But as I'm heading away from 4D, the door swings open.

"Young lady," comes a voice.

I turn to see a vast woman filling the door frame like bread in a loaf pan, holding the small, cellophaned muffin.

"What is your name? And what is this adorable little treat?" she asks. The muffin looks like an egg, nested in her palm.

"Mackenzie," I say, stepping forward. "Mackenzie Bishop. My family just moved in to 3F, and we're renovating the coffee shop on the ground floor."

"Well, lovely to meet you, Mackenzie," she says, engulfing my hand with hers. She is made up of low tones and bells and the sound of ripping fabric. "My name is Ms. Angelli."

"Nice to meet you." I slide my hand free as politely as possible.

And then I hear it. A sound that makes my skin crawl. A faint meow behind the wall that is Ms. Angelli, just before a clearly desperate cat finds a crack somewhere near the woman's feet and squeezes through, tumbling out into the hall. I jump back.

"Jezzie," scorns Ms. Angelli. "Jezzie, come back here." The cat is small and black, and stands just out of reach, gauging its owner. And then it turns to look at me.

I hate cats.

Or really, I just hate *touching* them. I hate touching any animal, for that matter. Animals are like people but fifty times worse—all id, no ego; all emotion, no rational thought—which makes them a bomb of sensory input wrapped in fur.

Ms. Angelli frees herself from the doorway and nearly stumbles forward onto Jezzie, who promptly flees toward me. I shrink back, putting the basket of muffins between us.

"Bad kitty," I growl.

"Oh, she's a lover, my Jezzie." Ms. Angelli bends to fetch the cat, which is now pretending to be dead, or is paralyzed by fear, and I get a glimpse of the apartment behind her.

Every inch is covered with antiques. My first thought is, *Why would anyone have so much stuff?*

"You like old things," I say.

"Oh, yes," she says, straightening. "I'm a collector." Jezzie is now tucked under her arm like a clutch purse. "A bit of an artifact historian," she says. "And what about you, Mackenzie—do you like old things?"

Like is the wrong word. They're *useful*, since they're more likely to have memories than new things.

"I like the Coronado," I say. "That counts as an old thing, right?"

"Indeed. A wonderful old place. Been around more than a century, if you can believe it. Full of history, the Coronado."

"You must know all about it, then."

Ms. Angelli fidgets. "Ah, a place like this, no one can know everything. Bits and pieces, really, rumors and tales . . ." She trails off.

"Really?" I brighten. "Anything unusual?" And then, worried my enthusiasm is a little too strong, I add, "My friend is convinced a place like this has to have a few ghosts, skeletons, secrets."

66

Ms. Angelli frowns and sets Jezzie back in the apartment, and locks the door.

"I'm sorry," she says abruptly. "You caught me on my way out. I've got an appraisal in the city."

"Oh," I fumble. "Well, maybe we could talk more, some other time?"

"Some other time," she echoes, setting off down the hall at a surprising pace.

I watch her go. She clearly knows *something*. It never really occurred to me that someone would know and not want to share. Maybe I should stick to reading walls. At least they can't refuse to answer.

My footsteps echo on the concrete stairs as I ascend to the fifth floor, where not a single person appears to be home. I leave a trail of muffins in my wake. Is this place empty? Or just unfriendly? I'm already reaching for the stairwell door at the other end of the hall when it swings open abruptly and I run straight into a body. I stumble back, steadying myself against the wall, but I'm not fast enough to save the muffins.

I cringe and wait for the sound of the basket tumbling, but it never comes. When I look up, a guy is standing there, the basket safely cradled in his arms. Spiked hair and a slanted smile. My pulse skips.

The third-floor lurker from last night.

"Sorry about that," he says, passing me the basket. "No harm, no foul?"

"Yeah," I say, straightening. "Sure."

He holds out his hand. "Wesley Ayers," he says, waiting for me to shake.

I'd rather not, but I don't want to be rude. The basket's in my right hand, so I hold out my left awkwardly. When he takes it, the sounds rattle in my ears, through my head, deafening. Wesley is made like a rock band, drums and bass and interludes of breaking glass. I try to block out the roar, to push back, but that only makes it worse. And then, instead of shaking my hand, he gives a theatrical bow and brushes his lips against my knuckles, and I can't breathe. Not in a pleasant, butterflies-and-crushes way. I literally cannot breathe around the shattering sound and the bricklike beat. My cheeks flush hot, and the frown must have made its way onto my face, because he laughs, misreading my discomfort, and lets go, taking all the noise and pressure with him.

"What?" he says. "That's custom, you know. Right to right, hand-shake. Left to right, kiss. I thought it was an invitation."

"No," I say curtly. "Not exactly." The world is quiet again, but I'm still thrown off and having trouble hiding it. I shuffle past him toward the stairs, but he turns to face me, his back to the hall.

"Ms. Angelli, in Four D," he continues. "She always expects a kiss. It's hard with all the rings she wears." He holds up his left hand, wiggles his fingers. He's got a few of his own.

"Wes!" calls a young voice from an open doorway halfway down the hall. A small, strawberry-blond head pops out of 5C. I want to be annoyed that she didn't answer when I knocked, but I'm still resisting the urge to sit down on the checkered carpet. Wesley makes a point of ignoring her, his attention trained on me. Up close I can confirm that his light brown eyes are ringed with eyeliner.

"What were you doing in the hall last night?" I ask, trying to bury my unease. His expression is blank, so I add, "The third-floor hall. It was late."

"It wasn't *that* late," he says with a shrug. "Half the cafés in the city were still open."

"Then why weren't you in one of them?" I ask.

He smirks. "I like the third floor. It's so . . . yellow."

"Excuse me?"

"It's yellow." He reaches out and taps the wallpaper with a painted black nail. "Seventh is purple. Sixth is blue. Fifth"—he gestures around us—"is clearly red."

I wouldn't go so far as to say it's clearly any color.

"Fourth is green," he continues. "Third is yellow. Like your bandana. Retro. Nice."

I bring a hand up to my hair. "What's second?" I ask.

"It's somewhere between brown and orange. Ghastly."

I almost laugh. "They all look a bit gray to me."

"Give it time," he says. "So, you just move in? Or do you enjoy roaming the halls of apartment buildings, hocking"—he peers into the basket—"baked goods?"

"Wes," the girl says again, stamping her foot, but he ignores her pointedly, winking at me. The girl's face reddens, and she disappears into the apartment. A moment later she emerges, weapon in hand.

She sends the book spinning through the air with impressive aim, and I must have blinked, or missed something, because the next minute, Wesley's hand has come up and the book is resting in it. And he's still smiling at me.

"Be right there, Jill."

He brushes the book off and lets it fall to his side while he peers into the muffin basket. "This basket nearly killed me. I feel I deserve compensation." His hand is already digging through the cellophane, past ribbons and tags.

"Help yourself," I say. "You live here, then?"

"Can't say that I do— Oooooh, blueberry." He lifts a muffin and reads the label. "So you are a Bishop, I presume."

"Mackenzie Bishop," I say. "Three F."

"Nice to meet you, Mackenzie," he says, tossing the muffin into the air a few times. "What brings you to this crumbling castle?"

"My mother. She's on a mission to renovate the café."

"You sound so enthused," he says.

"It's just old . . ." *That's enough sharing,* warns a voice in my head.

One dark eyebrow arches. "Afraid of spiders? Dust? Ghosts?"

"No. Those things don't worry me." *Everything is loud here, like you.*

His smile is teasing, but his eyes are sincere. "Then what?"

I'm spared by Jill, who emerges with another book. Part of me wants to see this Wesley try to stave off a second blow while holding a book and a blueberry muffin, but he turns away, conceding.

"All right, all right, I'm coming, brat." He tosses the first book back to Jill, who fumbles it. And then he casts one last look at me with his crooked smile. "Thanks for the muffin, Mac." He just met me and he's already using a nickname. I'd kick his ass, but there's a slight affection to the way he says it, and for some reason I don't mind.

"See you around."

Several moments after the door to 5C has closed, I'm still standing there when the scratch of letters in my pocket brings me to my senses. I head for the stairs and pull the paper from my jeans.

Jackson Lerner. 16.

This History is old enough that I can't afford to put it off. They slip so much faster the older they get—distress to destruction in a matter of hours; minutes, even. I get back to the third floor, ditching the basket in the stairwell, and pocket my ring as I reach the painting of the sea. I pull the key's cord over my head, wrapping it several times around my wrist as my eyes adjust to make out the keyhole in the faint wall crack. I slot the key and turn. A hollow click; the door floats to the surface, lined in light, and I head back into the forever night of the Narrows.

I close my eyes and press my fingertips against the nearest wall, reaching until I catch hold of the memories, and behind my eyes the Narrows reappear, bleak and bare and grayer, but the same. Time rolls away beneath my touch, but the memory sits like a picture, unchanging, until the History finally flickers in the frame, blink-and-you-miss-it quick. The first time, I *do* miss it, and I have to drag time to a stop and turn it forward, breathing out slow, slow, inching frame by frame until I see him. It goes like *empty empty empty empty empty empty body empty empty*—gotcha. I focus, holding the memory long enough to identify the shape as a teenage boy in a green hoodie—it must be Jackson—and then I nudge the memory forward and watch him walk past from right to left, and turn the first corner. Right.

I blink, the Narrows sharpening around me as I pull back from the wall, and follow Jackson's path around the corner. Then I start again, repeating the process at each turn until I close the gap, until I'm nearly walking in his wake. Just as I'm reading the fourth or fifth wall, I hear *him*, not the muddled sounds of the past but the shuffling steps of a body in the now. I abandon the memory and track the sound down the hall, whipping around the corner, where I find myself face-to-face with—

Myself.

Two distorted reflections of my sharp jaw and my yellow bandana pool in the black that's spreading across the History's eyes, eating up the color as he slips.

Jackson Lerner stands there staring at me with his head cocked, a mop of messy reddish brown hair falling against his cheeks. Beneath his bright green hoodie, he has that gaunt look boys sometimes get in their teens. Like they've been stretched. I take a small step back.

"What the hell's going on here?" he snaps, hands stuffed into his jeans. "This some kind of fun house or something?"

I keep my tone empty, even. "Not really, no."

"Well, it blows," he says, a thin layer of bravado masking the fear in his voice. Fear is dangerous. "I want to get out of here."

He shifts his weight, as solid as flesh and blood on the stained floor. Well, as solid as flesh, anyway. Histories don't bleed. He shifts again, restless, and then his blackening eyes drift down to my hand, to the place where my key dangles from the cord wrapped around my wrist. The metal glints.

"You got a key." Jackson points, gaze following the key's small, swinging movements. "Why don't you just let me out? Huh?"

I can hear the change in tone. Fear twists into anger.

"All right." Da would tell me to stay steady. *The Histories will slip; you can't afford to.* I glance around at the nearest doors.

But they all have chalk X's.

"What are you waiting for?" he growls. "I said, let me out."

"All right," I say again, sliding back. "I'll take you to the right door."

I steal another step away. He doesn't move.

"Just open this one," he says, pointing to the nearest outline, X and all.

"I can't. We need to find one with a white circle and then—"

"Open the damn door!" he yells, lunging for the key around my wrist. I dodge.

"Jackson," I snap, and the fact that I know his name causes him to pause. I try a different approach. "You have to tell me where you want to go. These doors all go to different places. Some don't even open. And some of them do, but the places they lead are very bad."

The anger written across his face fades into frustration, a crease between his shining eyes, a sadness in his mouth. "I just want to go home."

"Okay," I say, letting a small sigh of relief escape. "Let's go home."

He hesitates.

"Follow me," I press. The thought of turning my back on him sends off a slew of warning lights in my head, but the Narrows are too, well, *narrow* for us to pass through side by side. I turn and walk, searching for a white circle. I catch sight of one near the end of the hall, and pick up my pace, glancing back to make sure Jackson is with me.

He's not.

He's stopped, several feet back, and is staring at the keyhole of a door set into the floor. The edge of an X peeks out beneath his shoe.

"Come on, Jackson," I say. "Don't you want to go home?"

He toes the keyhole. "You aren't taking me home," he says.

"I am."

He looks up at me, his eyes catching the thin stream of light coming from the keyhole at his feet. "You don't know where my home is."

That is, of course, a very good point. "No, I don't." A wave of anger washes over his face when I add, "But the doors do."

I point to the one at his feet. "It's simple. The X means it's not your door." I point to the one just ahead, the filled-in circle drawn on its front. "That one, with the chalk circle. That's your door. That's where we're going."

Hope flickers in him, and I might feel bad about lying if I had any choice. Jackson catches up, then pushes past me.

"Hurry up," he says, waiting by the door, running a finger over the chalk as his gaze continues down the hall. I reach out to slide the key into the lock.

"Wait," he says. "What's that?"

I look up. He's pointing at another door, one at the very end of the hall. A white circle has been drawn above the keyhole, large enough to see from here. Damn.

"Jackson——"

He spins on me. "You lied. You're not taking me home." He steps forward, and I step back, away from the door.

"I didn't——"

He doesn't give me a chance to lie again, but lunges for the key. I twist out of the way, catching his sleeved wrist as he reaches out. I wrench it behind his back, and he yelps, but somehow, by some combination of fighter's luck and sheer will, twists free. He turns to run, but I catch his shoulder and force him forward, against the wall.

I keep my arm firmly around his throat, pulling back and up with enough force to make him forget that he is six inches taller than I am, and still has two arms and two legs to fight with.

"Jackson," I say, trying to keep my voice level, "you're being ridiculous. Any door with a white circle can take you——"

And then I see metal, and jump back just in time, the knife in his hand arcing through the air, fast. This is wrong. Histories never have weapons. Their bodies are searched when they're shelved. So where did he get it?

I kick up and send him reeling backward. It only buys a moment, but a moment is long enough to get a good look at the blade. It gleams in the dark, well-kept steel as long as my hand, a hole drilled in the grip so it can be spun. It is a *lovely* weapon. And there is no way it belongs to a punk teen with a worn-out hoodie and a bad attitude.

But whether it's his, or he stole it, or someone gave it to him—a possibility I don't even want to consider—it doesn't change the fact that right now he's the one holding a knife.

And I've got nothing.

SEVEN

I AM ELEVEN, and you are stronger than you look.

You take me out into the summer sun to show me how to fight. Your limbs are weapons, brutally fast. I spend hours figuring out how to avoid them, how to dodge, roll, anticipate, react. It's get out of the way or get hit.

I'm sitting on the ground, exhausted and rubbing my ribs where you got a touch, even though I saw you try to pull back.

"You said you'd teach me how to fight," I say.

"I am."

"You're only showing me how to defend."

"Trust me. You need to know that first."

"I want to learn how to attack." I cross my arms. "I'm strong enough."

"Fighting isn't really about using your strength, Kenzie. It's about using theirs. Histories will always be stronger. Pain doesn't stick, so you can't hurt them, not really. They don't bleed, and if you kill them, they don't stay dead. They die, they come back. You die, you don't."

"Can I have a weapon?"

"No, Kenzie," you snap. "Never carry a weapon. Never count on anything that's not attached to you. It can be taken. Now, get back up."

• • •

There are times when I wish I'd broken Da's rules. Like right now, staring at the sharp edge of a knife in the hands of a slipping History. But I don't break Da's rules, not ever. Sometimes I break the Archive's rules, or bend them a bit, but not his. And they must work, because I'm still alive.

For now.

Jackson fidgets with the knife, and I can tell by the way he holds it he's not used to the weapon. Good. Then at least I stand a chance of getting it away from him. I tug the yellow bandana from my hair and pull it tight between my hands. And I force my mouth to smile, because he might have the advantage as far as sharp things go, but even when the game turns physical, it never stops being mental.

"Jackson," I say, pulling the fabric taut. "You don't need to——"

Something moves in the hall beyond him. A shadow there and then gone, a dark shape with a silver crown. Sudden enough to catch my attention, dragging it from Jackson for only a second.

Which is, of course, the second he lunges.

His limbs are longer than mine, and it's all I can do to get out of the way. He fights like an animal. Reckless. But he's holding the knife wrong, too low, leaving a gap on the hilt between his hand and the blade. The next slice comes blindingly quick, and I lean back but hold my ground. I have an idea, but it means getting close, which is always risky when the other person has a knife. He jabs again, and I try to twist my body to get my arms to one side, one above and one below the knife; but I'm not fast enough, and the blade skims my forearm. Pain burns over my skin, but I've almost got this—and sure enough, on the next try he jabs wrong and I dodge right, lifting one arm and lowering the other so the knife slices into the circle of space made by my limbs and the bandana. He sees the trap too late, jerks back; but I swing my hand down, looping the fabric around the knife, the gap on the hilt. I snap it tight and bring my boot to the front of his green hoodie as hard as I can, and he stumbles, losing his hold on the knife.

The fabric goes slack and the blade tumbles into my grip, handle hitting my palm right as he dives forward, tackling me around the waist and sending us both to the floor. He knocks the air from my lungs like a brick to the ribs, and the blade goes skittering into the dark.

At least it's a fair fight now. He might be strong, made stronger by slipping, but he clearly didn't have a grandfather who saw combat training as a bonding opportunity. I free my leg from under him and manage to get my foot against the wall, for once thankful that the Narrows are so narrow. Pushing off, I roll on top of Jackson, just in time to dodge a clumsily thrown fist.

And then I see it on the floor, right above his shoulder.

A keyhole.

I never marked it, so I don't know where it leads, or if my key will even work, but I have to do something. Ripping my wrist and my key free of his grip, I drive the metal teeth down into the gap and turn, holding my breath until I hear it click. I look down into Jackson's wild eyes just before the door falls open, plunging us both downward.

Space changes, suddenly, and instead of falling down we fall forward, sprawling onto the cold marble of the Archive's antechamber floor.

I can see the front desk in the corner of my eye, a QUIET PLEASE sign and a stack of papers and a green-eyed girl looking over it.

"This is not the Returns room," she says, her voice edged with amusement. She has hair the color of sun and sand.

"I realize that," I growl as I try to pin a hissing, cussing, clawing Jackson to the floor. "A little help?"

I've got him down for all of two seconds before he somehow gets his knee and then his shoe between our bodies.

The young Librarian stands up as Jackson uses his boot to pry me off, sending me backward to the hard floor. I'm still on the ground, but Jackson is halfway to his feet when the Librarian rounds the desk and cheerfully plunges something thin and sharp and shining into his back. His eyes widen, and when she twists the weapon there's a noise, like a lock turning or a bone breaking, and all the life goes out of Jackson Lerner's eyes. She withdraws, and he crumples to the floor with the sickening thud of dead weight. I can see now that what she holds is not a weapon exactly, but a kind of key. It's gleaming gold and has a handle and a stem, but no teeth.

"That was fun," she says.

There's something like a giggle in the corners of her voice. I've seen her around the stacks. She always catches my eye because she is so young. Girlish. Librarian is top rank, so the vast majority are older, seasoned. But this girl looks like she's twenty.

I drag myself to my feet. "I need a key like that."

She laughs. "You couldn't handle it. Literally." She holds it out, but the moment my fingers touch the metal, they go pins-and-needles numb. I pull back, and her laugh trails off as the key vanishes into the pocket of her coat.

"Stumble through the wrong door?" she asks just before the large doors behind the desk fly open.

"What is going on?" comes a very different voice. Patrick storms in, the eyes behind his black glasses flicking from the Librarian to Jackson's body on the floor to me.

"Carmen," he says, his attention still leveled on me. "Please take care of that."

The girl smiles and, despite her size, hauls the body up and through

79

a pair of doors built right into the curving walls of the antechamber. I blink. I never noticed those before. And the moment they've closed behind her, I can't seem to focus on them. My eyes roll off.

"Miss Bishop," Patrick says tersely. The room is quiet except for my heavy breathing. "You're bleeding on my floor."

I look down and realize he's right. Pain rolls up my arm as my eyes slide over the place where Jackson's knife cut through fabric and grazed skin. My sleeve is stained red, a narrow line running down my hand and over my key before dripping to the floor. Patrick is gazing distastefully at the drops as they hit the granite.

"Did you have a problem with the doors?" asks Patrick.

"No," I say, aiming for a joke. "The doors were fine. I had a problem with the *History*."

Not even a smile.

"Do you need medical attention?" he asks.

I feel dazed, but I know better than to show it. Certainly not in front of him.

Every branch staffs a medically trained Librarian in the interest of keeping work-related injuries quiet, and Patrick is the man for this branch. If I say yes, then he'll treat me; but he'll also have an excuse to report the incident, and there won't be anything Roland can do to keep it off the books. I don't have a clean record, so I shake my head.

"I'll live." A swatch of yellow catches my eye, and I recover my bandana from the floor and wrap it around the cut. "But I really liked this shirt," I add as lightly as possible.

He frowns and I think he's going to chew me out or report me, but when he speaks it's only to say, "Go clean up."

I nod and turn back to the Narrows, leaving a trail of red behind.

EIGHT

I AM A MESS.

I scoured the Narrows, but Jackson's knife was nowhere to be found. As for the strange shadow I saw during the fight, the one with the silvery crown . . . maybe my eyes were playing tricks on me. That happens, now and then, with the ring off. Press against a surface wrong and you can see the present and past at once. Things can get tangled.

I wince, focusing on the task at hand.

The cut on my arm is deeper than I thought, and it bleeds through the gauze before I can get the bandage on. I toss another ruined wrap into the plastic bag currently serving as the bathroom trash bin and run the cut under cool water, digging through the extensive first-aid kit I've assembled over the years. My shirt is sitting in a heap on the floor, and I take in my reflection, the web of fine scars across my stomach and arms, and the bruise blossoming on my shoulder. I am never without the marks of my job.

Pulling my forearm from the water, I dab the cut, finally getting it gauzed and wrapped. Red drops have made a trail along the counter and into the sink.

"I christen thee," I mutter to the sink as I finish bandaging the cut. I take the trash bag and add it to the larger one in the kitchen, making sure all evidence of my first aid is buried, just as Mom appears, a slightly smooshed but still cellophaned muffin in one hand, and the basket in the other. The muffins inside have cooled, a film of condensation fogging up the wrappers. Damn. I knew I forgot something.

"Mackenzie Bishop," she says, dropping her purse on the dining room table, which is the only fully assembled piece of furniture. "What is this?"

"A Welcome muffin?"

She drops the basket with a thud.

"You said you would *deliver* them. Not drop them on people's doormats and leave the basket in the stairwell. And where have you been?" she snaps. "This couldn't have taken you all morning. You can't just disappear. . . ." She's an open book: anger and worry too thinly veiled behind a tight-lipped smile. "I asked for your help."

"I knocked, but nobody was home," I snap back, pain and fatigue tightening around me. "Most people have jobs, Mom. Normal jobs. Ones where they get up and go to the office and come home."

She rubs her eyes, which means that she's been rehearsing whatever she's about to say. "Mackenzie. Look. I was talking to Colleen, and she said that you'd need to grieve in your own way—"

"You're kidding me."

"—and when you add that to your age, and the natural desire for rebellion—"

"Stop." My head is starting to hurt.

"—I know you need space. But you also need to learn discipline. Bishop's is a family business."

"But it wasn't a family *dream*."

She flinches.

I want to be oblivious to the hurt written on her face. I want to be selfish and young and normal. M would be that way. She would need space to grieve. She would rebel because her parents were simply uncool, not because one was wearing a horrifying happy mask and the other was a living ghost. She'd be distant because she was preoccupied with boys or school, not because she's tired from hunting down the Histories of the dead, or distracted by her new hotel-turned-apartment, where the walls are filled with crimes.

"Sorry," I say, adding, "Colleen's right, I guess." The words try to crawl back down my throat. "Maybe I just need a little time to adjust. It's a lot of change. But I didn't mean to bail."

"Where were you?"

"Talking to a neighbor," I say. "Ms. Angelli. She invited me in, and I didn't want to be rude. She seemed kind of lonely, and she had this amazing place full of old stuff, and so I just stayed with her for a while. We had tea, and she showed me her collections."

Da would call that an extrapolation. It's easier than a straight lie because it contains seeds of truth. Not that Mom would be able to tell if I told her a blatant lie, but it makes me feel a fraction less guilty.

"Oh. That was . . . sweet of you," she says, looking wounded because I'd rather have tea with a stranger than talk to her.

"I should have kept better track of time"—and then, feeling guiltier—"I'm sorry." I rub my eyes and begin to lean toward the bedroom. "I'm going to go unpack a little."

"This will be good for us," she promises. "This will be an adventure." But while it sounded cheerful coming from Dad, it leaves her lips like a breath being knocked out of her. Desperate. "I promise, Mac. An adventure."

"I believe you," I say. And because I can tell she wants more, I manage a smile and add, "I love you."

The words taste strange, and as I make my way to my room and then to my waiting bed, I can't figure out why. When I pull the sheet over my head, it hits me.

It's the only thing I said that wasn't a lie.

I'm twelve, six months shy of becoming a Keeper, and Mom is mad at you because you're bleeding. She accuses you of fighting, of drinking, of refusing to age gracefully. You light a cigarette and run your fingers through your shock of peppered hair and let her believe it was a bar fight, let her believe you were looking for trouble.

"Is it hard?" I ask when she storms out of the room. "Lying so much?"

You take a long drag and flick ash into the sink, where you know she'll see it. You're not supposed to smoke anymore.

"Not hard, no. Lying is easy. But it's lonely."

"What do you mean?"

"When you lie to everyone about everything, what's left? What's true?"

"Nothing," I say.

"Exactly."

The phone wakes me.

"Hey, hey," says Lyndsey. "Daily check-in!"

"Hey, Lynds." I yawn.

"Were you sleeping?"

"I'm trying to fulfill your mother's image of me."

"Don't mind her. So, hotel update? Found me any ghosts yet?"

I sit up, swing my legs off the bed. I've got the bloodstained boy in my walls, but I don't think that's really shareable. "No ghosts yet, but I'll keep looking."

"Look harder! A place like that? It's got to be full of creepy things. It's been around for, like, a hundred years."

"How do you know that?"

"I looked it up! You don't think I'd let you move into some haunted mansion without scoping out the history."

"And what did you find?"

"Weirdly, nothing. Like, *suspiciously* nothing. It was a hotel, and the hotel was converted into apartments after World War Two, a big boom time moneywise. The conversion was in a ton of newspapers, but then a few years later the place just falls off the map . . . no articles, nothing."

I frown, getting up from the bed. Ms. Angelli admitted that this place was full of history. So where is it? Assuming *she* can't read walls, how did she learn the Coronado's secrets? And why was she so defensive about sharing them?

"I bet it's like a government conspiracy," Lynds is saying. "Or a witness protection program. Or one of those horror reality films. Have you checked for cameras?"

I laugh, but silently wonder—glancing at the blood-spotted floor—if the truth is worse.

"Have you at least got tenants who look like they belong in a Hitchcock film?"

"Well, so far I've met a morbidly obese antiques hoarder, and a boy who wears eyeliner."

"They call that guyliner," she says.

"Yes. Well." I stretch and head for the bedroom door. "I'd call it stupid, but he's rather nice to look at. I can't tell if the eyeliner makes him attractive, or if he's good-looking in spite of it."

"At least you've *got* nice things to look at."

I step around the ghostly drops on the floor and venture out into the apartment. It's dusk, and none of the lights are on.

"How are *you* doing?" I ask. Lyndsey possesses the gift of normalcy. I bathe in it. "Summer courses? College prep? Learning new languages? New instruments? Single-handedly saving countries?"

Lyndsey laughs. It's so easy for her. "You make me sound like an overachiever."

I feel the scratch of letters and pull the list from my jeans.

Alex King. 13.

"That's because you *are* an overachiever," I say.

"I just like to stay busy."

Come over here, then, I think, pocketing the list. *This place would keep you busy.*

I distinctly hear the thrum of guitar strings. "What's that noise?" I ask.

"I'm tuning, that's all."

"Lyndsey Newman, do you actually have me on speaker just so you can talk and tune a guitar at the same time? You're jeopardizing the sanctity of our conversations."

"Relax. The parents have vacated. Some kind of gala. They left in fancy dress an hour ago. What about yours?"

I find two notes on the kitchen counter.

My mother's reads: *Store! Love, Mom.*

My father's reads: *Checking in at work. —D*

"Similarly out," I say, "but minus the fancy dress and the togetherness."

I retreat to the bedroom.

"The place to yourself?" she says. "I hope you're having a party."

"I can barely hear over the music and drinking games. I better tell them to quiet down before someone calls the cops."

"Talk soon, okay?" she says. "I miss you." She really means it.

"I miss you, Lynds." I mean it too.

The phone goes dead. I toss it onto the bed and stare down at the faded spots on my floor.

Questions eat at me. What happened in this room? Who was the boy? And whose blood was he covered in? Maybe it's not my job, maybe it's an infraction to find out, a misuse of power, but every member of the Archive takes the same oath.

We protect the past. And the way I see it, that means we need to understand it.

And if neither Lyndsey's search engines nor Ms. Angelli are going to tell me anything, I'll have to see for myself. I tug the ring from my finger, and before I can chicken out, I kneel, press my hands to the floor, and reach.

NINE

THERE IS A GIRL sitting on a bed, knees pulled up beneath her chin.

I run the memories back until I find the small calendar by the bed that reads MARCH, the blue dress on the corner chair, the black book on the table by the bed. Da was right. *Bread crumbs and bookmarks.* My fingers found their way.

The girl on the bed is thin in a delicate way, with light blond hair that falls in waves around her narrow face. She is younger than I am, and talking to the boy with the bloodstained hands, only right now his hands are still clean. Her words are a murmur, nothing more than static, and the boy won't stand still. I can tell by the girl's eyes that she's talking slowly, insistently, but the boy's replies are urgent, punctuated by his hands, which move through the air in sweeping gestures. He can't be much older than she is, but judging by his feverish face and the way he sways, he's been drinking. He looks like he's about to be sick. Or scream.

The girl sees it too, because she slides from the bed and offers him a glass of water from the top of the dresser. He knocks the glass away hard and it shatters, the sound little more than a crackle. His fingers dig into her arm. She pushes him away a few times before he loses his grip and stumbles back into the bed frame. She turns, runs. He's up, swiping a large shard of glass from the floor. It cuts into his hand as he lunges for her. She's at the door when he reaches her, and they tumble into the hall.

I drag my hand along the floor until I can see them through the doorway, and then I wish I couldn't. He's on top of her, and they are a tangle of glass and blood and fighting limbs, her slender bare feet kicking under him as he pins her down.

And then the struggle slows. And stops.

He drops the shard beside her body and staggers to his feet, and I can see her, the lines carved across her arms, the far deeper cut across her throat. The shard pressed into her own palm. He stands over her a moment before turning back toward the bedroom. Toward me. He is covered in blood. *Her* blood. My stomach turns, and I have to resist the urge to scramble away. He is not here. I am not there.

You killed her, I whisper. Who are you? Who is she?

He staggers into the room, and for a moment he breaks, slides into a crouch, rocking. But then he gets back up. He looks down at himself, the glitter of broken glass at his feet, and over at the body, and begins to wipe his bloody hands slowly and then frantically on his bloody shirt. He scrambles over to the closet and yanks a black coat from a hook, forcing it on and pulling it closed. And then he runs, and I'm left staring at the girl's body in the hall.

The blood is soaking into her pale blond hair. Her eyes are open, and in that moment, all I want is to cross to her and close them.

I pull my hands from the floor and open my eyes, and the memory shatters into the now, taking the body with it. The room is my room again, but I still see her in that horrible light-echo way, like she's burned into my vision. I shove my ring on, tripping over half the boxes as I focus on the simple need to get the hell out of this apartment.

I slam the door to 3F behind me and sag against it, sliding to the floor and pressing my palms to my eyes, breathing into the space between my chest and knees.

Revulsion claws up my throat and I swallow hard and picture Da taking one look at me and laughing through smoke, telling me how silly I look. I picture the council who inducted me seeing straight through the worlds and declaring me unfit. I am not M, I think. Not some silly squeamish girl. I am more. I am a Keeper. I am Da's replacement.

It's not the blood, or even the murder, though both turn my stomach. It's the fact that he *ran*. All I can think is, did he get away? Did he get away with that?

Suddenly I need to move, to hunt, to do *something*, and I get up, steadying myself against the door, and pull the list from my pocket, thankful to have a name.

But the name is gone. The paper is blank.

"You look like you could use a muffin."

I shove the paper back in my jeans and look up to find Wesley Ayers at the other end of the hall, tossing a still-wrapped *Welcome!* muffin up and down like a baseball. I don't feel like doing this right now, like putting on a face and acting normal.

"You still have that?" I ask wearily.

"Oh, I ate mine," he says, heading toward me. "I swiped this one from Six B. They're out of town this week."

I nod.

When he reaches me, his face falls. "You all right?"

"I'm fine," I lie.

He sets the muffin on the carpet. "You look like you need some fresh air."

What I need are answers. "Is there a place here where they keep records? Logs, anything like that?"

Wesley's head tilts when he thinks. "There's the study. Mostly old books, classics, anything that looks, well, like it belongs in a study.

But it might have something. It's kind of the opposite of fresh air, though, and there's this garden I was going to show——"

"Tell you what. Point me to the study, and then you can show me whatever you want."

Wesley's smile lights up his face, from his sharp chin all the way to the tips of his spiked hair. "Deal."

He bypasses the elevator and leads me down the flight of concrete steps to the grand staircase, and from there down into the lobby. I keep my distance, remembering the last time we touched. He's several steps below me, and from this angle, I can just see beneath the collar of his black shirt. Something glints, a charm on a leather cord. I lean, trying to see——

"Where are you going?" comes a small voice. Wesley jumps, grabs his chest.

"Jeez, Jill," he says. "Way to scare a guy in front of a girl."

It takes me several seconds to find Jill, but finally I spot her in one of the leather high-backed chairs in a front corner, reading a book. The book comes up to the bridge of her nose. She skims the pages with sharp blue eyes, and every now and then turns her attention up, as if she's waiting for something.

"He spooks easily," she calls behind her book.

Wesley runs his fingers through his hair and manages a tight laugh. "Not one of my proudest traits."

"You should see what happens when you really surprise him," offers Jill.

"That's enough, brat."

Jill turns a page with a flourish.

Wesley casts a glance back at me and offers his arm. "Onward?"

I smile thinly but decline to take it. "After you," I say.

He leads the way across the lobby. "What are you looking for, anyway?"

"Just wanted to learn about the building. Do you know much about it?"

"Can't say I do." He guides me down a hall on the other side of the grand stairs.

"Here we are," he says, pushing open the door to the study. It's stuffed to the brim with books. A corner desk and a few leather chairs furnish the space, and I scan the spines for anything useful. My eyes trail over encyclopedias, several volumes of poetry, a complete set of Dickens. . . .

"Come on, come on," he says, crossing the room. "Keep up."

"Study first," I say. "Remember?"

"I pointed it out." He gestures to the room as he reaches a pair of doors at the far side of the study. "You can come back later. The books aren't going anywhere."

"Just give me a—"

He flings the doors open. Beyond them, there's a garden flooded with twilight and air and chaos. Wesley steps out onto the moss-covered rocks, and I drag my attention from the books and follow him out.

The dying light lends the garden a glow, shadows weaving through vines, colors dipping darker, deeper. The space is old and fresh at once, and I forget how much I've missed the feel of green. Our old house had a small yard, but it was nothing like Da's place. He had the city at his front but the country at his back, land that stretched out in a wild mass. Nature is constantly growing, changing, one of the few things that can't hold memories. You forget how much clutter there is in the world, in the people and things, until you're surrounded by green. And even if they don't hear and see and feel the past the way

I do, I wonder if normal people feel this too—the quiet.

"'The sun retreats,'" Wes says softly, reverently. "'The day, out-lived, is o'er. It hastens hence and lo, a new world is alive.'"

My eyebrows must be creeping up, because when he glances over his shoulder at me, he gives me his slanted smile.

"What? Don't look so surprised. Beneath this shockingly good hair is something vaguely resembling a brain." He crosses the garden to a stone bench woven over with ivy, and brushes away the tendrils to reveal the words etched into the rock.

"It's *Faust*," he says. "And it's possible I spend a good deal of time here."

"I can see why." It's bliss. If bliss had gone untouched for fifty years. The place is tangled, unkempt. And perfect. A pocket of peace in the city.

Wesley slides onto the bench. He rolls up his sleeves and leans back to watch the streaking clouds, blowing a blue-black chunk of hair from his face.

"The study never changes, but this place is different every moment, and really best at sun fall. Besides"—he waves a hand at the Coronado—"I can give you a proper tour some other time."

"I thought you didn't live here," I say, looking up at the dimming sky.

"I don't. But my cousin, Jill, does, with her mom. Jill and I are both only children, so I try to keep an eye on her. You have any siblings?"

My chest tightens, and for a moment I don't know how to answer. No one's asked that, not since Ben died. In our old town, everyone knew better, skipped straight to pity and condolences. I don't want either from Wesley, so I shake my head, hating myself even as I do, because it feels like I'm betraying Ben, his memory.

"Yeah, so you know how it is. It can get lonely. And hanging around this old place is better than the alternative."

"Which is?" I find myself asking.

"My dad's. New fiancée. Satan in a skirt, and all. So I end up here more often than not." He arches back, letting his spine follow the curve of the bench.

I close my eyes, relishing the feel of the garden, the cooling air and the smell of flowers and ivy. The horror hidden in my room begins to feel distant, manageable, though the question still whispers in my mind: *Did he get away?* I breathe deep and try to push it from my thoughts, just for a moment.

And then I feel Wesley stand and come up beside me. His fingers slide through mine. The noise hits a moment before his rings knock against mine, the bass and beat thrumming up my arm and through my chest. I try to push back, to block him out, but it makes it worse, the sound of his touch crushing even though his fingers are feather-light on mine. He lifts my hand and gently turns it over.

"You look like you lost a fight with the moving equipment," he says, gesturing to the bandage on my forearm.

I try to laugh. "Looks like it."

He lowers my hand and untangles his fingers. The noise fades, my chest loosening by degrees until I can breathe, like coming up through water. Again my eyes are drawn to the leather cord around his neck, the charm buried beneath the black fabric of his shirt. My gaze drifts down his arms, past his rolled sleeves, toward the hand that just let go of mine. Even in the twilight I can see a faint scar.

"Looks like you've lost a couple fights of your own," I say, running my fingers through the air near his hand, not daring to touch. "How did you get that?"

"A stint as a spy. I wasn't much good."

A crooked line runs down the back of his hand. "And that?"

"Scuff with a lion."

Watching Wesley lie is fascinating.

"And that?"

"Caught a piranha bare-handed."

No matter how absurd the tale, he says it steady and simple, with the ease of truth. A scratch runs along his forearm. "And that?"

"Knife fight in a Paris alley."

I search his skin for marks, our bodies drawing closer without touching.

"Dove through a window."

"Icicle."

"Wolf."

I reach up, my fingers hovering over a nick on his hairline.

"And this?"

"A History."

Everything stops.

His whole face changes right after he says it, like he's been punched in the stomach. The silence hangs between us.

And then he does an unfathomable thing. He smiles.

"If you were clever," he says slowly, "you would have asked me what a History was."

I am still frozen when he reaches out and brushes a finger over the three lines etched into the surface of my ring, then twists one of his own rings to reveal a cleaner but identical set of lines. The Archive's insignia. When I don't react—because no fluid lie came to me and now it's too late—he closes the gap between us, close enough that I can *almost* hear the bass again, radiating off his skin. His thumb hooks under the cord around my throat and guides my key out from under my shirt. It glints in the twilight. Then he fetches the key from around his own neck.

"There," he says cheerfully. "Now we're on the same page."

"You knew," I say at last.

His forehead wrinkles. "I've known since the moment you came into the hall last night."

"How?"

"Your eyes went to the keyhole. You did a decent job of hiding the look, but I was watching for it. Patrick told me there would be a new Keeper here. Wanted to see for myself."

"Funny, because Patrick didn't tell *me* there was an old one."

"The Coronado isn't really my territory. It hasn't been anyone's for ages. I like to check in on Jill, and I keep an eye on the place while I'm at it. It's an old building, so you know how it goes." He taps a nail against his key. "I even have special access. Your doors are my doors."

"You're the one who cleared my list," I say, the pieces fitting together. "There were names on my list, and they just disappeared."

"Oh, sorry." He rubs his neck. "I didn't even think about that. This place has been shared for so long. They always keep the Coronado doors unlocked for me. Didn't mean any harm."

A moment of quiet hangs between us.

"So," he says.

"So," I say.

A smile begins to creep up the side of Wesley's face.

"What?" I ask.

"Oh, come on, Mac . . ." He blows at a chunk of hair hanging in his face.

"Come on, what?" I say, still sizing him up.

"You don't think it's cool?" He gives up and fixes his hair with his fingers. "To meet another Keeper?"

"I've never met one except for my grandfather." It sounds naive, but it never occurred to me to think of others. I mean, I knew they existed, but out of sight, out of mind. The territories, the branches of the Archive—I think they're all designed to make you feel like an only child. Unique. Or solitary.

"Me either," Wes is saying. "What a broadening experience this is." He squares his shoulders toward me. "My name is Wesley Ayers, and I am a Keeper." He breaks out into a full grin. "It feels good to say it out loud. Try."

I look up at him, the words caught in my throat. I have spent four years with this secret bottled in me. Four years lying, hiding, and bleeding, to hide what I am from everyone I meet.

"My name is Mackenzie Bishop," I say. Four years since Da died, and not a single slip. Not to Mom or Dad, not to Ben, or even to Lynds. "And I am a Keeper."

The world doesn't end. People don't die. Doors don't open. Crew don't pour out and arrest me. Wesley Ayers beams enough for both of us.

"I patrol the Narrows," he says.

"I hunt Histories," I say.

"I return them to the Archive."

It becomes a game, whispered and breathless.

"I hide who I am."

"I fight with the dead."

"I lie to the living."

"I am alone."

And then I get why Wes can't stop smiling, even though it looks silly with his eyeliner and jet-black hair and hard jaw and scars. I am not alone. The words dance in my mind and in his eyes and against our rings and our keys, and now I smile too.

"Thank you," I say.

"My pleasure," he says, looking up at the sky. "It's getting late. I'd better go."

For one silly, nonsensical moment, I'm scared of his leaving, scared he'll never come back and I'll be left with this, this . . . loneliness. I swallow the strange panic and force myself not to follow him to the study door.

Instead I keep still and watch him tuck his key beneath his shirt, roll his ring so the three lines are hidden against his palm. He looks exactly the same, and I wonder if I do too and how that's possible, considering how I feel—like some door in me has been opened and left ajar.

"Wesley," I call after him, instantly berating myself when he stops and glances back at me.

"Good night," I say lamely.

He smiles and closes the gap between us. His fingers brush over my key before they curl around it, and guide it under the collar of my shirt, the metal cold against my skin.

"Good night, Keeper," he says.

And then he's gone.

TEN

I **LINGER A MOMENT** in the garden after Wes is gone, savoring the taste of our confessions on my tongue, the small defiance of sharing a secret. I focus on the coolness creeping into the air around me, and the hush of the evening.

Da took me onto the stretch of green behind his house once and told me that building walls—blocking out people and their noise— should feel like this. An armor of quiet. Told me that walls were just like a ring but better because they were in my head, and because they could be strong enough to silence anything. If I could just learn to build them.

But I couldn't. I sometimes think that maybe, if I could remember what it felt like, touching people and feeling nothing but skin . . . But I can't, and when I try to block out their noise, it just gets worse, and I feel like I'm in a glass box under the ocean, the sound and pressure cracking in. Da ran out of time to teach me, so all I have are frustrating memories of him wrapping his arm around people without even flinching, making it look so easy, so normal.

I would give anything to be normal.

The thought creeps in, and I force it away. No I wouldn't. I wouldn't give anything. I wouldn't give the bond I had with Da. I wouldn't give the time I have with Ben's drawer. I wouldn't give Roland, and I wouldn't give the Archive, with its impossible light and the closest thing I've ever felt to peace. This is all I have. This is all I am.

I head for the study doors, thinking of the murdered girl and the bloodstained boy. I have a job. SERVAMUS MEMORIAM. I push the doors open, and stiffen when I see the large woman behind the desk in the corner.

"Ms. Angelli."

Her eyebrows inch into a nest of hair I strongly suspect is a wig, and a moment of surprise passes before recognition spreads across her broad face. If she's upset to see me after this morning, she doesn't show it, and I wonder for once if I read too much into her rush to leave. Maybe she really was late for an appraisal.

"Mackenzie Bishop, of the baked goods," she says. Her voice is quieter here in the study, almost reverent. Several large texts are spread before her, the corners of the pages worn. A cup of tea sits nestled in the space between two books.

"What are you reading?" I ask.

"Histories, mostly." I know she only means the kind in books, the *little h* kind, as Da would say. Still, I flinch.

"Where did they all come from?" I ask, gesturing toward the volumes stacked on the table and lining the walls.

"The books? Oh, they appeared over time. A resident took one and left two behind. The study simply grew. I'm sure they stocked it when the Coronado was first converted, leather-bound classics and atlases and encyclopedias. But these days it's a delightful mix of old and new and odd. Just the other night I found a romance novel mixed in with the directories! Imagine."

My pulse skips. "Directories?"

Something nervous shifts in her face, but she points a ringed finger over her shoulder. My eyes skim the walls of books behind her until they land on a dozen or so slightly larger than the rest, more uniform. In the place of a title, each spine has a set of dates.

"They chronicle the residents?" I ask casually, eyes skimming the years. The dates go all the way back to the earliest parts of the past century. The first half of the books are red. The second half are blue.

"They were first used while the Coronado was still a hotel," she explains. "A kind of guestbook, if you will. Those red ones, those are from the hotel days. The blue ones are from the conversion on."

I round the table to the shelf that bears the books' weight. Pulling the most recent one from the wall and flipping through, I see that each directory comprises five years' worth of residential lists, an ornate page dividing each year. I go to the last divider, the most recent year, and turn until I get to the page for the third floor. In the column for 3F, someone has crossed out the printed word *Vacant* and added *Mr. and Mrs. Peter Bishop* in pencil. Flipping back through, I find that 3F has been vacant for two years, and was rented before that to a *Mr. Bill Lighton*. I close the book, return it to the shelf, and immediately take up the previous directory.

"Looking for something?" Ms. Angelli asks. There's a subtle tension in her voice.

"Just curious," I say, again searching for 3F. Still *Mr. Lighton*. Then *Ms. Jane Olinger*. I pause, but I know from reading the walls that it was more than ten years ago, and besides, the girl was too young to be living alone. I reshelve the book and pull the next one down.

Ms. Olinger again.

Before that, *Mr. and Mrs. Albert Locke*. Still not far enough.

Before that, *Vacant*.

Is this how normal people learn the past?

Next, a *Mr. Kenneth Shaw*.

And then I find what I'm looking for. The wall of black, the dead space between most of the memories and the murder. I run my finger down the column.

Vacant.

Vacant.

Vacant.

Not just one set, either. There are whole books of *Vacant*. Ms. Angelli watches me too intently, but I keep pulling the books down until I reach the last blue book, the one that starts with the conversion: 1950 – 54.

The 1954 book is marked *Vacant*, but when I reach the divider marked *1953*, I stop.

3F is missing.

The entire floor is missing.

The entire *year* is missing.

In its place is a stack of blank paper. I turn back through 1952 and 1951. Both are blank. There's no record of the murdered girl. There's no record of *anyone*. Three entire years are just . . . missing. The inaugural year, 1950, is there, but there's no name written under 3F. What did Lyndsey say? There was nothing on record. *Suspiciously* nothing.

I drop the blue book open on the table, nearly upsetting Ms. Angelli's tea.

"You look a touch pale, Mackenzie. What is it?"

"There are pages missing."

She frowns. "The books are old. Perhaps something fell out. . . ."

"No," I snap. "The years are deliberately blank."

Apartment 3F sat vacant for nearly two decades after the mysterious missing chunk of time. The murder. It had to have happened in those years.

"Surely," she says, more to herself than to me, "they must be archived somewhere."

"Yeah, I——" And it hits me. "You're right. You're totally right." Whoever did this tampered with evidence in the Outer, but they can't tamper with it in the Archive. I'm already out of the leather chair. "Thanks for your help," I say, scooping up the directory and returning it to its shelf.

Ms. Angelli's eyebrows inch up. "Well, I didn't really do——"

"You did. You're brilliant. Thanks. Good night!" I'm at the door, then through it, into the Coronado's lobby, and pulling the key from my neck and the ring from my finger before I even reach the door set into the stairs.

"What brings you to the Archive, Miss Bishop?"

It's Lisa at the desk. She looks up, pen hovering over a series of ledgers set side by side behind the QUIET PLEASE sign, which I'm pretty sure is her contribution. Her black bob frames her face, and her eyes are keen but kind—two different shades—behind a pair of green horn-rimmed glasses. Lisa is a Librarian, of course, but unlike Roland, or Patrick, or most of the others, for that matter, she really looks the part (aside from the fact that one of her eyes is glass, a token from her days as Crew).

I fiddle with the key around my wrist.

"Couldn't sleep," I lie, even though it's not that late. It's my default response here, the way people always answer *How are you?* with *Good* or *Great* or *Fine*, even when they're not. "Those look nice," I say, gesturing to her nails. They're bright gold.

"You think so?" she asks, admiring them. "Found the polish in the closets. Roland's idea. He says they're all the rage right now."

I'm not surprised. In addition to his public addiction to trashy magazines, Roland has a private addiction to stealing glances at newly added Histories. "He would know."

Her smile thins. "What can I do for you tonight, Miss Bishop?" she asks, two-toned eyes leveled on me.

I hesitate. I could tell Lisa what I'm looking for, of course, but I've already used up my quota of Lisa-issued rule-bending coupons this month, what with the visits to Ben's shelf. And I don't have any bartering chips, no tokens from the Outer that she might like. I'm comfortable with Lisa, but if I ask her and she says no, I'll never make it past the desk.

"Is Roland around?" I ask casually. Lisa's gaze lingers, but then she goes back to writing in the ledgers.

"Ninth wing, third hall, fifth room. Last time I checked."

I smile and round the desk to the doors.

"Repeat it," orders Lisa.

I roll my eyes, but parrot, "Nine, three, five."

"Don't get lost," she warns.

My steps slow as I cross into the atrium. The stained glass is dark, as if the sky beyond—if there were a sky—had slipped to night. But still the Archive is bright, well-lit despite the lack of lights. Walking through is like wading into a pool of water. Cool, crisp, beautiful water. It slows you and holds you and washes over you. It is dazzling. Wood and stone and colored glass and calm. I force myself to look down at the dark wood floor, and find my way out of the atrium, repeating the numbers *nine three five, nine three five, nine three five*. It is too easy to go astray.

The Archive is a patchwork, pieces added and altered over the years, and the bit of hall I wander down is made of paler wood, the ceilings still high but the placards on the front of the shelves worn. I reach the fifth room, and the style shifts again, with marble floors and a lower ceiling. Every space is different, and yet in all of them, that steady quiet reigns.

Roland is standing in front of an open drawer, his back to me and his fingertips pressed gently into a man's shoulder.

When I enter the room, his hands shift from the History to its drawer, sliding it closed with one fluid, silent motion. He turns my way, and for a moment his eyes are so . . . sad. But then he blinks and recovers.

"Miss Bishop."

"'Evening, Roland."

There's a table and a pair of chairs in the center of the room, but he doesn't invite me to sit. He seems distracted.

"Are you all right?" I ask.

"Of course." An automatic reply. "What brings you here?"

"I need a favor." His brows knit. "Not Ben. I promise."

He looks around the space, then leads me into the hall beyond, where the walls are free of shelves.

"Go on . . ." he says slowly.

"Something horrible happened in my room. A murder."

A brow arches. "How do you know?"

"Because I read it."

"You shouldn't be reading things unnecessarily, Miss Bishop. The point of that gift is not to indulge in——"

"I know, I know. The perils of curiosity. But don't pretend you're immune to it."

His mouth quirks.

"Look, isn't there any way you can . . ." I cast my arm wide across the room, gesturing at the walls of bodies, of lives.

"Any way I can *what*?"

"Do a search? Look for residents of the Coronado. Her death

would have been in March. Sometime between 1951 and 1953. If I can find the girl here in the Archive, then we can read her and find out who she was, and who *he* was—"

"Why? Just to slake your interest? That's hardly the purpose of these files—"

"Then what is?" I snap. "We're supposed to protect the past. Well, someone is trying to erase it. Years are missing from the Coronado's records. Years in which a girl was *murdered*. The boy who killed her *left*. He ran. I need to find out what happened. I need to know if he got away, and I can't—"

"So that's what this is about," he says under his breath.

"What do you mean?"

"This isn't just about understanding a murder. It's about Ben."

I feel like I've been slapped. "It's not. I—"

"Don't insult me, Miss Bishop. You're a remarkable Keeper, but I know why you can't stand leaving a name on your list. This isn't just about curiosity, it's about closure—"

"Fine. But that doesn't change the fact that something horrible happened in my room, and someone tried to cover it up."

"People do bad things," Roland says quietly.

"Please." Desperation creeps in with the word. I swallow. "Da used to say that Keepers needed three things: skill, luck, and intuition. I have all three. And my gut says something is *wrong*."

He tilts his head a fraction. It's a tell. He's bending.

"Humor me," I say. "Just help me find out who she was, so I can find out who *he* was."

He straightens but pulls a small pad from his pocket and begins to make notes.

"I'll see what I can do."

I smile, careful not to make it broad—I don't want him to think he was conned—just wide enough to read as grateful. "Thank you, Roland."

He grunts. I feel the telltale scratch of letters in my pocket, and retrieve the list to find a new name. *Melanie Allen. 10.* I rub my thumb over the number. Ben's age.

"All well?" he asks casually.

"Just a kid," I say, pocketing the list.

I turn to go, but hesitate. "I'll keep you apprised, Miss Bishop," says Roland in answer to my pause.

"I owe you."

"You always do," he says as I leave.

I wind my way back through the halls and the atrium and into the antechamber, where Lisa is flipping through the pages of her ledgers, eyes narrowed in concentration.

"Going so soon?" she asks as I pass.

"Another name," I say. She should know. She gave it to me. "The Coronado is certainly keeping me busy."

"Old buildings—"

"I know, I know."

"We've been diverting traffic, so to speak, as best we could, but it will be better now that you're on the premises—"

"Joy."

"It's safe to say you'll experience a higher number of Histories here than in your previous territory. Maybe two to three times. No more—"

"Two to three *times?*"

Lisa folds her hands. "The world tests us for reasons, Miss Bishop," she says sweetly. "Don't you want to be Crew?"

I hate that line. I hate it because it is the Librarians' way of saying *deal with it.*

She locks eyes with me over her horn-rimmed glasses, daring me to press the issue. "Anything else, Miss Bishop?"

"No," I grumble. It's rare to see Lisa so rigid. "I think that's all."

"Have a nice night," she calls, offering a small, gold-flecked wave before taking up her pen. I head back into the Narrows to find Melanie.

There's this moment when I step into the Narrows, right after the Archive door closes behind me and before I start hunting; this little sliver of time where the world feels still. Not quiet, of course, but steady, calm. And then I hear a far-off cry or the shuffle of steps or any one of a dozen sounds, and all of them remind me it's not the calm that keeps me still. It's fear. Da used to say that only fools and cowards scorned fear. Fear keeps you alive.

My fingers settle on the stained wall, the key on my wrist clinking against it. I close my eyes and press down, reach until I catch hold of the past. My fingers, then palms, then wrists go numb. I'm just about to roll the memories back in search of Melanie Allen, when I'm cut off by a sound, sharp like metal against rock.

I blink and draw back from the wall.

The sound is too close.

I follow the noise down the corridor and around the corner.

The hall is empty.

Pausing, I slide the Archive list from my pocket, checking it again, but ten-year-old Melanie is the only name there.

The sound comes a second time, grating as nails, from the end of the hall, and I hurry down it, turn left and—

The knife comes out of nowhere.

It slashes, and I drop the paper and jerk back, the blade narrowly missing my stomach as it carves a line through the air. I recover and dodge sideways as the knife slices the air again, clumsy but fast. The hand holding the knife is massive, the knuckles scarred, and the History behind the knife looks just as rough. He is height and muscle, filling the hall, his eyes half buried beneath thick, angry brows, the irises fully black. He's been out long enough to slip. Why wasn't he listed? My stomach sinks when I recognize the knife in his hand as Jackson's. A blade of folded metal the length of my hand running into a dark hilt and—somewhere hidden by his palm—a hole drilled into the grip.

He slashes again, and I drop to a crouch, trying to think; but he's fast, and it's all I can do to stay on my feet and in one piece. The hall is too narrow to take out his legs, so I spring up, get a foot on the wall, and push off, crushing his face into the opposite wall with my boot. His head connects with a sound like bricks, but he barely flinches, and I hit the ground and roll just in time to avoid another slice.

Even as I dodge and duck, I can tell I'm losing ground, being forced backward.

"How do you have that key, Abbie?"

He's already slipped. He's looking at me but seeing someone else, and whoever this Abbie is, he doesn't seem too happy with her.

I scan him desperately for clues as I duck. A faded jacket with a small nameplate sewn into the front reads *Hooper*.

He swings the knife like an ax, chopping the air. "Where did you get the key?"

Why isn't he on my list?

"Give it to me," he growls. "Or I'll cut it from your pretty wrist."

He slashes with so much force that the knife hits a door and sticks, the metal embedded in the wood. I seize the chance and kick him as hard as I can in the chest, hoping the momentum will force him to let go of the blade. It doesn't. Pain rolls up my leg from the blow, which knocks Hooper back just hard enough to help him free his weapon from the Narrows wall. His grip tightens on the handle.

I know I'm running out of room.

"I need it," he groans. "You know I need it."

I need to pause this whole moment until I can figure out what a full-grown History is doing in my territory and how I'm going to get out of here without considerable blood loss.

Another step back and a wall comes up to meet my shoulders.

My stomach twists.

Hooper presses forward, and the cool tip of the knife comes up just below my chin, so close that I'm afraid to swallow.

"The key. Now."

ELEVEN

YOU HOLD OUT the slip of paper you keep rolled behind your ear.

I tap the small 7 beside the boy's name. "Are they all so young?"

"Not all," you say, smoothing the paper, an unlit cigarette between your teeth. "But most."

"Why?"

You take the cigarette out, jabbing the air with the unlit tip. "That is the most worthless question in the world. Use your words. Be specific. *Why* is like *bah* or *moo* or that silly sound pigeons make."

"Why are most of the ones that wake so young?"

"Some are—were—troubled. But most are restless. Didn't live enough, maybe." Your tone shifts. "But everyone has a History, Kenzie. Young and old." I can see you testing the words in your mouth. "The older the History, the heavier they sleep. The older ones that wake have something in them, something different, something dark. Troubled. Unstable. They're bad people. Dangerous. They're the ones who tend to get into the Outer. The ones who fall into the hands of Crew."

"Keeper-Killers," I whisper.

You nod.

I straighten. "How do I beat them?"

"Strength. Skill." You run a hand over my hair. "And luck. Lots of luck."

My back presses against the wall as the tip of the knife nicks my throat, and I really don't want to die like this.

"Key," Hooper growls again, his black eyes dancing. "God, Abbie, I just want out. I want out and he said you had it, said I had to get it—so give it to me now."

He?

The knife bites down.

My mind is suddenly horribly blank. I take a shallow breath.

"Okay," I say, reaching for the key. The cord is looped three times around my wrist, and I'm hoping that somewhere between untangling it and motioning toward him, I can get the knife away.

I unloop it once.

And then something catches my eye. Down the hall, beyond Hooper's massive form, a shadow moves. A shape in the dark. The form slips silently forward, and I can't see his face, only his outline and a sweep of silver-blond hair. He slides up behind the History as I unloop the cord a second time.

I unloop the cord a final time, and Hooper is snatching the key, the knife retreating a fraction from my throat, when the stranger's arm coils around the History's neck.

The next moment Hooper is slammed backward onto the ground, the knife tumbling from his grasp. The motion is clean, efficient. The stranger catches the blade and drives it down toward the History's broad chest, but he's a beat too slow, and Hooper grabs hold of him and flings him into the nearest wall with an audible crack.

And then I see it, glittering on the floor between us.

My key.

I dive for it as Hooper sees, and lunges too. He reaches it first, but between one blink and the next, the blond man has his hands around Hooper's jaw, and swiftly breaks his neck.

Before Hooper can sag forward, the stranger catches his body and slams it against the nearest door, driving the knife straight through his chest, the blade and most of the hilt buried deep enough to pin his body against the wooden door. I stare at the History's limp form, chin against his chest, wondering how long it will take him to recover from that.

The stranger is staring, too, at the place where his hand meets the knife and the knife meets Hooper's body, the wound bloodless. He curls and uncurls his fingers around the handle.

"He won't stay like that," I say, desperate to keep the tremor from my voice as I rewrap the key cord around my wrist.

His voice is quiet, low. "I doubt it."

He lets go of the knife, and Hooper's body hangs against the door. I feel a drop of blood running down my throat. I wipe it away. I wish my hands would stop shaking. My list is a spot of white on the blackened floor. I recover it, muttering a curse.

Right below Melanie Allen's name sits a new one in clean print.

Albert Hooper. 45.

A little late. I look up as the stranger brings a hand to the slope of his neck and frowns.

"Are you hurt?" I ask, remembering how hard he hit the wall.

He rolls his shoulder first one way and then the other, a slow testing motion. "I don't think so."

He's young, late teens, maybe, whitish blond hair long enough to drift into his eyes, across his cheekbones. He's dressed in all black, not punk or goth, but simple, well-fitting. His clothing blurs into the dark around him.

The moment is surreal. I can't shake the feeling that I've seen him before, but I know I'd remember if I did. And now we're standing in the Narrows, the body of a History hanging like a coat on the door between us. He doesn't seem bothered by that. If his combat skills aren't enough to mark him as a Keeper, his composure is.

"Who are you?" I ask, trying to force as much authority into my voice as possible.

"My name's Owen," he says. "Owen Chris Clarke."

His eyes meet mine as he says it, and my chest tightens. Everything about him is calm, even. His movements when fighting were fluid, efficient to the point of elegant. But his eyes are piercing. Wolfish. Eyes like one of Ben's drawings, sketched out in a stark, pale blue.

I feel dazed, both by Hooper's sudden attack and Owen's equally sudden appearance, but I don't have time to collect myself, because Hooper's body shudders against the door.

"What's your name?" Owen asks. And for some reason, I tell him the truth.

"Mackenzie."

He smiles. He has the kind of smile that barely touches his mouth.

"Where did you come from?" I ask, and Owen glances over his shoulder, when Hooper's eyelids flutter.

The door he's braced against is marked with white, the edge of the chalk circle peering out from his back, and that's all I have time to notice before Hooper's black eyes snap open.

I spring into action, driving the key into the door and turning the lock as I grip the knife in the History's chest and pull. The door falls open and the knife comes out; and I drive my boot into Hooper's stomach, sending him back a few steps, just enough. His shoes hit the white of the Returns, and I catch the door and slam it shut between us.

I hear Hooper beat against it once before falling deathly silent. I spin to face the Narrows, only seconds having passed, but Owen Chris Clarke is gone.

I slump down onto the worn runner of the Coronado's stairs and slide my ring back on, dropping the knife and the list onto the steps beside me. Hooper's name is gone now. Little good it did, since it didn't show up until I was halfway through the fight. I should report it, but to who? The Librarians would probably just turn it into a lecture on making Crew, on being prepared. But how could I have been prepared?

My eyes burn as I replay the fight. Clumsy. Weak. Caught off guard. I should never, ever be off guard. I know he'd lecture, I know he'd scold; but for the first time in years, the memories are not enough. I wish I could talk to Da.

"I nearly lost."

It is a whispered confession to an empty lobby, the strength leaching from my voice. Behind my eyes, Owen Chris Clarke breaks Hooper's neck. "I didn't know how to fight him, Da. I felt helpless." The word scratches my throat. "I've been doing this for years and I've never felt that." My hands tremble faintly.

I turn my thoughts from Hooper to Owen as my fingers drift toward the knife. His fluid movements, the ease with which he handled the weapon and the History. Wesley said the territory had been shared. Maybe Hooper was on Owen's list first. Or maybe Owen, like Wesley, had nothing better to do and happened to be in the right place at the right time.

I turn the knife absently between my fingers, and stop. There's something etched into the metal, right above the hilt. Three small lines. The Archive mark. My stomach twists. The weapon belonged to a member of the Archive—Keeper, Crew, Librarian—so how did it end up in the hands of a History? Did Jackson swipe it when he escaped?

I rub my eyes. It's late. I tighten my grip on the knife. Maybe I'll need it. I drag myself to my feet, and I'm about to go upstairs when I hear it.

Music.

It must have been playing all along. I turn my head from side to side, trying to decipher where it's coming from, and see that a sheet of paper has been tacked beneath the café sign: *Coming Soon!* announced in the cleanest, most legible version of my mother's script. I head for the sign, but then I remember that I'm holding a large, unsheathed, and very conspicuous knife. There's a planter in the corner where the grand stairs meet the wall, and I set the weapon carefully inside before crossing the lobby. The music grows. Into the hall, and it's louder still, then through the door on the right, down a step and through another door, the notes leading me like bread crumbs.

I find my mother kneeling in a pool of light.

It's not light, I realize, but clean, pale stone. Her head is bent as she scours the floor, the tiles of which, it turns out, are not gray at all, but a stunning pearlescent white marble. One section of the counter, too, where Mom has already asserted her cleaning prowess, is gleaming white granite, run through with threads of black and gold. These spots glitter, like gems across coal. The radio blasts, a pop song that peaks then trails off into commercials, but Mom doesn't seem to register anything but the *whoosh* of her sponge and the spreading pool of white. In the middle of the floor, partially revealed, is a rust-colored pattern. A rose, petal after petal of inlaid stone, an even, earthy red.

"Wow," I say.

She looks up suddenly. "Mackenzie, I didn't see you there."

She gets to her feet. She looks like a human cleaning rag, as if she simply transferred all the dirt from the café onto herself. On one of the counters a bag of groceries sits, forgotten. Condensation makes the plastic bag cling to the once-cold contents.

"It's amazing," I say. "There's actually something underneath the dust."

She beams, hands on her hips. "I know. It's going to be perfect."

Another pop song starts up on the radio, but I reach over and turn it off.

"How long have you been down here, Mom?"

She blinks several times, looks surprised. As if she hadn't thought about time and its penchant for moving forward. Her eyes register the darkness beyond the windows, then travel back to the neglected groceries. Something in her sags. And for a moment, I see her. Not the watts-too-bright, smile-till-it-hurts her, but the real one. The mother who lost her little boy.

"Oh, I'm sorry, Mac," she says, rubbing the back of her hand across her forehead. "I completely lost track of time." Her hands are red and raw. She isn't even wearing plastic gloves. She tries to smile again, but it falters.

"Hey, it's fine," I say. I hoist the soap-filled bucket onto the counter, wincing as the weight sends pain through my bandaged arm, and dump its contents into the sink. The sink, by the looks of it, could use it. I hook the empty container on my elbow. "Let's go upstairs."

Mom suddenly looks exhausted. She picks up the groceries from the counter, but I take them from her.

"I got it," I say, my arm aching. "Are you hungry? I can heat you up some dinner."

Mom nods wearily. "That would be great."

"All right," I say. "Let's go home."

Home. The word still tastes like sandpaper in my mouth. But it makes Mom smile—a tired, true smile—so it's worth it.

I'm so tired my bones hurt. But I can't sleep.

I press my palms against my eyes, going through the fight with Hooper over and over and over again, scouring the scene for what I could have—should have—done differently. I think of Owen, the swift, efficient movements, the breaking of the History's neck, the plunging of the knife into his chest. My fingers drift to my sternum, then inch down until they rest on the place where it ends.

I sit up, reach beneath the bed, and free the knife from the lip of bed frame, where I hid it. Once Mom was settled, I went back to the lobby and rescued it from the planter. Now it glints wickedly in the darkened room, the Archive mark like ink on the shining metal. Whose was it?

I slide off my ring, letting it fall to the comforter, and close my hand over the hilt. The hum of memories buzzes against my palm. Weapons, even small ones, are easy to read because they tend to have such vivid, violent pasts. I close my eyes and catch hold of the thread inside. Two memories roll backward, the more recent one with Hooper—I watch myself pressed against the wall, eyes wide— and the older one with Jackson. But before Jackson brought it into the Narrows, there's . . . *nothing.* Only flat black. This blade should be filled to the brim with stories, and instead it's like it doesn't have a past. But the three marks on the metal say otherwise. What if Jackson didn't steal it? What if someone sent him into the Narrows armed?

I blink, trying to dispel my growing unease along with the matte black of missing memories.

The only bright side is that, wherever this weapon came from, it's mine now. I hook my finger through the hole in the handle and twirl the blade slowly. I close my hand around the handle, stopping its path, and the hilt hits my palm with a satisfying snap, the metal tracing the line up my forearm. I smile. It is an amazing weapon. In fact, I'm fairly certain I could kill myself with it. But having it, holding it, makes me feel better. I'll have to find a way to bind it to my calf, to keep it from sight, from reach. Da's warnings echo in my head, but I quiet them.

I put my ring back on and return the knife to its hidden lip beneath the bed, promising myself I won't *use* it. I tell myself I won't need to. I lie back, less shaken, but no closer to sleep. My eyes settle on the blue bear propped on my side table, the black glasses perched on its nose. Nights like this I wish I could sit and talk to Ben, wear my mind out, but I can't go back to the stacks so soon. I think of calling Lyndsey, but it's late, and what would I say?

How was your day? . . . Yeah? Oh, mine?

I got attacked by a Keeper-Killer.

I know! And saved by a stranger who just vanished—

And that guyliner boy, he's a Keeper!

. . . No, Keeper *with a capital* K.

And there's the murder in my room. Someone tried to cover it up, ripped the pages right out of the history books.

Oh, and I almost forgot. Someone in the Archive might be trying to get me killed.

I laugh. It's a strained sound, but it helps.

And then I yawn, and soon, somehow, I find sleep.

TWELVE

THE NEXT DAY *Melanie Allen. 10.* has been joined by *Jena Greeth. 14.* but the moment I emerge from my room to hunt, Mom appears with an apron and a revived high-wattage smile, thrusts a box of cleaning supplies into my hands, and drops a book on top.

"Coffee shop duty!"

She says it like I've been given a prize, a reward. My forearm still aches dully, and the box bulges in my arms, threatening to crumble.

"I have a vague idea of what cleaning supplies do, but what's with the book?"

"Your father picked up your school's reading list."

I look at my mother, then at the calendar on the kitchen wall, then at the sunlight streaming in the window. "It's summer."

"Yes, it's a *summer* reading list," she says cheerfully. "Now, off with you. You can clean or you can read, or you can clean and then read, or read and then clean, or——"

"I got it." I could beg off, lie, but I'm still feeling shaky from last night and I wouldn't mind a couple hours as M right now, a taste of normalcy. Besides, there's a Narrows door *in* the coffee shop.

Downstairs, the overhead lights blink sleepily on. I drop the box on the counter, letting it regain its composure as I dig out the book. Dante's *Inferno*. You've got to be kidding me. I consider the cover, which features a good deal of hellfire and proudly announces that this is the SAT prep edition, complete with starred vocabulary. I turn to the first page and begin to read.

In the midway of this our mortal life, I found me in a gloomy wood, astray . . .

No, thank you.

I toss Dante onto a pile of folded sheets by the wall, where it lands with a plume of dust. Cleaning it is, then. The whole room smells faintly of soap and stale air, and the stone counters and floor make it feel cold, despite the summer air beyond the windows. I throw them open, then switch the radio on, crank up the volume, and get to work.

The soapy mixture I concoct smells strong enough to chew right through my plastic gloves, to peel back skin and polish bone. It is beautiful bluish stuff, and when I smear it across the marble, it shimmers. I think I can hear it chewing away at the grime on the floor. A few vigorous circles and my corner of the floor even begins to resemble Mom's.

"I don't believe it."

I look up to find Wesley Ayers sitting backward on a metal chair, a relic unearthed from beneath one of the folded sheets. Most of the furniture has been moved onto the patio, but a few chairs dot the room, including this one. "There's actually a room under all this dust!" He drapes his arms over the chair and rests his chin on the arching metal. I never heard him come in.

"Good morning," he adds. "I don't suppose there's a pot of coffee down here."

"Alas, not yet."

"And you call yourself a coffee shop."

"To be fair, the sign says 'Coming Soon.' So," I say, getting to my feet, "what brings you to the future site of Bishop's Coffee Shop?"

"I've been thinking."

"A dangerous pursuit."

"Indeed." He raises one eyebrow playfully. "I got it into my head to save you from the loneliness born of rainy days and solitary chores."

"Oh, did you?"

"Magnanimous, I know." His gaze settles on the discarded book. He leans, reaching until his fingertips graze Dante's *Inferno*, still on its bed of folded sheets.

"What have we here?" he asks.

"Required reading," I say, starting to scrub the counter.

"It's a shame they do that," he says, thumbing through the pages. "Requirement ruins even the best of books."

"Have you read it?"

"A few times." My eyebrows arch, and he laughs. "Again with the skepticism. Looks can be deceiving, Mac. I'm not *all* beauty and charm." He keeps turning the pages. "How far in are you?"

I groan, making circular motions on the granite. "About two lines. Maybe three."

Now it's his turn to raise a brow. "You know, the thing about a book like this is that it's meant to be heard, not read."

"Oh, really."

"Honest. I'll prove it to you. You clean, I'll read."

"Deal."

I scrub as he rests the book on the top of the chair. He doesn't start from the beginning, but turns to a page somewhere in the middle, clears his throat, and begins.

"'Through me you pass into the city of woe.'"

His voice is measured, smooth.

"'Through me you pass into eternal pain. . . .'"

He slips to his feet and rounds the chair as he reads, and I try to listen, I do, but the words blur in my ears as I watch him step toward me, half his face in shadow. Then he crosses into the light and stands there, only a counter between us. Up close, I see the scar along his collar, just beneath the leather cord; his square shoulders; the dark lashes framing his light eyes. His lips move, and I blink as his voice dips low, private, forcing me to listen closer, and I catch the end.

"'Abandon all hope, ye who enter here.'"

He looks up at me and stops. The book slips to his side.

"Mackenzie." He flashes a crooked smile.

"Yeah?"

"You're spilling soap on everything."

I look down and realize he's right. The soap is dripping over the counter, making bubble-blue puddles on the floor.

I laugh. "Well, can't hurt," I say, trying to hide my embarrassment. Wesley, on the other hand, seems to relish it. He leans across the counter, drawing aimless patterns in the soap.

"Got lost in my eyes, did you?"

He leans farther forward, his hands in the dry spaces between soap slicks. I smile and lift the sponge, intending to ring it out over his head, but he leans back just in time, and the soapy mix splashes onto the already flooded counter.

He points a painted black nail at his hair. "Moisture messes up the 'do." He laughs good-naturedly as I roll my eyes. And then I'm laughing, too. It feels good. It's something M would do. Laugh like this.

I want to tell Wes that I dream of a life filled with these moments.

"Well," I say, trying to sop up the soap, "I have no idea what you were reading about, but it sounded nice."

"It's the inscription on the gates of Hell," says Wes. "It's my favorite part."

"Morbid, much?"

He shrugs. "When you think about it, the Archive is kind of like a Hell."

The cheerful moment wobbles, cracks. I picture Ben's shelf, picture the quiet, peace-filled halls. "How can you say that?" I ask.

"Well, not the Archive so much as the Narrows. After all, it is a place filled with the restless dead, right?"

I nod absently, but I can't shake the tightness in my chest. Not just at the mention of Hell, but at the way Wesley went from reciting homework to musing on the Archive. As if it's all one life, one world—but it's not, and I'm stuck somewhere between my Keeper world and my Outer world, trying to figure out how Wesley has one foot so comfortably in each.

You use your thumbnail to dig out a sliver of wood from the railing on the porch. It needs to be painted, but it never will be. It's our last summer together. Ben didn't come this year; he's at some sleepaway camp. And when the house goes on the market this winter, the rail will still be crumbling.

You're trying to teach me how to split myself into pieces.

Not messy, like tearing paper into confetti, but clean, even: like cutting a pie. You say that's you how you lie and get away with it. That's how you stay alive.

"Be who you need to be," you say. "When you're with your brother, or your parents, or your friends, or Roland, or a History. Remember what I taught you about lying?"

"You start with a little truth," I say.

"Yes. Well, this is the same." You throw the sliver of wood over the rail and start working on another. Your hands are never still. "You start with you. Each version of you isn't a total lie. It's just a twist."

It's quiet and dark, a too-hot summer even at night, and I turn to go inside.

"One more thing," you say, drawing me back. "Every now and then, those separate lives, they intersect. Overlap. That's when you have to be careful, Kenzie. Keep your lies clean, and your worlds as far apart as possible."

Everything about Wesley Ayers is messy.

My three worlds are kept apart by walls and doors and locks, and yet here he is, tracking the Archive into my life like mud. I know what Da would say, I know, I know, I know. But the strange new overlap is scary and messy and welcome. I can be careful.

Wesley fiddles with the book, doesn't go back to reading. Maybe he can feel it, too, this place where lines smudge. Quiet settles over us like dust. Is there a way to do this? Last night in the dark of the garden it was thrilling and terrifying and wonderful to tell the truth, but here in the daylight it feels dangerous, exposed.

Still. I want him to say the words again. *I am a Keeper. I hunt Histories . . .* I'm about to ask something, anything, to break the quiet, when Wesley beats me to it.

"Favorite Librarian?" As if he's asking about my favorite food, or song, or movie.

"Roland," I say.

"Really?" He drops the book.

"You sound surprised."

"I pictured you as a Carmen fan. But I do appreciate Roland's taste in shoes."

"The red Chucks? He says he found them in the closets, but I'm pretty sure he swiped them from a History."

"Weird to think of closets in the Archive."

"Weird to think of Librarians *living* there," I say. "It just seems unnatural."

"I left a ball of Oreo filling out for months one time," says Wesley. "It never got hard. Lot of unnatural things in the world."

A laugh escapes my lips, echoes off the granite and glass of the hollowed coffee shop. The laugh is easy, and it feels so, so good. And then Wes picks up the book, and I pick up my sponge, and he promises to read as long as I keep cleaning. I turn back to my work as he clears his throat and starts. I scrub the counter four times just so he won't stop.

For an hour, the world is perfect.

And then I look down at the frosted blue of the soap, and my mind drifts, of all things, to Owen. Who is he? And what's he doing in my territory? Some small part of me thinks he was a phantom, that maybe I've split myself into one too many pieces. But he seemed real enough, driving the knife into Hooper's chest.

"Question," I say, and Wes's reading trails off. "You said you covered the Coronado's doors. That this place was shared." Wes nods. "Were there any other Keepers covering it?"

"Not since I got my key last year. There was a woman at first, but she moved away. Why?"

"Just curious," I say automatically.

His mouth quirks. "If you're going to lie to me, you'll have to try a bit harder."

"It's not a big deal. There was an incident in my territory. I've just been thinking about it." My words skirt around Owen and land on Hooper. "There was this adult—"

His eyes go wide. "Adult *History*? Like a *Keeper-Killer*?"

I nod. "I took care of it, but . . ."

He misreads my question about the Keepers on patrol.

"Do you want me to go with you?"

"Where?"

"In the Narrows. If you're worried—"

"I'm not—" I growl.

"I could go with you, for protect—"

I lift the sponge. "Finish that word," I say, ready to pitch it at his head. To his credit, he backs down, the sentence fading into a crooked smile. Just then, something scratches my leg. I drop the sponge back to the counter, tug off the plastic gloves, and dig out the list. I frown. The two names, *Melanie Allen. 10.* and *Jena Greeth. 14.* hover near the top of the page, but instead of a third name below them, I find a note.

Miss Bishop, please report to the Archive. —R

R, for Roland. Wesley is lounging in the chair, one leg over the side. I turn the paper for him to see.

"A summons?" he asks. "Look at you."

My stomach sinks, and for a moment I feel like I'm sitting in the back of English class when the intercom clicks on, ordering me to the principal's office. But then I remember the favor I asked of Roland, and my heart skips. Did he find the murdered girl?

"Go on," says Wesley, rolling up his sleeves and reaching for my discarded plastic gloves. "I'll cover for you."

"But what if Mom comes in?"

127

"I'm going to meet Mrs. Bishop eventually. You do realize that."

I can dream.

"Go on now," he presses.

"Are you sure?"

He's already taking up the sponge. He cocks his head at me, silver glinting in his ears. He paints quite a picture, decked in black, a teasing smile and a pair of lemon-yellow gloves.

"What's the matter?" he asks, wielding the sponge like a weapon. "Doesn't it look like I know what I'm doing?"

I laugh, pocket the list, and head for the closet in the back of the café. "I'll be back as soon as I can." I hear the slosh of water, a muttered curse, the sounds of a body slipping on a slick floor.

"Try not to hurt yourself," I call, vanishing among the brooms.

THIRTEEN

CLASSICAL MUSIC WHISPERS through the circular antechamber of the Archive.

Patrick is sitting at the desk, trying to focus on something while Roland leans over him, wielding a pen. A Librarian I've never spoken to—though I've heard her called Beth—is standing at the entrance to the atrium, making notes, her reddish hair plaited down her back. Roland looks up as I step forward.

"Miss Bishop!" he says cheerfully, dropping the pen on top of Patrick's papers and coming to meet me. He guides me off in the direction of the stacks, making small talk, but as soon as we turn down a wing on the far side of the atrium, his features grow stern, set.

"Did you find the girl?" I ask.

"No," he says, leading me through a tight corridor and up a flight of stairs. We cross a landing and end up in a reading room that's blue and gold and smells like old paper, faded but pleasant. "There's no one in the branch that fits your description or the time line."

"That's not possible; you must not have searched wide—" I say.

"Miss Bishop, I scrounged up whatever I could on every female resident—"

"Maybe she wasn't a resident. Maybe she was just visiting."

"If she died in the Coronado, she'd be shelved in this branch. She isn't."

"I know what I saw."

"Mackenzie—"

She has to be here. If I can't find her, I can't find her killer. "She existed. I *saw* her."

"I'm not questioning that you did."

Panic claws through me. "How could someone have erased her from *both* places, Roland? And why did you call me here? If there's no record of this girl——"

"I didn't find her," says Roland, "but I found someone else." He crosses the room and opens one of the drawers, gesturing to the History on the shelf. From his receding hairline to his slight paunch to his worn loafers, the man looks . . . ordinary. His clothes are dated but clean, his features impassive in his deathlike sleep.

"This is Marcus Elling," Roland says quietly.

"And what does he have to do with the girl I saw?"

"According to his memories, he was also a resident on the third floor of the Coronado from the hotel's conversion in 1950 until his death in 1953."

"He lived on the same floor as the girl, and died in the same time frame?"

"That's not all," says Roland. "Put your hand on his chest."

I hesitate. I've never read a History. Only the Librarians are allowed to read the dead. Only they know *how*, and it's an infraction for anyone else to even try. But Roland looks shaken, so I put my hand on Elling's sweater. The History feels like every other History. Quiet.

"Close your eyes," he says, and I do.

And then Roland puts his hand over mine and presses down. My fingers instantly go numb, and it feels like my mind is being shoved into someone else's body, pushed into a shape that doesn't fit my own. I wait for the memories to start, but they don't. I'm left in total darkness. Typically, memories start with the present and rewind, and

I've been told the lives of Histories are no different. They begin with their end, their most recent memory. Their death.

But Marcus Elling has no death. I spin back for ten solid seconds of flat black before the dark dissolves into static, and then the static shifts into light and motion and memory. Elling carrying a sack of groceries up the stairs.

The weight of Roland's hand lifts from mine, and Elling vanishes. I blink.

"His death is missing," I say.

"Exactly."

"How is that even possible? He's like a book with the last pages torn out."

"That is, in effect, exactly what he is," says Roland. "He's been altered."

"What does that mean?"

He scuffs one sneaker against the floor. "It means removing a memory, or memories. Carving the moments out. It's occasionally done in the Outer to protect the Archive. Secrecy, you have to understand, is key to our existence. Only a select few members of Crew are capable of and trained to do alterations, and only when absolutely necessary. It's neither an easy nor a pleasant task."

"So Marcus Elling had some kind of contact with the Archive? Something that merited wiping the end of his memory?"

Roland shakes his head. "No, altering is sanctioned only in the *Outer*, and only to shield the Archive from exposure. If he were dead or dying, there'd be no risk of exposure. In this case, the History was altered *after* he was shelved. The alteration's old—you can tell by the way the edges are fraying—so it was probably right after he arrived."

"But that means that whoever did it wanted Elling's death hidden from people here in the *Archive*."

Roland nods. "And the severity of the implication . . . the fact that this happened . . . it's . . ."

I say what he won't. "Only a Librarian possesses the skills to read a History, so only a Librarian would be able to alter one."

His voice slides toward a whisper. "And to do so goes against the principles of this establishment. Altering is used to modify the memories of the living, not bury the lives of the dead."

I stare down at Marcus Elling's face, as if his body can tell me something his memories couldn't. We now have a girl with no History, and a History with no death. I thought I was being paranoid, thought that Hooper could have been a glitch, that maybe Jackson stole the knife. But if a Librarian was willing to do *this*, to break the cardinal oath of the Archive, then maybe a Librarian was behind the malfunctioning list and the weapon too. But whoever altered Elling would be long gone by now . . . right?

Roland looks down at the body, a deep crease forming between his brows. I've never seen him look so worried.

And yet he is the one who asks me if I'm all right. "You seem quiet," he adds.

I want to tell him about the Keeper-Killer and the Archive knife, but one has been returned and the other is strapped to my calf beneath my jeans, so instead I ask, "Who would do this?"

He shakes his head. "I honestly don't know."

"Don't you have a file or something on Elling? Maybe there are clues—"

"He *is* the file, Miss Bishop."

With that he closes the drawer on Elling and leads me from the reading room back to the stairs.

"I'll keep looking into this," he says, pausing at the top of the steps. "But Mackenzie, if a Librarian was responsible for this, it's possible they were acting alone, defying the Archive. Or it's possible they had a reason. It's even possible they were following orders. By investigating these deaths, we're investigating the Archive itself. And that is a dangerous pursuit. Before we go any further, you need to understand the risks."

There's a long pause, and I can see Roland searching for words. "Altering is used in the Outer to eliminate witnesses. But it's also used on members of the Archive if they choose to leave service . . . or if they're deemed unfit."

My heart lurches in my chest. I'm sure the shock is written on my face. "You mean to tell me that if I lose my job, I lose my *life?*"

He won't look at me. "Any memories pertaining to the Archive and any work done on its behalf—"

"That *is* my life, Roland. Why wasn't I told?" My voice gets louder, echoing in the stairs, and Roland's eyes narrow.

"Would it have changed your mind?" he asks quietly.

I hesitate. "No."

"Well, it would change some people's minds. Numbers in the Archive are thin as it is. We cannot afford to lose more."

"So you lie?"

He manages a sad smile. "An omission is not the same thing as a lie, Miss Bishop. It's a manipulation. You as a Keeper should know the varying degrees of falsehood."

I clench my fists. "Are you trying to make a joke about this? Because I don't find the prospect of being erased, or altered, or whatever the hell you want to call it very funny."

My trial plays back like a reel in my head.

If she proves herself unfit in any way, she will forfeit the position.

And if she proves unfit, you, Roland, will remove her yourself.

Would he really do that to me, carve the Keeper out of me, strip away my memories of this world, of this life, of Da? What would be left?

And then, as if he can read my thoughts, Roland says, "I'd never let it happen. You have my word."

I want to believe him, but he's not the only Librarian here. "What about Patrick?" I ask. "He's always threatening to report me. And he mentioned someone named Agatha. Who is she, Roland?"

"She's an . . . assessor. She determines if a member of the Archive is fit." Before I can open my mouth, he adds, "She *won't* be a problem. I promise. And I can handle Patrick."

I run my fingers through my hair, dazed. "Aren't you breaking a rule just by telling me this?"

Roland sighs. "We are breaking a great many rules right now. That's the point. And you need to grasp that before this goes any further. You can still walk away."

But I won't. And he knows it.

"I'm glad you told me." I'm not, not at all, I'm still reeling; but I have to focus. I have my job, and I have my mind, and I have a mystery to solve.

"But what about Librarians?" I ask as we descend the steps. "You talk about retiring. About what you'll do when you're done serving. But you won't even remember. You'll just be a man full of holes."

"Librarians are exempt," he says when he reaches the base of the steps, but there's something hollow in his voice. "When we retire, we get to keep our memories. Call it a reward." He tries to smile and doesn't quite manage it. "Even more reason for you to work hard and move up those ranks, Miss Bishop. Now, if you're certain—"

"I am."

We head down the corridor back to the atrium.

"So what now?" I ask softly as we pass a QUIET PLEASE sign on the end of a line of stacks.

"*You're* going to do your job. *I'm* going to keep looking—"

"Then I'll keep looking, too. You look here, and I'll look in the Outer—"

"Mackenzie—"

"Between the two of us we'll find out who's—"

The sound of footsteps stops me midsentence as we round a set of stacks and nearly collide with Lisa and Carmen. A third Librarian, the one with the red braid, is walking a few steps behind them, but when we all pull up short, she continues on.

"Back so soon, Miss Bishop?" asks Lisa, but the question lacks Patrick's scorn.

"Hello, Roland," says Carmen, and then, warming when she sees me, "Hello, Mackenzie." Her sun-blond hair is pulled back, and once again I'm struck by how young she looks. I know that age is an illusion here, that she's older now than she was when she arrived, even if it doesn't show, but I still don't get it. I can see why some of the older Librarians choose the safety of this world over the constant danger of Keeper or Crew. But why would she?

"Hello, Carmen," says Roland, smiling stiffly. "I was just explaining to Miss Bishop"—he accentuates the formality—"how the different sections work." He reaches out and touches the name card on the nearest shelf. "White stacks, red stacks, black stacks. That sort of thing."

The placards are color-coded—white cards for ordinary Histories, red for those who've woken, black for those who've made it to the Outer—but I've only ever seen white stacks. The red and black are kept separately, deep within the branch, where the quiet is thick. I've known about the color system for a full two years, but I simply nod.

"Stay out of seven, three, five," says Lisa. As if on cue, there's a low sound, like far-off thunder, and she cringes. "We're having a slight technical difficulty."

Roland frowns but doesn't question. "I was just leading Miss Bishop back to the desk."

The two women nod and walk on. Roland and I return to the front desk in silence. Patrick glances back through the doors and sees us coming, and gathers up his things.

"Thank you," says Roland, "for standing in."

"I even left your music going."

"How kind of you," Roland says, managing a shadow of his usual charm. He takes a seat at the desk as Patrick strides off, a folder tucked under his arm. I head for the Archive door.

"Miss Bishop."

I look back at Roland. "Yes?"

"Don't tell anyone," he says.

I nod.

"And please," he adds, "be careful."

I force a smile. "Always."

I step into the Narrows, shivering despite the warm air. I haven't hunted since the incident with Hooper and Owen, and I feel stiff, more on edge than usual. It's not just the hunt that has me coiled, it's also the new fear of failing the Archive, of being found unfit. And at the same time, the fear of not being able to leave. I wish Roland had never told me.

Abandon all hope, ye who enter here.

My chest tightens, and I force myself to take a long, steadying breath. The Narrows is enough to make me claustrophobic on a good day, and I can't afford to be distracted like this right now, so I resolve to put it out of my mind and focus on clearing my list and keeping my job. I'm about to bring my hands to the wall when something stops me.

Sounds—the stretched-out, far-off kind—drift through the halls, and I close my eyes, trying to break them down. Too abstract to be words; the tones dissolve into a breeze, a thrum, a . . . melody?

I stiffen.

Somewhere in the Narrows, someone is humming.

I blink and push off the wall, thinking of the two girls still on my list. But the voice is low and male, and Histories don't sing. They shout and cry and scream and pound on walls and beg, but they don't sing.

The sound wafts through the halls; it takes me a moment to figure out which direction it's coming from. I turn a corner, then another, the notes taking shape until I round a third and see him. A shock of blond hair at the far end of the hall. His back is to me, his hands in his pockets and his neck craned as if he's looking up at the ceilingless Narrows, in search of stars.

"Owen?"

The song dies off, but he doesn't turn.

"Owen," I call again, taking a step toward him.

He glances over his shoulder, startling blue eyes alight in the dark, just as something slams into me, *hard*. Combat boots and a pink sundress, and short brown hair around huge blackening eyes. The History collides with me, and then she's off again, sprinting down the hall. I'm up and after her, thankful the pink of her dress is bright and the metal on her shoes is loud, but she runs fast. I finally chance a shortcut and catch her, but she thrashes and fights, apparently convinced I'm some kind of monster, which—as I'm half carrying, half dragging her to the nearest Returns door—maybe I am.

I pull the list from my pocket and watch as *Jena Street E. 14.* fades from the page.

The fight has done one thing—scraped the film of fear away, and as I lean, breathing heavy, against the Returns door, I feel like myself again.

I retrace my steps to the spot where I saw Owen, but he's nowhere to be found.

Shaking my head, I go in search of Melanie Allen. I read the walls and track her down, and send her back, all the while listening for Owen's song. But it never starts again.

FOURTEEN

LIST CLEARED, I head back to the coffee shop, ready to save Wesley Ayers from the perils of domestic labor. I use the Narrows door in the café closet, and freeze.

Wesley isn't alone.

I creep to the edge of the closet and chance a look out. He's engaged in lively conversation with my dad, talking about the perks of a certain Colombian coffee while he mops the floor. The whole place glitters, polished and bright. The rust-red rose, roughly the diameter of a coffee table, gleams in the middle of the marble floor.

Dad is juggling a mug and a paint roller, waving both as he sloshes dark roast and finishes a large color swatch—burnt yellow—on the far wall. His back is to me as he chats, but Wesley catches sight of me and watches as I slide from the closet and along the wall until I'm near the café door.

"Hey, Mac," he says. "Didn't hear you come in."

"There you are," says Dad, jabbing the air with his roller. He's standing straighter, and there's a light in his eyes.

"I told Mr. Bishop I offered to cover while you ran upstairs to get some food."

"I can't believe you put Wesley here to work so fast," says Dad. He sips his coffee, seems surprised to find so little left, and sets it down. "You'll scare him off."

"Well," I say, "he does scare easily."

Wesley wears a look of mock affront.

"Miss Bishop!" he says, and I have to fight back a smile. His impersonation of Patrick is spot-on. "Actually," he admits to my father, "it's true. But no worries, Mr. Bishop, Mac's going to have to do better than assign chores if she means to scare me off."

Wesley actually winks. Dad smiles. I can practically see the marquee in his head: *Relationship Material!* Wesley must see it too, because he capitalizes on it, and sets the mop aside.

"Would you mind if I borrowed Mackenzie for a bit? We've been working on her summer reading."

Dad *beams*. "Of course," he says, waving his paint roller. "Go on, now."

I half expect him to add *kids* or *lovebirds*, but thankfully he doesn't.

Meanwhile, Wes is trying to tug off the plastic gloves. One snags on his ring, and when he finally manages to wrest his hand free, the metal band flies off, bouncing across the marble floor and underneath an old oven. Wes and I go to recover it at the same time, but he's stopped by Dad's hand, which comes down on his shoulder.

Wes goes rigid. A shadow crosses his face.

Dad's saying something to Wes, but I'm not listening as I drop to the floor before the oven. The metal grate at the base digs into the cut on my arm as I reach beneath, stretching until my fingers finally close around the ring, and I get to my feet as Wesley bows his head, jaw clenched.

"You okay there, Wesley?" asks Dad, letting go. Wes nods, a short breath escaping as I drop the ring into his palm. He slides it on.

"Yeah," he says, voice leveling. "I'm fine. Just a little dizzy." He forces a laugh. "Must be the fumes from Mac's blue soap."

"Aha!" I say. "I told you cleaning was bad for your health."

"I should have listened."

"Let's get you some fresh air, okay?"

"Good idea."

"See you, Dad."

The café door closes behind us, and Wesley slumps back against it, looking a little pale. I know the feeling.

"We have aspirin upstairs," I offer. Wesley laughs and rolls his head to look at me.

"I'm fine. But thank you." I'm struck by the change in tone. No jokes, no playful arrogance. Just simple, tired relief. "Maybe a little fresh air, though."

He straightens up and heads through the lobby, and I follow. Once we reach the garden, he sinks down on his bench and rubs his eyes. The sun is bright, and he was right, this is a different place in daylight. Not a lesser place, really, but open, exposed. At dusk there seemed so many places to hide. At midday, there are none.

The color is coming back into Wesley's face, but his eyes, when he stops rubbing them, are distant and sad. I wonder what he saw, what he felt, but he doesn't say.

I sink onto the other end of the bench. "You sure you're okay?"

He blinks, stretches, and by the time he's done, the strain is gone and Wes is back: the crooked smile and the easy charm.

"I'm fine. Just a bit out of practice, reading people."

Horror washes over me. "You *read* the living? But how?"

Wesley shrugs. "The same way you read anything else."

"But they're not in order. They're loud and tangled and—"

He shrugs. "They're *alive*. And they may not be organized, but the important stuff is there, on the surface. You can learn a lot, at a touch."

My stomach turns. "Have you ever read *me?*"

Wes looks insulted but shakes his head. "Just because I know how doesn't mean I make a sport of it, Mac. Besides, it's against Archive policy, and believe it or not, *I'd* like to stay on their good side."

You and me both, I think.

"How can you stand to read them?" I ask, suppressing a shudder. "Even with my ring on, it's awful."

"Well, you can't go through life without touching anyone."

"Watch me," I say.

Wesley's hand floats up, a single, pointed finger drifting through the air toward me.

"Not funny."

But he keeps reaching.

"I. Will. Cut. Your. Fingers. Off."

He sighs and lets his hand drop to his side. Then he nods at my arm. Red has crept through the bandage and the sleeve where the bottom of the oven dug in.

I look down at it. "Knife."

"Ah," he says.

"No, it really was a teenage boy with a really big knife."

He pouts. "Keeper-Killers. Kids with knives. Your territory was never that much fun when I worked there."

"I'm just lucky, I guess."

"You sure I can't give you a hand?"

I smile, more at the way he offers this time—tiptoeing through the question—than the prospect; but the last thing I need is another complication in my territory.

"No offense, but I've been doing this for quite a while."

"How's that?"

I should backtrack, but it's too late to lie when the truth is half-way up my throat. "I became a Keeper at twelve."

His brow furrows. "But the age requirement is sixteen."

I shrug. "My grandfather petitioned."

Wesley's face hardens as he grasps the meaning. "He passed the job to a kid."

"It wasn't——" I warn.

"What kind of sick bastard would——" The words die on his lips as my fingers tangle in his collar, and I shove him back against the stone bench. For a moment he is just a body and I am a Keeper, and I don't even care about the deafening noise that comes with touching him.

"Don't you dare," I say.

Wesley's face is utterly unreadable as my hands loosen and slide away from his throat. He brings his fingers to his neck but never takes his eyes from mine. We are, both of us, coiled.

And then he smiles.

"I thought you hated touching."

I groan and shove him, slumping back into my corner of the bench.

"I'm sorry," I say. The words seem to echo through the garden.

"One thing's for certain," he says. "You keep me on my toes."

"I shouldn't have——"

"It wasn't my place to judge," he says. "Your grandfather obviously did something right."

I try to shape a tight laugh, and it dies in my throat. "This is new to me, Wes. Sharing. Having someone I *can* share with. And I really appreciate your help—— That sounds lame. I've never had someone like . . . This is a mess. There's finally something good in my life and I'm already making a mess of it." My cheeks go hot, and I have to clench my teeth to stop the rambling.

"Hey," he says, knocking his shoe playfully against mine. "It's the same for me, you know? This is all new to me. And I'm not going anywhere. It takes at least three assassination attempts to scare me off. And even then, if there are baked goods involved, I might come back." He hoists himself up from the bench. "But on that note, I retreat to tend my wounded pride." He says it with a smile, and somehow I'm smiling, too.

How does he do that, untangle things so easily? I walk with him back through the study and into the lobby. As the revolving doors groan to a stop after him, I close my eyes and sink back against the stairs. I've been mentally berating myself for all of ten seconds when I feel the scratch of letters and dig my list from my pocket to see a new name scrawl itself across my paper.

Angela Price. 13.

It's getting harder to keep this list clear. I am heading for the Narrows door set into the side of the stairs when I hear a creak and turn to see Ms. Angelli coming in, struggling with several bags of groceries. For an instant, I'm back in the Archive, watching the last moment of Marcus Elling's recorded life as he performed the exact same task. And then I blink, and the large woman from the fourth floor comes back into focus as she reaches the stairs.

"Hi, Ms. Angelli," I say. "Can I give you a hand?" I hold out my hands, and she gratefully passes two of the four bags over.

"Obliged, dear," she says.

I follow her up, choosing my words. She knows about the Coronado's past, its secrets. I just have to figure out how to get her to share. Coming at it head-on didn't work, but maybe a more oblique path will. I think of her living room, brimming with antiques.

"Can I ask you something," I say, "about your job?"

"Of course," she says.

"What made you want to be a collector?" I understand clinging to one's own past, but when it comes to the pasts of other people, I don't get it.

She gives a winded laugh as she reaches the landing. "Everything is valuable, in its own way. Everything is full of history." *If only she knew.* "Sometimes you can feel it in them, all that life. I can always spot a fake." She smiles, but then her face softens. "And . . . I suppose . . . it gives me purpose. A tether to other people in other times. As long as I have that, I'm not alone. And they're not really gone."

I think of Ben's box of hollow things in my closet, the bear and the black plastic glasses, a tether to my past. My chest hurts. Ms. Angelli shifts her grip on the groceries.

"I haven't got much else," she adds quietly. And then the smile is back, bright as her rings, which have torn tiny holes in the grocery bags. "I suppose that might sound sad. . . ."

"No," I lie. "I think it sounds hopeful."

She turns and heads past the elevators, into the north stairwell. I follow, and our footsteps echo as we climb.

"So," she calls back, "did you find what you were looking for?"

"No, not yet. I don't know if there are other records about this place, or if it's all lost. It seems sad, doesn't it, for the Coronado's history to be forgotten? To fade away?"

She is climbing the stairs, and while I can't see her face, I watch her shoulders stiffen. "Some things should be allowed to fade."

"I don't believe that, Ms. Angelli," I say. "Everything deserves to be remembered. You think so too, or you wouldn't do what you do. I think you probably know more than anyone else in this building when it comes to the Coronado's past."

She glances back, her eyes dancing nervously.

"Tell me what happened here," I say. We reach the fourth floor and step out into the hall. "Please. I know that you know."

She drops her groceries onto a table in the hall and digs around for her keys. I set my bags beside hers.

"Children are so morbid these days," she mutters. "I'm sorry," she adds, unlocking the door. "I just don't feel comfortable talking about this. The past is past, Mackenzie. Let it rest."

And with that, she scoops up her groceries, steps into her apartment, and shuts the door in my face.

Instead of dwelling on the irony of Ms. Angelli telling me to let the past rest, I go home.

The phone is ringing when I get there. I'm sure it's Lyndsey, but I let it ring. A confession: I am not a good friend. Lyndsey writes letters, Lyndsey makes calls. Lyndsey makes plans. Everything I do is in reaction to everything she does, and I'm terrified of the day she decides not to pick up the phone, not to take the first step. I'm terrified of the day Lyndsey outgrows my secrets, my ways. Outgrows me.

And yet. Some part of me—a part I wish were smaller—wonders if it would be better to let it go. Let her go. One less thing to juggle. One less set of lies, or at least omissions. I hate myself as soon as the thought forms. I reach for the phone.

"Hey!" I say, trying to sound breathless. "Sorry! I just walked in."

"Have you been out finding me some ghosts or exploring forbidden corners and walled-up rooms?"

"The search continues."

"I bet you're too busy getting close to Guyliner."

"Oh, yeah. If I could just keep my hands off him long enough to look around . . ." But despite the joke, I smile—a small genuine thing that she obviously can't see.

"Well, don't get too close until I can inspect him. So, how goes it in the haunted mansion?"

I laugh, even as a *third* name scratches itself into the list in my pocket. "Same old, same old." I dig the list out, unfold it on the counter. My stomach sinks.

Angela Price. 13.
Eric Hall. 15.
Penny Walker. 14.

"Pretty boring, actually," I add, running my fingers over the names. "How about you, Lynds? I want stories." I crumple the list, shove it back in my jeans, and head into my room.

"Bad day?" she asks.

"Nonsense," I say, sagging onto my bed. "I live for your tales of adventure. Regale me."

And she does. She rambles, and I let myself pretend we're sitting on the roof of her house, or crashed on my couch. Because as long as she talks, I don't have to think about Ben, or the dead girl in my room, or the missing pages in the study, or the Librarian erasing Histories. I don't have to wonder if I'm losing my mind, dreaming up Keepers, or acting paranoid, twisting glitches and bad luck into dangerous schemes. Because as long as she talks, I can be somewhere else, some*one* else.

But soon she has to leave, and hanging up feels like letting go. The world sharpens the way it does when I pull out of a memory and back into the present, and I examine the list again.

The Histories' ages have been going up.

I noticed it before and thought it was a blip, a rash of double digits, but now everyone on my list is in their teens. I can't afford to wait. I pull on some workout pants and a fresh black shirt, the knife still strapped carefully to my calf. I won't use it, but I can't bring myself to leave it behind. The metal feels good against my skin. Like armor.

I head into the living room right as Mom comes through the front door with her arms full of bags.

"Where are you off to?" she asks, dropping everything on the table as I continue toward the door.

"Going for a run," I say, adding, "Might go out for track this year." If my list doesn't settle down, I'll need a solid excuse for being gone so often anyway, and I used to run, back in middle school when I had spare time. I like running. Not that I actually plan to go running tonight, but still.

"It's getting dark," says Mom. I can see her working through the pros and cons. I head her off.

"There's still a little light left, and I'm pretty out of shape. Won't go far." I pull my knee to my chest in a stretch.

"What about dinner?"

"I'll eat when I get back."

Mom squints at me, and for a moment, part of me begs for her to see through this, a flimsy, half-concocted lie. But then she turns her attention to her bags. "I think it's a good idea, you joining track."

She always tells me she wishes I'd join a club, a sport, be a part of something. But I *am* a part of something.

"Maybe you could use some structure," she adds. "Something to keep you busy."

I almost laugh.

The sound crawls up my throat, a near hysterical thing, and I end up coughing to hold it back. Mom tuts and gets me a glass of water. Staying busy isn't exactly a problem right now. But last time I checked, the Archive didn't offer PE credits for catching escaped Histories.

"Yeah," I say, a little too sharply. "I think you're right."

In that moment, I want to shout.

I want to show her what I go through.

I want to throw it in her face.

I want to tell her the *truth*.

But I can't.

I would never.

I know better.

And so I do the only thing I can.

I walk out.

FIFTEEN

A NGELA PRICE is easy enough to find, and despite her being
very upset, and mistaking me for her dead best friend, which
of course only adds to her distress, I usher her back to Returns with
little more than cunning lies and a few hugs.

Eric Hall is scrawny, albeit a little . . . hormonal, and I get him to
the nearest Returns door with a giggle, a girlish look, and promises
I'll never have to keep.

By the time I finish hunting down and delivering Penny Walker,
I feel like I really have gone for a run. I have a headache from reading walls, my muscles burn from being constantly on guard, and
I think I might actually be able to sleep tonight. I'm making my
way back toward the cluster of numbered doors when something
catches my eye.

The white chalk circle on the front of one of the Returns doors
has been disturbed, altered. Two vertical lines and one horizontal
curve have been drawn into the chalk, turning my marker into a kind
of . . . smiley face? I bring my hand to the door and close my eyes,
and I've barely skimmed the surface of the memories when a form
appears right in front of me, lean and dressed in black, his silvery-
blond hair standing out against the dark.

Owen.

I let the memory roll forward, and his hand dances languidly
across the chalk, drawing the face. And then he dusts the white from
his fingers, puts his hands back in his pockets, and ambles down the

hall. But when he reaches the end, he doesn't continue around the corner. He turns on his heel and doubles back.

What is he doing here? He's not tracking, not hunting. He's . . . pacing.

I watch him come all the way down the hall, toward me, eyes on the floor. He walks until he's inches from my face. And then he stops and looks up, his eyes finding mine, and I can't shake the feeling that he *sees* me even though he's alone in the past and I'm alone in the now.

Who are you? I ask his wavering form.

It doesn't answer, only stares unblinking off into the dark beyond me.

And then I hear it.

Humming. Not the humming of the walls beneath my hands, not the sound of memories, but an actual human voice, somewhere nearby.

I pull away from the door and blink, the Narrows refocusing around me. The melody weaves through the halls, close. It's coming from the same direction as my numbered doors, and I round the corner to find Owen leaning against the door with the I above its handle.

His eyes are closed. But when I step closer, they drift open and turn to consider me. Crisp and blue.

"Mackenzie."

I cross my arms. "I was beginning to wonder if you were real."

An eyebrow arches. "What else would I be?"

"A phantom?" I say. "An imaginary friend?"

"Well then, am I all that you imagined?" The very corner of his mouth curls up as he pushes off the door. "You really doubt my existence?"

I don't take my eyes off him, don't even blink. "You have a way of disappearing."

He spreads his arms. "Well, here I am. Still not convinced?"

My eyes trail from the top of his white-blond hair over his sharp jaw, down his black clothes. Something's off.

"Where's your key?" I ask.

Owen pats his pockets. "I don't have one."

That's not possible.

I must have said it aloud, because his eyes narrow. "What do you mean?"

"A Keeper can't get into the Narrows without a key. . . ."

Unless he's not a Keeper. I close the gap between us. He doesn't retreat, not as I come toward him, and not as I press my hand flush against his chest and see . . .

Nothing. Feel nothing. Hear nothing.

Only quiet. Dead quiet. My hands fall away, and the quiet vanishes, replaced by the low hum of the hall.

Owen Chris Clarke isn't a Keeper. He's not even alive.

He's a *History*.

But that can't be. He's been here for days, and he hasn't started slipping. The blue of his eyes is so pale that I'd notice even the slightest change, and his pupils are crisp and black. And everything about him is level, normal, human. But he's not.

Behind my eyes I see him break Hooper's neck, and I take a step back.

"What's wrong?" he says.

Everything, I want to say. Histories have a pattern. From the moment they wake up, they devolve. They become more distressed, frightened, destructive. Whatever they're feeling at the moment of waking becomes worse and worse. But they never, ever become rational, or self-possessed, or calm. Then how does Owen behave like a person in a hallway rather than a History in the Narrows? And why isn't he on my list?

"I need you to come with me," I say, trying to picture the nearest Returns door. Owen takes a single small step back.

"Mackenzie?"

"You're dead."

His brow creases. "Don't be ridiculous."

"I can prove it to you." Prove it to both of us. My hand itches for the knife that's hidden against my leg, but I think better of it. I've seen Owen use it. Instead I grip Da's key. The teeth are rusted but sharp enough to break the skin, with pressure.

"Hold out your hand."

He frowns but doesn't hesitate, offering his right hand. I press the key against his palm—putting a key in the hands of a History; Da would kill me—and drag it quick across his skin. Owen hisses and pulls back, cradling his hand to his chest.

"Alive enough to feel that," he grumbles, and I'm afraid I've made a mistake until he looks down at his hand and his expression changes, shifts from pain to surprise.

"Let me see," I say.

Owen turns his palm toward me. The slash across his hand is a thin dark line, the skin clearly broken, but the cut doesn't bleed. His eyes float up to mine.

"I don't . . ." he starts, before his gaze drops back to his hand. "I don't understand . . . I felt it."

"Does it still hurt?"

He rubs at the line on his palm. "No." And then, "What am I?"

"You're a History," I say. "Do you know what that means?"

He pauses, looks down over his arms, his wrists and hands, his clothes. A shadow flits across his face, but when he answers, it's with a tight "No."

"You're a record of the person you were when you were alive."

"A ghost?"

"No, not exactly. You—"

"But I *am* a ghost," he cuts in, his voices inching louder, and I brace myself for the slip. "I'm not flesh and blood, I'm not human, I'm not alive, I'm not *real* . . ." And then he checks himself. Swallows hard and looks away. When his eyes find mine, he's calm. Impossible.

"You have to go back," I say again.

"Go where?"

"To the Archive. You don't belong here."

"Mackenzie," he says, "I don't belong there either."

And I believe him. He's not on my list, and if it weren't for the irrefutable proof, I'd never believe he's a History. I force myself to focus. He *will* slip; he has to—and then I'll have to deal with him. I should deal with him now.

"How did you get here?" I ask.

He shakes his head. "I don't know. I was asleep, and then I was awake, and then I was walking." He seems to remember only as he says it. "And then I saw you, and I knew you needed help. . . ."

"I didn't *need* help," I snap, and he does the one thing I've never seen a History do.

He *laughs*. It's a soft, choked sound—but still.

"Yes, well," he says, "you *looked like* you might appreciate a hand, then. How did *you* get here?"

"Through a door."

His eyes go to the numbered ones. "One of those?"

"Yes."

"Where do they go?"

"Out."

"Can *I* go out?" he asks. There's no apparent strain in the question, only curiosity.

"Not through those doors," I say. "But I can take you through one with a white circle—"

"Those doors don't go out," he says shortly. "They go back. I'd rather stay here than go back there." A flicker of anger again, but he's already regaining composure, despite the fact that Histories don't *have* composure.

"You need to go back," I say.

His eyes narrow a fraction.

"I confuse you," he says. "Why is that?"

Is he actually trying to *read* me?

"Because you're—"

The sound of footsteps cuts through the hall.

I pull the list from my pocket, but it's still blank. Then again, I'm standing right beside a History who, according to this same slip of paper, doesn't exist, so I'm not sure how much I trust the system right now.

"Hide," I whisper.

Owen holds his ground and stares past me down the hall. "Don't make me go back."

The steps are getting closer, only a few corridors away. "Owen, hide now."

His gaze shifts back to me. "Promise me you won't—"

"I can't do that," I say. "My job—"

"Please, Mackenzie. Give me one day."

"Owen—"

"You owe me." It's not a challenge. When he says it, there's a careful absence in his voice. No accusation. No demand. Just simple, empty observation. "You do."

"Excuse me?"

"I helped you with that man, Hooper." I can't believe a History is trying to bargain. "Just one day."

The steps are too close.

"Fine," I hiss, pointing to a corridor. "Now, hide."

Owen takes a few silent strides backward, vanishing into the dark as I spin and make my way briskly to the bend in the hall where the steps are growing louder and closer—

And then they stop.

I press myself against the corner and wait, but judging by the way the footsteps paused, the other person is waiting too.

Someone has to move, so I turn the corner.

The fist comes out of nowhere, narrowly missing my cheek. I duck and cross behind my attacker. A pole swipes toward my stomach, but my foot finds its way up at the same time, boot connecting with stick. The pole tumbles toward the damp floor. I catch it and bring it up to the attacker's throat, pinning him against the wall. It's only then that I look at his face, and I'm met by a crooked smile. My grip loosens.

"That's twice in one day you've assaulted me."

I let the pole fall away, and Wesley straightens.

"What the hell, Wes?" I growl. "I could have hurt you."

"Um," he says, rubbing his throat, "you kind of did."

I shove him, but the moment my hands meet his body, his crashing rock band sound shatters into *got to get away from there from her from them massive house giant stairs high laughter and glass escape* before the pressure forces me back, knocking the air from my lungs. I feel

156

ill. With Owen, I forgot about the inextricable link between touch and sight—he may act like a living being, but his quiet says he's not. And Wes is anything but quiet. Did *he* see anything when our skin met? If he did, it doesn't show.

"You know," he says, "for someone who doesn't like touching people, you keep finding ways to put your hands on me."

"What are you even doing here?" I say.

He nods at the numbered doors. "I forgot my bag in the café. Thought I'd run back and get it."

"Using the Narrows."

"How do you think I go back and forth? I live on the other side of the city."

"I don't know, Wes! A cab? A bus? On foot?"

He raps a knuckle against the wall. "Condensed space, remember? The Narrows, fastest transportation around."

I offer up the pole. "Here's your stick."

"*Bō* staff." He takes the pole and twirls it a few times. There's something in his eyes, not his usual grin, but a kind of happiness nonetheless, an excitement. Boys. He flicks his wrist and the pole collapses into a short cylinder, like the batons sprinters pass off in relay races.

He watches, obviously waiting for me to be impressed.

"Ooooooh," I say halfheartedly, and he grumbles and puts the stick away. I turn back toward my numbered doors, eyes scanning the dark beyond for Owen, but he's gone.

"How's the hunting?" asks Wes.

"It's getting worse," I say. I can already feel a new name writing itself on the paper in my pocket. I leave the list there. "Was it this bad when you covered the territory?"

"I don't think so, no. A bit irregular, but never unmanageable. I don't know if I had the full picture, or if I was only being given names here and there."

"Well, it's bad now. I cross one History off my list, and three more show up. It's like that Greek beast . . ."

"Hydra," he answers; then, reading my surprise, adds, "Again with the skepticism. I took a trip to the Smithsonian. You should try it sometime. Get your hands on a few ancient artifacts. Worlds faster than reading books."

"Aren't all those things behind glass?"

"Yes, well . . ." He shrugs as we reach the door. "You done for the night?"

I think of Owen somewhere in the dark. But I already promised him a day. And I really, really want a shower.

"Yeah," I say finally. "Let's go."

Wes and I part ways in the lobby, and I'm about to hit the stairs when I get this gut feeling and find myself making a detour to the study.

Angelli was no help at all, what with her *let the past rest* speech—but I can't, not until I know what happened—and there's got to be something here. I don't know where I'll find it, but I've got an idea where to start.

The directories fill a shelf, a block of red, then a block of blue. I swipe the oldest blue directory, the one from the first years of the conversion, shuffling the books a bit to hide the gap. And then I head upstairs to find Mom experimenting in the kitchen, Dad hiding in a corner of the living room with a book, and a box of pizza open on the table. I field a few questions on the length and quality of my run, finally enjoy a glorious shower, and then sink onto my bed with a slice of cold pizza and the Coronado's log, flipping through as I eat. There has to be *something*. Names fill the inaugural year, but the three missing years that follow are a wall of white in the middle of the book. I scan 1954, hoping that some clue—one of the names, maybe—will catch my eye.

In the end it's not the names that strike me as odd, but the lack of them. In the inaugural year, every room is rented out, and there's a wait list at the back of the section. The year the records come back, the word *Vacant* is written into more than a dozen spots. Was a murder enough to empty the Coronado? What about *two* murders? I think of Marcus Elling on his shelf, the stretch of black where his death should have been. His name is among the ones that fill the original roster. Three years later, his room is among the ones marked *Vacant*. Did people leave in reaction to the deaths? Or could more of them be victims? I dig up a pen and pull my Archive list from my pocket. Turning it over, I scribble out the names of the other residents whose apartments were marked *Vacant* when the records resumed.

I sit back to read over the names, but I've only reached the third one when they begin to *disappear*. One by one, from top to bottom, the words soak into the paper and fade away until the page is blank, erasing themselves the way names do when I've returned the Histories. I've always thought of the paper as a one-way street, a way for the Archive to send notices, not a place for dialogue.

But a moment later, new words write themselves across the page.

Who are these people? —R

After a brief period of stunned silence, I force myself to scribble out an explanation of the directory: the missing pages and the vacancies. I watch as each word dissolves into the paper, and hold my breath until Roland responds.

Will investigate.

And then . . .

Paper is not safe. Do not use again. —R

I can feel the end of the discussion in Roland's handwriting as it dissolves. As if he's set the pen aside and closed the book. I've seen the ancient ledger they keep on the front desk, the one they use to send out names and notes and summons, a different page for every Keeper, every Crew. I hold my slip of Archive paper, wondering why I never knew that it could carry messages both ways.

Four years of service, and the Archive is still so full of secrets—some big, like altering; some small, like this. The more of them I learn, the more I realize how little I know, and the more I wonder about the things I *have* been told. The rules I have been taught.

I turn the Archive paper over. There are three new names. None of them is Owen's. The Archive teaches us that Histories share a common want, a need, to get out. It is a primal, vital thing, an all-consuming hunger: as if they are starved and all the food is on the other side of the Narrows' walls. All the air. All the life. That need causes panic, and the History spirals and shatters and slips.

But Owen isn't slipping, and when he asked for one thing, it wasn't a way out.

It was time.

Don't make me go back.

Promise me you won't.

Please, Mackenzie. Give me one day.

I press my palms into my eyes. A History who's not on my list and doesn't slip and wants only to stay awake.

What kind of History is that?

What is Owen?

And then, somewhere in my tangled, tired thoughts, the *what* becomes a far more dangerous word.

Who.

"Don't you ever wonder about the Histories?" I ask. "Who they are?"

"Were," you correct. "And no."

"But . . . they're people . . . were people. Don't you—"

"Look at me." You knock my chin up with your finger. "Curiosity is a gateway drug to sympathy. Sympathy leads to hesitation. Hesitation will get you killed. Do you understand?"

I nod halfheartedly.

"Then repeat it."

I do. Over and over again, until the words are burned into my memory. But unlike your other lessons, this one never quite sticks. I never stop wondering about the *who* and the *why*. I just learn to stop admitting it.

SIXTEEN

I **CAN'T EVEN TELL** if the sun is up yet.

Rain taps against the windows, and when I look out, all I see is gray. The gray of clouds and of wet stone buildings and wet streets. The storm drags its stomach over the city, swelling to fill the spaces between buildings.

I had a dream.

In it, Ben was stretched out on the living room floor, drawing pictures with his blue pencils and humming Owen's song. When I came in, he looked up, and his eyes were black; but as he got to his feet, the black began to shrink, twist back into the centers, leaving only warm brown.

"I won't slip," he said, drawing an *X* on his shirt in white chalk. "Cross my heart," he said. And then he reached out and took my hand, and I woke up.

What if?

It is a dangerous thought, like a nag, like an itch, like a prickle where my head meets my neck, where my thoughts meet my body.

I swing my legs off the bed.

"All Histories slip," I say aloud.

But not Owen, whispers another voice.

"Yet." I say the word aloud and shake away the clinging threads of the dream.

Ben is gone, I think, even though the words hurt. *He's gone.* The pain is sharp enough to bring me to my senses.

I promised Owen a day, and as I get dressed in the half dark, I wonder if I've waited long enough. I almost laugh. Making deals with a History. What would Da say? It would probably involve an admirable string of profanity.

It's just a day, whispers the small, guilty voice in my head.

And a day is long enough for a grown History to slip, growls Da's voice.

I pull my running shoes on.

Then why hasn't he?

Maybe he has. Harboring a History.

Not harboring. He's not on my——

You could lose your job. You could lose your life.

I shove the voices away and reach for the slip of Archive paper on my bedside table. My hand hovers above it when I see the number sandwiched between the other two.

Evan Perkins. 15.

Susan Lank. 18.

Jessica Barnes. 14.

As if on cue, a fourth name adds itself to the list.

John Orwell. 16.

I swear softly. Some small part of me thinks that maybe if I stop clearing the names, they will stop appearing. I fold the list and shove it in my pocket. I know the Archive doesn't work that way.

Out in the main room, Dad is sitting at the table.

It must be Sunday.

Mom has her rituals—the whims, the cleaning, the list-making. Dad has his too. One of them is commandeering the kitchen table every Sunday morning with nothing but a pot of coffee and a book.

"Where are you off to?" he asks without looking up.

"Going for a run." I do a few impromptu stretches. "Might go out for track this year," I add. One of the keys to lying is consistency.

Dad sips his coffee and offers an absent nod and a hollow "That's nice."

My heart sinks. I guess I should be glad he doesn't care, but I'm not. He's *supposed* to care. Mom cares so much, it's smothering; but that doesn't mean he's allowed to do this, to check out. And suddenly I need him to care. I need him to give me something so I know he's still here, still Dad.

"I've been working on those summer reading books." Even though it's a crime against nature to do homework in July.

He looks up, face brightening a little. "Good. It's a good school. Wesley's been helping you, right?" I nod, and Dad says, "I like that boy."

I smile. "I like him too." And since Wes seems to be the trick to coaxing signs of life out of my father, I add, "We've really got a lot in common."

Sure enough, Dad gets brighter still. "That's great, Mac." Now that I've got his attention, it lingers. His eyes search mine. "I'm glad you're making a friend here, honey. I know this isn't easy. None of this is easy." My chest tightens. Dad can't voice what *this* is any more than Mom can, but it's written across his tired face. "And I know you're strong, but sometimes you seem . . . lost."

It feels like the most he's said to me since we buried Ben.

"Are you . . ." he starts and stops, searching for the words. "Is everything . . ."

I spare him by taking a breath and wrapping my arms around his shoulders. Noise fills my head, low and heavy and sad, but I don't let go, not even when he returns the hug and the sound redoubles.

"I just want to know if you're okay," he says, so soft I barely hear it through the static.

I'm not, not at all; but his worry gives me the strength I need to lie. To pull back and smile and tell him I'm fine.

Dad wishes me a good run, and I slip away to find Owen and the others.

According to my paper, Owen Chris Clarke doesn't exist.

But he's here in the Narrows, and it's time to send him back.

I wrap the key cord around my wrist and look up and down a familiar, dimly lit passageway.

It occurs to me that I need to find him first. Which turns out not to be a problem, because Owen isn't hiding. He's sitting on the ground with his back against a wall near the end of the corridor, legs stretched out lazily, one knee bent up to support an elbow. His head is slumped forward, hair falling into his eyes.

He's supposed to be distressed, supposed to be banging on the doors, tearing at himself, at the Narrows, at everything, searching for a way out. He's supposed to be slipping. He's not supposed to be *sleeping*.

I take a step forward.

He doesn't move.

I take another step, fingers tightening around my key.

I reach him, and he still hasn't budged. I crouch down, wondering what's wrong with him, and I'm just about to stand up when I feel something cool against my hand, the one clutching the key.

Owen's fingers slide over my wrist, bringing with them . . . nothing. No noise.

"Don't do that," he says, head still bowed.

I let the key slide from my grip, back to the end of its length of cord, and straighten, looking down at him.

He tips his head up. "Good evening, Mackenzie."

A bead of cold sweat runs down my spine. He hasn't slipped at all. If anything, he seems calmer. Grounded and human and alive. *Ben could be like this,* the dangerous thought whispers through my mind. I push it back.

"Morning," I correct.

He stands then, the motion fluid, like sliding down the wall but in reverse.

"Sorry," he says, gesturing to the space around us. A smile flickers across his face. "It's kind of hard to tell."

"Owen," I say, "I came to . . ."

He steps forward and tucks a stray chunk of hair behind my ear. His touch is so quiet I forget to pull back. As his hand traces the edge of my jaw and comes to rest beneath my chin, I feel that same *silence.* That dead quiet that Histories have . . . I've never paid it any mind, always been too busy hunting. But it's not just the simple absence of sound and life. It is a *silence* that spreads behind my eyes, where memories should be. It is a *silence* that doesn't stop at our skin, but reaches into me, fills me with cottony quiet, spreads through me like calm.

"I don't blame you," he says softly.

And then his hand falls away, and for the first time in years, I have to resist the urge to reach out and touch someone back. Instead, I force myself to take a step away, put a measure of distance between us. Owen turns toward the nearest door and brings both hands up against it, splaying his fingers across the wood.

"I can feel it, you know," he whispers. "There's this . . . sense in the center of my body, like home is on the other side. Like if I could just get there, everything else would be okay." His hands stay up against the door, but he turns his head toward me. "Is that strange?"

The black in the center of his eyes stays contained, the pupils small and crisp despite the lack of light. What's more, there's a careful hollowness in his voice when he speaks about the draw of the doors, as if he's skirting strong emotion, holding on to control, holding on to himself. He looks at the door again, then closes his eyes, brings his forehead to rest against it.

"No," I say quietly. "It's not strange."

It's what all Histories feel. It's proof of what he is. But most Histories want help, want keys, want a way out. Most Histories are desperate and lost. And Owen is nothing like that. So why is he here?

"Most Histories wake up for a reason," I say. "Something makes them restless, and whatever it is, it's what consumes them from the moment they wake."

I want to know what happened to Owen Chris Clarke. Not just why he woke, but how he died. Anything that can shed light on what he's doing in my territory, clear-eyed and calm.

"Is there something consuming you?" I ask gently.

His eyes find mine in the semidark, and for a moment, sadness dulls the blue. But then it's gone, and he pushes off the door. "Can I ask you something?"

He's redirecting, but I'm intrigued. Histories don't tend to care about Keepers. They see us only as obstacles. Asking a question means he's curious. Curious means he cares. I nod.

"I know that you're doing something wrong," he says, his eyes brushing over my skin, working their way up to my face. "Letting me stay here. I can tell."

"You're right," I say. "I am."

"Then why are you doing it?"

Because you don't make sense, I want to say. Because Da told me to always trust my gut. *Stomach tells when you're hungry,* he'd say, *and when you're sick, and when you're right or wrong. Gut knows.* And my gut says there's a reason Owen is here now.

I try to shrug. "Because you asked for a day."

"That man with the knife asked for your key," says Owen. "You didn't give it to him."

"He didn't ask nicely."

He flashes me that ghost of a smile, a quirk of his lips, there and gone. He steps closer, and I let him. "Even the dead can have manners."

"But most don't," I say. "I answered your question. Now answer one of mine."

He gives a slight obliging bow. I look at him, this impossible History. What made him this way?

"How did you die?"

He stiffens. Not much, to his credit; but I catch the glimpse of tension in his jaw. His thumb begins to rub at the line I made on his palm. "I don't remember."

"I'm sure it's traumatic, to think—"

"No," he says, shaking his head. "It's not that. I don't remember. I *can't* remember. It's like it's just . . . blank."

My stomach twists. Could he have been altered, too?

"Do you remember your *life?*" I ask.

"I do," he says, sliding his hands into his pockets.

"Tell me."

"I was born up north, by the sea. Lived in a house on the cliffs in a small town. It was quiet, which I guess means I was happy." I know the feeling. My life before the Archive is a set of dull impressions, pleasant but distant and strangely static, as if they belong to someone else. "And then we moved to the city, when I was fourteen."

"Who's we?" I ask.

"My family." And there's that sadness again in his eyes. I don't realize how close we're standing until I see it, written across the blue. "When I think of living by the sea, it's all one picture. Blurred smooth. But the city, it was fractured, clear and sharp." His voice is low, slow, even. "I used to go up on the roof and imagine I was back on the cliffs, looking out. It was a sea of brick below me," he says. "But if I looked up instead of down, I could have been anywhere. I grew up there, in the city. It shaped me. The place I lived . . . it kept me busy," he adds with a small private smile.

"What was your house like?"

"It wasn't a house," he says. "Not really."

I frown. "What was it, then?"

"A hotel."

The air catches in my chest.

"What was it called?" I whisper.

I know the answer before he says it.

"The Coronado."

SEVENTEEN

I TENSE.

"What is it?" he asks.

"Nothing," I say, a fraction too fast. What are the odds of Owen's managing to make his way here, within arm's reach of the numbered doors that don't just lead out, but lead *home*?

I force myself to shrug. "It's unusual, isn't it? Living in a hotel?"

"It was incredible," he says softly.

"Really?" I ask before I can stop myself.

"You don't believe me?"

"It's not that," I say. "I just can't picture it."

"Close your eyes." I do. "First, you step into the lobby. It is glass and dark wood, marble and gold." His voice is smooth, lulling. "Gold traces the wallpaper, threads the carpet, it edges the wood and flecks the marble. The whole lobby glitters. It gleams. There are flowers in crystal vases: some roses the dark red of the carpet, others the white of stone. The place is always light," he says. "Sun streams in through the windows, the curtains always thrown back."

"It sounds beautiful."

"It was. We moved in the year after it was converted to apartments."

There's something vaguely formal about Owen—there is a kind of timeless grace about him, his movements careful, his words measured—but it's hard to believe he lived . . . and died . . . so long ago. But even more striking than his age is the date he's referring to: 1951. I didn't see the name *Clarke* in the directory, and now I know why. His family moved in during the time when the records are missing.

"I liked it well enough," he's saying, "but my sister loved it."

His eyes take on an unfocused quality—not slipping, not black, but haunted.

"It was all a game to Regina," he says quietly. "When we moved to the Coronado, she saw the whole hotel as a castle, a labyrinth, a maze of hiding places. Our rooms were side by side, but she insisted on passing me notes. Instead of slipping them under the door, she'd tear them up and hide the pieces around the building, tied to rocks, rings, trinkets, anything to weigh them down. One time she wrote me a story and scattered it all across the Coronado, wedged in garden cracks and under tiles, and in the mouths of statues. . . . It took me days to recover the fragments, and even then I never found the ending. . . ." His voice trails off.

"Owen?"

"You said you think there's a reason Histories wake up. Something that eats at them . . . us." He looks at me when he says it, and sadness streaks across his face, barely touching his features and yet transforming them. He wraps his arms around his ribs. "I couldn't save her."

My heart drops. I see the resemblance now, clear as day: their lanky forms, their silver-blond hair, their strange, delicate grace. The murdered girl.

"What happened?" I whisper.

"It was 1953. My family had lived at the Coronado for two years. Regina was fifteen. I was nineteen, and I'd just moved away," Owen says through gritted teeth, "a couple of weeks before it happened. Not far, but that day it might as well have been countries, worlds, because when she needed me, I wasn't there."

The words cut through me. The same words I've said to myself a thousand times when I think about the day Ben died.

"She bled out on our living room floor," he says. "And I wasn't there."

He leans back against the wall and slides down it until he's sitting on the ground.

"It was my fault," he whispers. "Do you think that's why I'm here?"

I kneel in front of him. "You didn't kill her, Owen." I know. I've seen who did.

"I was her big brother." He tangles his fingers in his hair. "It was my job to protect her. Robert was my friend first. I introduced them. I brought him into her life."

Owen's face darkens, and he looks away. I'm about to press when the scratch of letters in my pocket drags me back to the Narrows and the existence of other Histories. I pull the paper out, expecting a new name, but instead I find a summons.

Report at once. —R

"I have to go," I say.

Owen's hand comes to rest on my arm. For that moment, all the thoughts and questions and worries hush. "Mackenzie," he says, "is my day over?"

I stand, and his hand slides from my skin, taking the quiet with it.

"No," I say, turning away. "Not yet."

My mind is still spinning over Owen's sister—their resemblance is so strong, now that I know—as I step into the Archive. And then I see the front desk in the antechamber and come to a halt. The table is covered in files and ledgers, paper sticking out of the towering stacks of folders; and in the narrow alley between two piles, I can see Patrick's glasses. Damn.

"If you're trying to set a record for time spent here," he says without looking up from his work, "I'm pretty sure you've done it."

"I was just looking for—"

"You do know," he says, "that despite my title, this isn't *really* a library, right? We don't lend, we don't check out, we don't even have a reference-only reading area. These constant visits are not only tiresome, they're unacceptable."

"Yes, I know, but—"

"And are you not busy enough, Miss Bishop? Because last time I checked, you had"—he lifts a pad of paper from the table, flicks through several pages—"five Histories on your list."

Five?

"You do know why you *have* a list, correct?"

"Yes," I manage.

"And why it's imperative that you clear it?"

"Of course." There's a reason we constantly patrol, hoping to keep the numbers down, instead of just walking away, letting the Histories pile up in the Narrows. It's said that if enough Histories woke and got into the space between the worlds, they wouldn't need Keepers and keys to get through. They could force the doors open. *Two ways through any lock,* said Da.

"Then why are you still standing in front of—"

"Roland summoned me," I say, holding up my Archive paper.

Patrick huffs and sits back in his seat, examining me for a long moment.

"Fine," he says, returning to his work with little more than a gesture to the doors behind him.

I round the desk, slowing to watch him write in the ancient ledger sprawled open before him, and then, barely lifting his pen, in one of a half dozen smaller books. This is the first time I've ever seen the desk look *cluttered*.

"You seem busy," I say as I pass.

"That's because I am," he answers.

"Busier than usual."

"How astute."

"I'm busier too, Patrick. You can't tell me five names is standard, even for the Coronado."

He doesn't look up. "We're experiencing some minor technical difficulties, Miss Bishop. So sorry to inconvenience you."

I frown. "What kind of technical difficulties?" Glitching names? Armed Histories? Boys who don't slip?

"Minor ones," he snaps, making it clear as day that he's done talking.

I put the list away as I pass through the main doors in search of Roland.

Crossing into the warm light of the atrium, my spirits lift, and I feel that sense of peace Da always spoke of. The calm.

And then something crashes.

Not here in the atrium but down one of the branching halls, the metal sound of a shelf falling to the floor. Several Librarians rise from their work and hurry toward the noise, closing the doors behind them; but I stand very, very still, remembering that I am surrounded by the sleeping dead.

I hold my breath and listen. Nothing happens. The doors stay closed. No sound comes through.

And then a hand lands on my shoulder and I spin, twisting the arm back behind the body. In one fluid move, the arm and body are both gone, and somehow I'm the one being pinned, facedown, against a table.

"Easy, there," says Roland, letting go of my wrist and shoulder.

I take a few steadying breaths and lean against the table. "Why did you summon me? Did you find something? And did you hear that crash—"

"Not here," he murmurs, motioning toward a wing. I follow him, rubbing my arm.

The farther we get from the atrium, the older the Archive seems. Roland leads me down corridors that begin to twist and coil and shrink, laid out more like the Narrows than the stacks. The ceilings shift from arching overhead to dipping low, and the rooms themselves are smaller, cryptlike and dusty.

"What was that sound?" I ask as Roland leads the way; but he doesn't answer, only ducks into an oddly shaped alcove and turns again under a low stone arch. The room beyond is dim, and its walls are lined with worn, dated ledgers, not Histories. It is a cramped and faded version of the chamber in which I faced my trial.

"We have a problem," he says as soon as he's closed the door. "I looked through that list of names you sent. Most of them didn't tell me anything, but two of them did. Two more people died in the Coronado, both in August, both within a month of Marcus Elling. And both Histories were altered, their deaths removed."

I sink into a low leather chair, and Roland begins to pace. He looks exhausted, the lilt in his voice growing stronger as he talks. "I didn't find them at first because they'd been mis-shelved, the entry ledgers saying one place but the catalogs saying another. Someone didn't want them found."

"Who were they?"

"Eileen Herring, a woman in her seventies, and Lionel Pratt, a man in his late twenties. Both lived in the Coronado, and both lived alone, just like Elling, but that's the only connection I can find. I can't even be certain they died *in* the Coronado, but their last intact memories are of the building. Eileen leaving her apartment on the second floor. Lionel sitting on the patio, having a smoke. The moments are mundane to a fault. Nothing about them gives any indication of what caused their deaths, and yet both have been blacked out."

"Marcus, Eileen, and Lionel died in August. But Regina was murdered in March."

His eyes narrow. "I thought you didn't know her name."

The air snags in my lungs. I didn't. Not until Owen told me. But I can't exactly explain that I've been sheltering her brother.

"You're not the only one doing research, remember? I tracked down a resident of the Coronado, Ms. Angelli, who'd heard about the murder."

It's not a lie, I reason. Just a manipulation.

"What else did she know?" he presses.

I shake my head, trying to keep the spin as clean as I can. "Not much. She didn't seem eager to swap stories."

"Does Regina have a last name?"

I hesitate. If I give it, Roland will cross-reference her with Owen, who's notably absent. I know I should tell him about Owen—we're already breaking rules—but there are rules and there are Rules, and while Roland has gone far enough to break the former, I don't know how he'd handle my breaking the latter and harboring a History in the Narrows. And I've still got so many questions for Owen.

I shake my head. "Angelli wouldn't say, but I'll keep pressing." At least that lie will buy me a little time. I try to shift the focus back to the second set of deaths.

"Five months between Regina's murder and these three deaths,

Roland. How do we even know they're related?"

He frowns. "We don't. But it's a suspicious number of filing errors. At first I thought it might be a cleanup, but . . ."

"A cleanup?"

"Sometimes, if things go badly—if a History does commit atrocities in the Outer, and there are victims as well as witnesses—the Archive does what it can to minimize the risk of exposure."

"Are you saying the Archive actively covers up murders?"

"Not all evidence can be buried, but most can be twisted. Bodies can be disposed of. Deaths can be made to appear natural." I must look as appalled as I feel, because he keeps talking. "I'm not saying it's right, Miss Bishop; I'm just saying the Archive cannot afford to have people learning about Histories. About us."

"But would they ever hide evidence from their own?"

He frowns again. "I've seen certain measures taken in the Outer. Surfaces altered. I've known members of the Archive who think the past should be sheltered here, in these walls, but not beyond them. People who think the Outer isn't sacred. People who think there are things that Keepers and Crew should not see. But even they would never approve of this, of altering Histories, keeping the truth from *us*." When he says *us*, he doesn't mean me. He means the Librarians. He looks wounded. Betrayed.

"So someone here went rogue," I say. "The question is why."

"Not just why. *Who*." Roland slides down into a chair. "Remember when I said we had a problem? Right after I found Eileen and Lionel, I went back to review Marcus's History. I couldn't. Someone had tampered with him. Erased him entirely."

I grip the arms of my chair. "But that means it was done by a current Librarian. Someone in the Archive *now*."

Suddenly I'm glad I've kept Owen a secret. If he is connected, then there's one big difference between the other victims and him: he's *awake*. I stand a better chance of learning what he knows by listening than by turning him back into a corpse. And if he *is* connected, then the moment I turn him in, our rogue Librarian will almost certainly erase what's left of his memories.

"And judging by the rush job," says Roland, "they know we're digging."

I shake my head. "But I don't get it. You said that Marcus Elling's death was first altered when he was brought in. That was more than sixty years ago. Why would a current Librarian be trying to cover up the work of an old one?"

Roland rubs his eyes. "They wouldn't. And they're not."

"I don't understand."

"Alterations have a signature. Memories that have been hollowed out by different hands both register as black, but there's a subtle difference in the way they read. The way they feel. The way Marcus Elling's History reads now is the same way it read before. The same way the other two read. They were all altered by the same person."

One person over the course of sixty-five years. "Can Librarians even serve that long?"

"There's not exactly mandatory retirement," he says. "Librarians choose the duration of their term. And since, as long as we're stationed here, we don't age . . ." Roland trails off, and I make a mental list of everyone I've seen in the branch. There have to be a dozen, two dozen Librarians here at any one time. I know only a few by name.

"It's clever," Roland says, half to himself. "Librarians are the one element of the Archive that isn't—can't be—fully recorded, kept track of. If they stayed too long in one place, a rogue action would have drawn attention, but Librarians are in a constant state of flux, of transfer. The staff is never together for very long. People come and go. They move freely through the branches. It's conceivable . . ."

I think of Roland, who's been here since my induction; but the others—Lisa and Patrick and Carmen—all came later.

"You stuck around," I say.

"Had to keep you out of trouble."

Roland's Chucks bounce nervously.

"What do we do now?" I ask.

"*We* aren't going to do anything." Roland's head snaps up. "*You're* going to stay away from this case."

"Absolutely not."

"Mackenzie, that's the other reason I summoned you. You've already taken too many chances—"

"If you're talking about the list of names—"

"You're lucky I'm the one who found it."

"It was an accident."

"It was reckless."

"Maybe if I'd known the paper could do that, maybe if the Archive didn't keep everything so damn secret—"

"Enough. I know you only want to help, but whoever is doing this is dangerous, and they clearly don't want to get caught. It's imperative that you stay out of—"

"—the way?"

"No, the crosshairs."

I think of Jackson's knife and Hooper's attack. *Too late.*

"Please," says Roland. "You have a lot more to lose. Let me take it from here."

I hesitate.

"Miss Bishop . . ."

"How long have you been a Librarian?" I ask him.

"Too long," he says. "Now, promise me."

I force myself to nod, and I feel a pinch of guilt as his shoulders visibly loosen because he believes me. He gets to his feet and heads to the door. I follow, but halfway there, I stop.

"Maybe you should let me see Ben," I say.

"Why's that?"

"You know, as a cover-up. In case our rogue Librarian is watching."

Roland almost smiles. But he still sends me home.

EIGHTEEN

MOM SAYS there's nothing a hot shower can't fix, but I've been steaming up the bathroom for half an hour and I'm no closer to fixing anything.

Roland sent me home with a last glance and a reminder not to trust *anyone*. Which isn't hard when you know that someone is trying to bury the past and possibly you with it. My mind immediately goes to Patrick, but as much as I dislike him, the fact is he's a model Librarian, and there are at least a dozen other Librarians in the Archive on a given day. It could be any of them. Where do you even start?

I turn the water all the way hot and let it burn my shoulders. After Roland, I went hunting. I wanted to clear my head. It didn't work, and I only managed to return the youngest two Histories, cutting my list in half for all of five minutes before three new names flashed up.

I hunted for Owen too, but without any luck. I'm worried now that I've scared him away, though *away* is a relative term in the Narrows. There can be only so many places to hide, but I haven't found them yet, and apparently he has. I've never met a History who didn't want to be found. And why shouldn't he hide? His bartered day is up, and I'm the one who means to send him back. And I will . . . but first I need to know what he knows, and to get that, I need to gain his trust.

How do you gain a History's trust?

Da would say you don't. But as the water scalds my shoulders, I think of the sadness in Owen's eyes when he spoke of Regina—not of her death, when his voice went hollow, but the time before, when he talked about the games she'd play, the stories she'd hide throughout the building.

One time she wrote me a story and scattered it all across the Coronado, wedged in garden cracks and under tiles, and in the mouths of statues. . . . It took me days to recover the fragments, and even then I never found the ending. . . .

I snap the water off.

That's my shot at Owen's trust. A token. A peace offering. Something to hold on to. My spirits start to sink. What are the odds of anything left for sixty-five years still being here? And then I think of the Coronado, its slow, unkempt decay, and I realize that maybe, maybe. Just maybe.

I dress quickly, glancing at the Archive paper on my bed (and grimacing at the five names, the oldest—*18*). I used to wait days in hopes of getting a name, relished the moment of reveal. Now I shove the slip into my pocket. A stack of books sits on a large box, Dante's *Inferno* on top of the pile. I tuck the paperback under my arm and head out.

Dad is still at the kitchen table, on his third or fourth cup of coffee, judging by the near-empty pot beside him. Mom is sitting beside him, making lists. She has at least five of them in front of her, and she keeps writing and rewriting and rearranging as if she can decode her life that way.

They both look up as I walk in.

"Where are you off to?" asks Mom. "I bought paint."

One of the cardinal rules of lying is to never, if it can be prevented, involve someone else in your story, because you can't control them. Which is why I want to punch myself when the lie that falls from my lips is, "To hang out with Wesley."

Dad beams. Mom frowns. I cringe, turning toward the door. And then, to my amazement, lie becomes truth when I open it to find a tall, black-clad shape blocking my way.

"Lo and behold," says Wesley, slouching in the doorway, holding an empty coffee cup and a brown paper bag. "I have escaped."

"Speak of the devil," says Dad. "Mac was just on her way—"

"Escaped what?" I ask, cutting Dad off.

"The walls of Chez Ayers, behind which I have been confined for days. Weeks. Years." He rests his forehead against the door frame. "I don't even know anymore."

"I just saw you yesterday."

"Well. It *felt* like years. And now I come begging for coffee and bearing sweets with the intent of rescuing you from your indentured servitude in the pit of . . ." Wesley's voice trails off as he sees my mother, arms crossed, standing behind me. "Oh, hello!"

"You must be the boy," says Mom. I roll my eyes, but Wesley only smiles. Not crookedly, either, but a genuine smile that should clash with his black spiked hair and dark-rimmed eyes, but doesn't.

"You must be the mom," he says, sliding past me into the room. He transfers the paper bag to his left hand and extends his right to her. "Wesley Ayers."

Mom looks caught off guard by the smile, the open, easy way he does it. I know I am.

He doesn't even flinch when she takes his hand.

"I can see why my daughter likes you."

Wesley's smile widens as his hand slips back to his side. "Do you think she's falling for my dashing good looks, my charm, or the fact I supply her with pastries?"

Despite herself, Mom laughs.

"'Morning, Mr. Bishop," says Wesley.

"It's a beautiful day," says Dad. "You two should go. Your mom and I can handle the painting."

"Great!" Wes swings his arm around my shoulder, and the noise slams into me. I push back, try to block him out, and make a mental note to punch him when we're alone.

Mom gets us two fresh coffees and walks us to the door, watching as we go. As soon as the door closes behind us, I knock Wesley's arm off my shoulders and exhale at the sudden lack of pressure. "Ass."

He leads the way down to the lobby.

"You, Mackenzie Bishop," he says as we hit the landing, "have been a very bad girl."

"How so?"

He rounds the banister at the base of the staircase. "You involved me in a lie! Don't think I didn't catch it."

We pass through the study to the garden door, and he throws it open and leads me into the dappled morning light. The rain has stopped, and as I look around, I wonder if Regina would hide a bit of story in a place like this. The ivy is overgrown and might keep a token safe, but I doubt a scrap of paper would survive the seasons, let alone the years.

Wes drops onto the Faust bench and takes a cinnamon roll out of the paper bag. "Where were you *really* going, Mac?" he asks, holding out the bag.

I drag my thoughts back to him, taking a roll as I perch on the arm of the bench.

"Oh, you know," I say dryly, "I thought I'd lie in the sun for a few hours, maybe read a book, savor my lazy summer."

"Still trying to clear your list?"

"Yep." And question Owen. And find out why a Librarian would want to cover up deaths that are decades upon decades old. All without letting the Archive know.

"You brought the book just to throw your folks off the trail? How very thorough of you."

I take a bite of the cinnamon roll. "I am, in fact, a master of deceit."

"I believe it," Wes says, taking another bite. "So, about your list . . ."

"Yes?"

"I hope you don't mind, but I took care of the History in your territory."

I stiffen. *Owen.* Is that why I couldn't find him this morning? Did Wesley already send him back? I force my voice level. "What do you mean?"

"A History? You know? One of those things we're supposed to be hunting?"

I fight to keep my shock from showing. "I told you. I didn't. Need. Help."

"A simple thanks will suffice, Mac. Besides, it's not like I went looking for her. She kind of ran into me."

Her? I dig the list from my pocket. *Susan Lank. 18.* is gone. A sigh of relief escapes, and I sag back against the bench.

"Luckily, I was able to use my charm," he's saying. "That, and she thought I was her boyfriend. Which, I'll admit, facilitated things a bit." He runs his hand through his hair. It doesn't move.

"Thanks," I say softly.

"It's a hard word to say, I know. It takes practice."

I throw the last bite of my roll at him.

"Hey," he warns, "watch the hair."

"How long does it take to make it stick up like that?" I ask.

"Ages," he says, standing. "But it's worth it."

"Is it really?"

"I'll have you know, Miss Bishop, that this"—he gestures from his spiked black hair all the way down to his boots—"is absolutely vital."

I raise an eyebrow and stretch out across the weather-pocked stone. "Let me guess," I say with a pout. "You just want to be seen." I give the line a dramatic flair so that he knows I'm teasing. "You feel invisible in your skin, and so you dress yourself up to get a reaction."

Wes gasps. "How did you know?" But he can't keep the smile off his face. "Actually, much as I love seeing my father's tortured expression, or his trophy soon-to-be wife's disdain, this does serve a purpose."

"And what purpose would that be?"

"Intimidation," he says with a flourish. "It scares the Histories. First impressions are very important, especially in potentially combative situations. An immediate advantage helps me control the situation. Many of the Histories don't come from the here and now. And this"—again he gestures to the length of himself—"believe it or not, can be intimidating."

He straightens and steps toward me, into a square of sunlight. His sleeves are rolled up, revealing leather bracelets that cut through some scars and cover others. His brown eyes are alive and warm, and the contrast between his tawny irises and his black hair is stark but pleasant. Beneath it all, Wesley Ayers is actually quite handsome. My eyes pan down over his clothes, and he catches me before I can look away.

"What's the matter, Mac?" he says. "Are you finally falling victim to my devilish good looks? I knew it was only a matter of time."

"Oh, yeah, that's it. . . ." I say, laughing.

He leans down, rests his hand on the bench beside my shoulder.

"Hey," he says.

"Hey."

"You okay?"

The truth sits on my tongue. I want to tell him. But Roland warned me not to trust anyone; and though it sometimes feels like I've known Wes for months instead of days, I haven't. Besides, even if I could tell Wesley parts but not the whole, partial truths are so much messier than whole lies.

"Of course," I say, smiling.

"Of course," he parrots, and pulls away. He collapses onto his own bench and tosses an arm over his eyes to block the sun.

I look back at the study doors and think of the directories. I've been so focused on the early years, I haven't taken a close look at the current roster. I've been focused on the dead, but I can't forget about the living.

"Who else lives here?" I ask.

"Hm?"

"Here in the Coronado," I press. I might not be able to tell Wes what's going on, but that doesn't mean he can't help. "I've only met you and Jill and Ms. Angelli. Who lives here?"

"Well, there's this new girl who just moved in on floor three. Her family's re-opening the café. I hear she likes to lie, and hit people."

"Oh yeah? Well, there's that strange goth guy, the one who's always lurking around Five C."

"Strangely hot in a mysterious way, though, right?"

I roll my eyes. "Who's the oldest person here?"

"Ah, that distinction goes to Lucian Nix up on the seventh floor."

"How old is he?"

Wes shrugs. "Ancient."

Just then, the study door flies open and Jill appears on the threshold.

"I thought I heard you," she says.

"How goes it, strawberry?" asks Wes.

"Your dad has been calling us nonstop for half an hour."

"Oh?" he says. "I must have forgotten." The way he says it suggests he knows exactly what time it is.

"That's funny," Jill says as Wes drags himself to his feet, "because your dad seems to think you snuck out."

"Wow," I chime in, "you weren't kidding when you said you escaped Chez Ayers."

"Yeah, well. Fix it." Jill turns and closes the study door on both of us.

"She's charming," I say.

"She's like my aunt Joan, but in miniature. It's spooky. All she needs is a cane and a bottle of brandy."

I follow him into the study, but stop, eyes drifting to the directories.

"Wish me luck," he says.

"Good luck," I say. And then, as he vanishes into the hall, "Hey, Wes?"

He reappears. "Yeah?"

"Thanks for your help."

He smiles. "See? It's getting easier to say."

And with that he's gone, and I'm left with a lead. Lucian Nix. How long has he lived in the building? I tug down the most recent directory, flipping through until I reach the seventh floor.

7E. Lucian Nix.

I pull down the next directory.

7E. Lucian Nix.

And the next.

7E. Lucian Nix.

All the way back, past the missing files, to the very first year of the first blue book. 1950.

He's been here all along.

I press my ear against the door of 7E.

Nothing. I knock. Nothing. I knock again, and I'm about to tug my ring off and listen for the sounds of any living thing when, finally, someone knocks back. There is a kind of scuffle on the other side of the door, joined by muttered cursing, and moments later the door swings open and collides with the metal side of a wheelchair. More cursing, and then the chair retreats enough so that the door can fully open. The man in the chair is, as Wesley put it, ancient. His hair is shockingly white, his milky eyes resting somewhere to my left. A thin stream of smoke drifts up from his mouth, where a narrow cigarette hangs, mostly spent. A scarf coils around his neck, and his clawlike fingers pluck at the fringe on the end.

"What are you staring at?" he asks. The question catches me off guard, since he's clearly blind. "You aren't saying anything," he adds, "so you must be staring."

"Mr. Nix?" I ask. "My name is Mackenzie Bishop."

"Are you a kiss-a-gram? Because I told Betty I didn't need girls being paid to come see me. Rather have no girls at all than that—"

I'm not entirely sure what a kiss-a-gram is. "I'm not a kiss—"

"There was a time when all I had to do was smile. . . ." He smiles now, flashing a pair of fake teeth that don't fit quite right.

"Sir, I'm not here to kiss you."

He adjusts his direction at the sound of my voice, pivoting in his chair until he's nearly facing me, and lifts his chin. "Then what are you knocking on my door for, little lady?"

"My family is renovating the coffee shop downstairs, and I wanted to introduce myself."

He gestures to his wheelchair. "I can't exactly go downstairs," he says. "Have everything brought up."

"There's . . . an elevator."

He has a sandpaper laugh. "I've survived this long. I've no plans to perish in one of those metal death traps." I decide I like him. His hand drifts shakily up to his mouth, removes the stub of his cigarette. "Bishop. Bishop. Betty brought in a muffin that was sitting in the hall. Suppose you're to blame for that."

"Yes, sir."

"More of a cookie person, myself. No offense to the other baked goods. I just like cookies. Well, suppose you want to come in."

He slides the wheelchair back several feet into the room, and it catches the edge of the carpet. "Blasted device," he growls.

"Would you like a hand?"

He throws both of his up. "I've got two of those. Need some new eyes, though. Betty's my eyes, and she's not here."

I wonder when Betty will be back.

"Here," I say, crossing the threshold. "Let me."

I guide the chair through the apartment to a table. "Mr. Nix," I say, sitting down beside him. I set the copy of the *Inferno* on the worn table.

"No *Mr.* Just Nix."

"Okay . . . Nix, I'm hoping you can help me. I'm trying to find out more about a series of"—I try to think of how to put this politely, but can't—"a series of deaths that happened here a very long time ago."

"What would you want to know about that for?" he asks. But the question lacks Angelli's defensiveness, and he doesn't feign ignorance.

"Curiosity, mostly," I say. "And the fact that no one seems to want to talk about it."

"That's because most people don't know about it. Not these days. Strange things, those deaths."

"How so?"

"Well, that many deaths so close together. No foul play, they said, but it makes you wonder. Weren't even in the paper. It was news around here, of course. For a while it looked like the Coronado wouldn't make it. No one would move in." I remember the string of vacancy listings in the directories. "Everyone thought it was cursed."

"You didn't, obviously," I say.

"Says who?"

"Well, you're still here."

"I may be stubborn. Doesn't mean I have the faintest idea what happened that year. String of bad luck, or something worse. Still, it's strange, how badly people wanted to forget about it."

Or how badly the Archive wanted them to.

"All started with that poor girl," says Nix. "Regina. Pretty thing. So cheerful. And then someone went and killed her. So sad, when people die so young."

Someone? Doesn't he know it was Robert?

"Did they catch the killer?" I ask.

Nix shakes his head sadly. "Never did. People thought it was her boyfriend, but they never found him."

Anger coils inside me at the image of Robert trying to wipe the blood off his hands, pulling on one of Regina's coats, and running.

"She had a brother, didn't she? What happened to him?"

"Strange boy." Nix reaches out to the table, fingers dancing until they find a pack of cigarettes. I take up a box of matches and light one for him. "The parents moved out right after Regina's death, but the boy stayed. Couldn't let go. Blamed himself, I think."

"Poor Owen," I whisper.

Nix frowns, blind eyes narrowing on me. "How did you know his name?"

"You told me," I say steadily, shaking out the match.

Nix blinks a few times, then taps the space between his eyes. "Sorry. I swear it must be going. Slowly, thanks be to God, but going all the same."

I set the spent match on the table. "The brother, Owen. How did he die?"

"I'm getting there," says Nix, taking a drag. "After Regina, well, things started to settle at the Coronado. We held our breaths. April passed. May passed. June passed. July passed. And then, just when we were starting to let out our air . . ." He claps his hands together, showering his lap with ash. "Marcus died. Hung himself, they said, but his knuckles were cut up and his wrists were bruised. I know because I helped cut the body down. Not a week later, Eileen goes down the south stairs. Broke her neck. Then, oh, what was his name, Lionel? Anyway, young man." His hand falls back into his lap.

"How did he die?"

"He was stabbed. Repeatedly. Found his body in the elevator. Not much use calling that one an accident. No motive, though, no weapon, no killer. No one knew what to make of it. And then Owen . . ."

"What happened?" I ask, gripping my chair.

Nix shrugs. "No one knows—well, I'm all that's left, so I guess I should say no one *knew*—but he'd been having a hard time." His milky eyes find my face and he points a bony finger up at the ceiling. "He went off the roof."

I look up and feel sick. "He jumped?"

Nix lets out a long breath of smoke. "Maybe. Maybe not. Depends on how you want to spin things. Did he jump or was he pushed? Did Marcus hang himself? Did Eileen trip? Did Lionel . . . well, there ain't much doubt about what happened to Lionel, but you see my point. Things stopped after that summer, though, and never started up again. No one could make sense of it, and it don't do any good to be thinking morbid thoughts, so the people here did the one thing they could do. They forgot. They let the past rest. You probably should too."

"You're right," I say softly, but I'm still looking up, thinking about the roof, about Owen.

I used to go up on the roof and imagine I was back on the cliffs, looking out. It was a sea of brick below me. . . .

My stomach twists as I picture his body going over the edge, blue eyes widening the instant before the pavement hits.

"I'd better be going." I push myself to my feet. "Thank you for talking to me about this."

Nix nods absently. I head for the door, but stop, turn back to see him still hunched over his cigarette, dangerously close to setting his scarf on fire.

"What kind of cookies?" I ask.

His head lifts, and he smiles. "Oatmeal raisin. The chewy kind."

I smile even though he can't see. "I'll see what I can do," I say, closing the door behind me. And then I head for the stairs.

Owen was the last to die, and one way or another, he went off the roof.

So maybe the roof has answers.

NINETEEN

I **TAKE THE STAIRWELL** up to the roof access door, which looks rusted shut, but it's not. The metal grinds against the concrete frame, and I step through a doorway of dust and cobwebs, past a crumbling overhang, and out into a sea of stone bodies. I had seen the statues from the street, gargoyles perched around the perimeter of the roof. What I couldn't see from there is that they cover the entire surface. Hunching, winged, sharp-toothed, they huddle here and there like crows, and glare at me with broken faces. Half of their limbs are missing, the rock eaten away by time and rain and ice and sun.

So this is Owen's roof.

I try to picture him leaning against a gargoyle, head tipped back against a stone mouth. And I can see it. I can see him in this place.

But I can't see him jumping.

There is something undeniably sad about Owen, something lost, but it wouldn't take this shape. Sadness can sometimes sap the fight from a person's features, but his are sharp. Daring. Almost defiant.

I trail my hand along a demon's wing, then make my way to the edge of the roof.

It was a sea of brick below me. But if I looked up instead of down, I could have been anywhere.

If he didn't jump, what happened?

A death is traumatic. Vivid enough to mark any surface, to burn in like light on photo paper.

I slide the ring from my finger, kneel, and press my hands flat to the weathered roof. My eyes slide shut, and I reach and reach. The thread is so thin and faint, I can barely grab hold. A distant tone tickles my skin, and finally I catch what little is left of the memory. My fingers go numb. I spin time back, past years and years of quiet. Decades and decades of nothing but an empty roof.

And then the rooftop plunges into black.

A flat, matte black I recognize immediately. Someone has reached into the roof itself and altered the memories, leaving behind the same dead space I saw in Marcus Elling's History.

And yet it doesn't *feel* the same. It's just like Roland said. Black is black, but it doesn't feel like the same hand, the same signature. And that makes sense. Elling was altered by a Librarian in the Archive. This roof was altered by someone in the Outer.

But the fact that multiple people tried to erase this piece of past is hardly comforting. What could have possibly happened to merit this?

. . . there are things that even Keepers and Crew should not see. . . .

I rewind past the black until the roof appears again, faded and unchanging, like a photo. And then finally, with a lurch, the photo flutters into life and lights and muddled laughter. This is the memory that hummed. I let it roll forward and see a night gala, with fairy lights and men in coattails and women in dresses with tight waists and A-line skirts, glasses of champagne and trays balanced on gargoyles' wings. I scan the crowd in search of Owen or Regina or Robert, but find none of them. A banner strung between two statues announces the conversion of the Coronado from hotel to apartments. The Clarkes don't live here yet. It will be a year until they move in. Three years until the string of deaths. I frown and guide the memory backward, watching the party dissolve into a faded, empty space.

Before that night there is nothing loud enough to hum, and I let go of the thread and blink, wincing in the sunlight on the abandoned roof. A stretch of black amidst the faded past. Someone erased Owen's death, carved it right out of this place, buried the past from both sides. What could have possibly happened that year to make the Archive—or someone in it—do this?

I weave through the stone bodies, laying my hands on each one, reaching, hoping one of them will hum. But they are all silent, empty. I'm nearly back to the rusted door when I hear it. I pause midstep, my fingers resting on an especially toothy gargoyle to my right.

He's whispering.

The sound is little more than an exhale through clenched teeth, but there it is, the faintest hum against my skin. I close my eyes and roll time back. When I finally reach the memory, it's faded, a pattern of light blurred to nearly nothing. I sigh and pull away, when something snags my attention—a bit of metal in the gargoyle's mouth. Its face is turned up to the sky, and time has worn away the top of its head and most of its features, but its fanged mouth hangs open an inch or two, intact, and something is lodged behind its teeth. I reach between stone fangs and withdraw a slip of rolled paper, bound by a ring.

One time she wrote me a story and scattered it across the Coronado, wedged in garden cracks and under tiles, and in the mouths of statues . . .

Regina.

My hands shake as I slide the metal off and uncurl the brittle page.

And then, having reached the top, the hero faced the gods and monsters that meant to bar his path.

197

I let the paper curl in on itself and look at the ring that held it closed. It's not jewelry—it's too big to fit a finger or a thumb—and clearly not the kind a young girl would wear anyway, but a perfect, rounded thing. It appears to be made of iron. The metal is cold and heavy, and one small hole has been drilled into the side of it; but other than that, the ring is remarkably undisturbed by scratches or imperfections. I slide it gently back over the paper and send up a silent thank-you to the long-dead girl.

I can't give Owen much time, and I can't give him closure.

But I can give him this.

"Owen?"

I wince at the sound of my own voice echoing through the Narrows.

"Owen!" I call again, holding my breath as I listen for something, anything. Still hiding, then. I'm about to reach out and read the walls—though they failed to lead me to him last time—when I hear it, like a quiet, careful invitation.

The humming. It is thin and distant, like threads of memory, just enough to take hold of, to follow.

I wind through the corridors, letting the melody lead me, and finally find Owen sitting in an alcove, a doorless recess, the lack of key light and outlines rendering the space even dimmer than the rest of the Narrows. No wonder I couldn't find him. My eyes barely register the space. Pressed against the wall, he is little more than a dark shape crowned in silver-blond, his head bowed as he hums and runs his thumb over the small dark line on his palm.

He looks up at me, the song trailing into the nothing. "Mackenzie."

His voice is calm but his eyes are tense, as if he's trying to steel himself. "Has it been a day?"

"Not quite," I say, stepping into the alcove. "I found something." I sink to my knees. "Something of yours."

I hold out my hand and uncurl my fingers. The slip of paper bound by the iron ring shines faintly in the dark.

Owen's eyes widen a fraction. "Where did you . . . ?" he whispers, voice wavering.

"I found it in a gargoyle's mouth," I say. "On the Coronado roof." I offer him the note and the ring, and when he takes it, his skin brushes mine and there is a moment of quiet in my head, a sliver, and then it's gone as he pulls back, examining my gift.

"How did you—"

"Because I live there now."

Owen lets out a shuddering breath. "So that's where the numbered doors lead?" he asks. Longing creeps into his voice. "I think I knew that."

He slides the fragile paper from its ring and reads the words despite the dark. I watch his lips move as he recites them to himself.

"It's from the story," he whispers. "The one she hid for me, before she died."

"What was it about?"

His eyes lose focus as he thinks, and I don't see how he can draw up a story from so long ago, until I remember that he's passed the decades sleeping. Regina's murder is as fresh to him as Ben's is to me.

"It was a quest. A kind of odyssey. She took the Coronado and made it grand, not just a building, but a whole world, seven floors full of adventure. The hero faced caves and dragons, unclimbable walls, impassable mountains, incredible dangers." A faint laugh crosses his lips as he remembers. "Regina could make a story out of anything." He closes his hand over the note and the ring. "Could I keep this? Just until the day's over?"

I nod, and Owen's eyes brighten—if not with trust, then with hope. Just like I wanted. And I hate to steal that flicker of hope from him so soon, but I don't have a choice. I need to know.

"When I was here before," I say, "you were going to tell me about Robert. What happened to him?"

The light goes out of Owen's eyes as if I blew out a candle's flame.

"He got away," he says through clenched teeth. "They let him get away. *I* let him get away. I was her big brother and I . . ." There's so much pain in his voice as it trails off; but when he looks at me, his eyes are clear, crisp. "When I first found my way here, I thought I was in Hell. Thought I was being punished for not finding Robert, for not tearing the world apart in search of him, for not tearing *him* apart. And I would have. Mackenzie, I really would have. He deserved that. He deserved worse."

My throat tightens as I tell Owen what I've told myself so many times, even though it never helps. "It wouldn't bring her back."

"I know. Trust me, I do. And I would have done far worse," he says, "if I'd thought there *was* a way to bring Regina back. I would have traded places. I would have sold souls. I would have torn this world apart. I would have done anything, broken any rule, just to bring her back."

My heart aches. I can't count the times I've sat beside Ben's drawer and wondered how much noise it would take to wake him up. And I can't deny how hard I've wished, since I met Owen, that he wouldn't slip: because if he could make it through, why not Ben?

"I was supposed to protect her," he says, "and I got her killed. . . ."

He must take my silence for simple pity, because he adds, "I don't expect you to understand."

But I do. Too well.

"My little brother is dead," I say. The words get out before I can stop them. Owen doesn't say *I'm sorry*. But he does shift closer, until we're sitting side by side.

"What happened?" he asks.

"He was killed," I whisper. "Hit and run. They got away. I would give anything to rewrite that morning, to walk Ben all the way to school, take an extra five seconds to hug him, to draw on his hand, do anything to change the moment when he crossed the street."

"And if you could find the driver . . ." says Owen.

"I would kill him." There is no doubt in my voice.

A silence falls around us.

"What was he like?" he asks, knocking his knee against mine. There is something so simple in it, as if I am just a girl, and he is just a boy, and we are sitting in a hallway—any hallway, not the Narrows—and I'm not talking about my dead brother with a History I'm supposed to have sent back.

"Ben? He was too smart for his own good. You couldn't lie to him, not even about things like Santa Claus or the Easter Bunny. He'd put on these silly glasses and cross-examine you until he found a crack. And he couldn't focus on anything unless he was drawing. He was really great at art. He made me laugh." I've never spoken this way about Ben, not since he died. "And he could be a real brat sometimes. Hated sharing. Would break something before he'd let you have it. This one time he broke an entire box of pencils because I wanted to borrow one. As if breaking pencils made them useless. So I pulled out this sharpener, one of those little plastic ones, and sharpened all the pencil halves and then we each had a set. Half as long as they were to start, but they still worked. It drove him mad."

A small laugh escapes, and then my chest tightens. "It feels wrong to laugh," I whisper.

"Isn't it strange? It's like after they die, you're only allowed to remember the good. But no one's all good."

I feel the scratch of letters in my pocket, but leave it.

"I've gone to see him," I say. "In the stacks. I talk to him, to his shelf, tell him what he's missing. Never the good stuff, of course. Just the boring, the random. But no matter how I hold on to his memory, I'm starting to forget him, one detail at a time. Some days I think the only thing that keeps me from prying open his drawer, from seeing him, from waking him, even, is the fact it's not him. Not really. They tell me there's no point because it wouldn't be him."

"Because Histories aren't people?" he asks.

I cringe. "No. That's not it at all." Even though most Histories *aren't* people, aren't human, not the way Owen is. "It's just that Histories have a pattern. They slip. The only thing that hurts me more than the idea of the thing in that drawer not being my brother is the idea of its being him, and my causing him pain. Distress. And then having to send him back to the stacks after all of it."

I feel Owen's hand drift toward mine, hover just above my skin. He waits to see if I'll stop him. When I don't, he curls his fingers over mine. The whole world quiets at his touch. I lean my head against the wall and close my eyes. The quiet is welcome. It dulls the thoughts of Ben.

"I don't feel like I'm slipping," says Owen.

"That's because you aren't."

"Well, that means it's possible, right? What if—"

"*Stop.*" I pull free of his touch and push myself to my feet.

"I'm sorry," he says, standing. "I didn't mean to upset you."

"I'm not upset," I say. "But Ben's gone. There's no bringing him back." The words are directed at myself more than at him. I turn to go. I need to move. Need to hunt.

"Wait," he says, taking my hand. The quiet floods in as he holds up the note in his other hand. "If you find any more of Regina's story, would you . . . would you bring it to me?" I hover at the edge of the alcove. "Please, Mackenzie. It's all I have left of her. What wouldn't you give, to have something, anything, of Ben's to hold on to?"

I think of the box of Ben's things, overturned on my bed, my hands shaking as I picked up each item and prayed there would be a glimpse, a fractured moment, anything. Clinging to a silly pair of plastic glasses with nothing more than a single, smudged memory.

"I'll keep an eye out," I say, and Owen pulls me into a hug. I flinch but feel nothing, only steady quiet.

"Thank you," he whispers against my ear, and my face flushes as his lips graze my skin. And then his arms slide away, taking the quiet and the touch, and he retreats into the alcove, the darkness swallowing everything but his silvery hair. I force myself to turn away, and hunt.

As nice as his touch was, it's not what lingers with me while I work. It's his words. Two words I tried to shut out, but they cling to me.

What if echoes in my head as I hunt.

What if haunts me through the Narrows.

What if follows me home.

TWENTY

I **PEER OUT** the Narrows door and into the hall, making sure the coast is clear before I step through the wall and back onto the third floor of the Coronado, sliding my ring on. I got the list down to two names before it shot back up to four. Whatever technical difficulty the Archive is experiencing, I hope they fix it soon. I am a horrible hollow kind of tired; all I want is quiet and rest.

There is a mirror across from me, and I check my reflection in it before heading home. Despite the bone-deep fatigue and the growing fear and frustration, I look . . . fine. Da always said he'd teach me to play cards. Said I'd take the bank, the way things never reach my eyes. There should be something—a tell, a crease between my eyes, or a tightness in my jaw.

I'm too good at this.

Behind my reflection I see the painting of the sea, slanting as if the waves crashing on the rocks have hit with enough force to tip the picture. I turn and straighten it. The frame makes a faint rattling sound when I do. Everything in this place seems to be falling apart.

I return home to 3F, but when I step through the door, I stop, eyes widening.

I'm braced for vacant rooms and scrounging through a pile of takeout flyers for dinner. I'm not braced for this. The moving boxes have been broken down and stacked in one corner beside several trash bags of packing material, but other than that, the apartment looks strikingly like, well, an apartment. The furniture has been assembled and arranged, Dad is stirring something on the stove, a book open on the counter. He pauses and pulls a pen from behind his ear to make a margin note. Mom is sitting at the kitchen table surrounded by enough paint swatches to suggest that she thoroughly raided that aisle of the home improvement store.

"Oh, hi, Mac!" she says, looking up from the chips.

"I thought you already painted."

"We started to," says Dad, making another note in his book.

Mom shakes her head, begins to stack the chips. "It's just wasn't quite right, you know? It has to be right. Just right."

"Lyndsey called," says Dad.

"How was Wes?" asks Mom.

"Fine. He's helping me with the *Inferno*."

"Is that what they call it?"

"Dad!"

Mom frowns. "Didn't you have it with you when you left?"

I look down at my empty hands, and rack my brain. Where did I leave it? The garden? The study? Nix's place? The roof? No, I didn't have it on the roof—

"Told you they weren't reading," whispers Dad.

"He has . . . character," adds Mom.

"You should see Mac around him. I swear I saw a smile!"

"Are you actually cooking?" I ask.

"Don't sound so surprised."

"Mac, what do you think of this green?"

"Food's up."

I carry plates to the table, trying to figure out why my chest hurts. And somewhere between pouring a glass of water and taking a bite of stir-fry, I realize why. Because this—the banter and the joking and the food—this is what normal families do. Mom isn't smiling too hard, and Dad isn't running away.

This is normal. Comfortable.

This is us moving on.

Without Ben.

My brother left a hole, and it's starting to close. And when it does, he'll be gone. Really and truly gone. Isn't this what I wanted? For my parents to stop running? For my family to heal? But what if I'm not ready to let Ben go?

"You okay?" asks Dad. I realize I've stopped with the fork halfway to my mouth. I open my mouth to say the three small words that will shatter everything. *I miss Ben.*

"Mackenzie?" asks Mom, the smile sliding from her face.

I blink. I can't do it.

"Sorry," I say. "I was just thinking. . . ."

Think think think.

Mom and Dad watch me. My mind stumbles through lies until I find the right one. I smile, even though it feels like a grimace. "Could we make cookies after dinner?"

Mom's brows peak, but she nods. "Of course." She twirls her fork. "What sort?"

"Oatmeal raisin. The chewy kind."

When the cookies are in the oven, I call Lyndsey back. I slip into my room and let her talk. She tunes her guitar and rambles about her parents and the boy at the gym. Somewhere between her description of her new music tutor and her lament over her mother's attempt to diet, I stop her.

"Hey, Lynds."

"Yeah?"

"I've been thinking. About Ben. A lot."

Oddly enough, we never talk about Ben. By some silent understanding he's always been off-limits. But I can't help it.

"Yeah?" she asks. I hear the hollow thud of the guitar being set aside. "I think about him all the time. I was babysitting a kid the other night, and he insisted on drawing with a green crayon. Wouldn't use anything else. And I thought about Ben and his love of blue pencils, and it made me smile and ache at the same time."

My eyes burn. I reach out for blue stuffed bear, the pair of black glasses still perched on its nose.

"But you know," says Lyndsey, "it kind of feels like he's not gone, because I see him in everything."

"I think I'm starting to forget him," I whisper.

"Nah, you're not." She sounds so certain.

"How do you know?"

"If you mean a few little things—the exact sound of his voice, the shade of his hair, then okay, yeah. You're going to forget. But Ben isn't those things, you know? He's your brother. He's made up of every moment in his life. You'll never forget all of that."

"Are you taking a philosophy course too?" I manage. She laughs. I laugh, a hollow echo of hers.

"So," she says, turning up the cheer, "how's Guyliner?"

I dream of Ben again.

Stretched out on his stomach on my bedroom floor, drawing with a blue pencil right on the hardwood, twisting the drops of blood into monsters with dull eyes. I come in, and he looks up. His eyes are black, but as I watch, the blackness begins to draw inward until it's nothing but a dot in the center of his bright brown eyes.

He opens his mouth to speak, but he only gets halfway through saying "I won't slip" before his voice fades away. And then his eyes fade, dissolving into air. And then his whole face fades. His body begins to fade, as if an invisible hand is erasing him, inch by inch.

I reach out, but by the time I touch his shoulder, he's only a vague shape.

An outline.

A sketch.

And then nothing.

I sit up in the dark.

I rest my head against my knees. It doesn't help. The tightness in my chest goes deeper than air. I snatch the glasses from the bear's nose and reach for the memory, watching it loop three or four times, but the faded impression of a Ben-like shape only makes it worse, only reminds me how much I'm forgetting. I pull on my jeans and boots, and shove the list in my pocket without even looking at the names.

I know this is a bad idea, a horrible idea, but as I make my way through the apartment, down the hall, into the Narrows, I pray that Roland is behind the desk. I step into the Archive, hoping for his red Chucks, but instead I find a pair of black leather boots, the heels kicked up on the desk before the doors, which are now closed. The girl has a notebook in her lap and a pen tucked behind her ear, along with a sweep of sandy blond hair, impossibly streaked with sun.

"Miss Bishop," says Carmen. "How can I help you?"

"Is Roland here?" I ask.

She frowns. "Sorry, he's busy. I'm afraid I'll have to do."

"I wanted to see my brother."

Her boots slide off the desk and land on the floor. Her green eyes look sad. "This isn't a cemetery, Miss Bishop." It feels weird for someone so young to refer to me this way.

"I know that," I say carefully, trying to pick my angle. "I was just hoping . . ."

Carmen takes the pen from behind her ear and sets it in the book to mark her place, then puts the book aside and interlaces her fingers on top of the desk. Each motion is smooth, methodical.

"Sometimes Roland lets me see him."

A faint crease forms between her eyes. "I know. But that doesn't make it right. I think you should—"

"Please," I say. "There's nothing of him left in my world. I just want to sit by his shelf."

After several long moments, she picks up a pad of paper and makes a note. We wait in silence, which is good, because I can barely hear over my pulse. And then the doors behind her open, and a short, thin Librarian strides through.

"I need a break," says Carmen, rolling her neck. The Librarian—Elliot, I remember—nods obediently and takes a seat. Carmen holds her hand toward the doors, and I pass through into the atrium. She follows and tugs them shut behind her.

We make our way through the room and down the sixth wing.

"What would you have done," she asks, "if I'd said no?"

I shrug. "I guess I would have gone home."

We cross through a courtyard. "I don't believe that."

"I don't believe you would have said no."

"Why's that?" she asks.

"Your eyes are sad," I say, "even when you smile."

Her expression wavers. "I may be a Librarian, Miss Bishop, but we have people we miss, too. People we want back. It can be hard to be so far from the living, and so close to the dead."

I've never heard a Librarian talk that way. It's like light shining through armor. We start up a short set of wooden stairs.

"Why did you take this job?" I ask. "It doesn't make sense. You're so young—"

"It was an honor to be promoted," she says, but the words have a hollow ring. I can see her drawing back into herself, into her role.

"Who did you lose?" I ask.

Carmen flashes a smile that is at once dazzling and sad. "I'm a Librarian, Miss Bishop. I've lost everyone."

Before I can say anything, she opens the door to the large reading room with the red rug and the corner chairs, and leads me to the wall of cabinets on the far side. I reach out and run my fingers over the name.

BISHOP, BENJAMIN GEORGE

I just want to see him. That's all. I *need* to see him. I press my hand flat against the face of the drawer, and I can almost feel the pull of him. The need. Is this the way the Histories feel, trapped in the Narrows with only the desperate sense that something vital is beyond the doors, that if they could just get out—

"Is there anything else, Miss Bishop?" Carmen asks carefully.

"Could I see him?" I ask quietly. "Just for a moment?"

She hesitates. And to my surprise, she steps up to the shelves and produces the same key she used to disable Jackson Lerner. Gold and sharp and without teeth, but when she slides it into the slot on Ben's drawer and turns, there is a soft click within the wall. The drawer opens an inch, and sits ajar. Something in me tightens.

"I'll give you a few minutes," Carmen whispers, "but no more."

I nod, unable to take my eyes off the sliver of space between the front of the drawer and the rest of the stacks, a strip of deep shadow. I listen to the sound of Carmen's withdrawing steps. And then I reach out, wrap my fingers over the edge, and slide my brother's drawer open.

TWENTY-ONE

I'M SITTING ON THE SWINGS in our backyard, rocking from heel to toe, heel to toe, while you pick slivers of wood off the frame.

"You can't tell anyone," you say. "Not your parents. Not your friends. Not Ben."

"Why not?"

"People aren't smart when it comes to the dead."

"I don't understand."

"If you told someone that there was a place where their mother, or their brother, or their daughter, still existed—in some form—they'd tear the world apart to get there."

You chew a toothpick.

"No matter what people say, they'd do anything."

"How do you know?"

"Because I'd do it. Trust me, you'd do it too."

"I wouldn't."

"Maybe not anymore, because you know what a History is. And you know I'd never forgive you if you tried to wake one up. But if you weren't a Keeper . . . if you lost someone and you thought they were gone forever, and then you learned you could get them back, you'd be there with the rest of them, clawing at the walls to get through."

• • •

My chest turns to stone when I see him, crushing my lungs and my heart.

Benjamin lies on the shelf, still as he was beneath the hospital sheet. But there's no sheet now, and his skin isn't bruised or blue. He's got the slightest flush in his cheeks, as if he's sleeping, and he's wearing the same clothes he had on that day, before they got ruined. Grass-stained jeans and his favorite black-and-red-striped shirt, a gift from Da the summer he died, an emblematic X over the heart because Ben always used to say "cross my heart" so solemnly. I was with him when Da gave it to him. Ben wore it for days until it smelled foul and we had to drag it off of him to be washed. It doesn't smell like anything now. His hands are at his sides, which looks wrong because he used to sleep on his side with both fists crammed under the pillow; but this way I can see the black pen doodle on the back of his left hand, the one I drew that morning, of me.

"Hi, Ben," I whisper.

I want to reach out, to touch him, but my hand won't move. I can't will my fingers to leave my side. And then that same dangerous thought whispers into the recesses of my mind, at the weak points.

If Owen can wake without slipping, why not Ben?

What if some Histories don't slip?

It's fear and anger and restlessness that make them wake up. But Ben was never afraid or angry or restless. So would he even wake? Maybe Histories who wouldn't wake wouldn't slip if they did . . . *But Owen woke,* a voice warns. Unless a Librarian woke him and tried to alter his memories. Maybe that's the trick. Maybe Owen isn't slipping because he didn't wake himself up.

I look down at Ben's body and try to remember that this isn't my brother.

It was easier to believe when I couldn't see him.

My chest aches, but I don't feel like crying. Ben's dark lashes rest against his cheeks, his hair curling across his forehead. When I see that hair tracing its way across his skin, my body unfreezes, my hand drifting up to brush it from his face, the way I used to do.

That's all I mean to do.

But when my fingers graze his skin, Ben's eyes float open.

TWENTY-TWO

I **GASP AND JERK MY HAND BACK,** but it's too late.
Ben's brown eyes—Mom's eyes, warm and bright and wide—
blink once, twice.

And he sits up.

"Mackenzie?" he asks.

The ache in my chest explodes into panic. My pulse shatters the
calmness I know I need to show.

"Hi, Ben," I choke out, the shock making it hard to breathe, to
speak.

My brother looks around at the room—the stacked drawers
reaching to the ceiling, the tables and dust and oddness—then
swings his legs over the edge of the shelf.

"What happened?" And then, before I can answer: "Where's
Mom? Where's Dad?"

He hops down from the shelf, sniffles. His forehead crinkles. "I
want to go home."

My hand reaches for his.

"Then let's go home, Ben."

He moves to take my hand, but stops. Looks around again.

"What's going on?" he asks, his voice unsteady.

"Come on, Ben," I say.

"Where am I?" The black at the center of his eyes wobbles. *No.*
"How did I get here?" He takes a small step back. Away from me.

"It's going to be okay," I say.

When his eyes meet mine, they are tinged with panic. "Tell me how I got here." Confusion. "This isn't funny." Distress.

"Ben, please," I say softly. "Let's just go home."

I don't know what I'm thinking. I can't think. I look at him, and all I know is that I can't leave him here. He's Ben, and I pinkie-swore a thousand times I'd never let anything hurt him. Not the ghosts under the bed or the bees in the yard or the shadows in his closet.

"I don't understand." His voice catches. His irises are darkening. "I don't . . . I was . . ."

This isn't supposed to happen. He didn't wake himself. He's not supposed to—

"Why . . ." he starts.

I step toward him, kneeling so I can take his hands. I squeeze them. I try to smile.

"Ben—"

"Why aren't you telling me what happened?"

His eyes hover on me, the black spreading too fast, blotting out the warm, bright brown. All I see in those eyes is the reflection of my face, caught between pain and fear and an unwillingness to believe that he's slipping. Owen didn't slip. Why does Ben have to?

This isn't fair.

Ben begins to cry, hitching sobs.

I pull him into a hug.

"Be strong for me," I whisper in his hair, but he doesn't answer. I tighten my grip as if I can hold the Ben I know—knew—in place, can keep him with me; but he pushes me away. A jarring strength for such a small body. I stumble, and another pair of arms catches me.

"Get back," orders the man holding me. Roland.

His eyes are leveled on Ben, but the words are meant for me. He pushes me out of his way and approaches my brother. *No, no, no, I* think, the word playing in my head like a metronome.

What have I done?

"I didn't . . ."

"Stay back," Roland growls, then kneels in front of Ben.

That's not Ben, I think. Looking at the History—its eyes black, where Ben's were brown.

Not Ben, I think, clutching my hands around my ribs to keep from shaking.

Not Ben, as Roland puts a hand on my brother's shoulder and says something too soft for me to hear.

Not Ben. Metal glints in Roland's other hand and he plunges a toothless gold key into Not Ben's chest and turns it.

Not Ben doesn't cry out, but simply sinks. His eyes fall shut and his head falls forward, and his body slumps toward the ground but never hits because Roland catches him, scoops him up, and returns him to his drawer. The pain goes out of his face, the tension goes out of his limbs. His body relaxes against the shelf, as if settling into sleep.

Roland slides the door shut, the dark devouring Not Ben's body. I hear the cabinet lock, and something in me cracks.

Roland doesn't look at me as he pulls a notepad from his pocket. "I'm sorry, Miss Bishop."

"Roland," I plead. "Don't do this." He scratches something onto the paper. "I'm sorry," I say. "I'm sorry, I'm sorry, but please don't—"

"I don't have a choice," he says as the card on the front of Ben's drawer turns red. The mark of the restricted stacks.

No, no, no come the metronome cries, each one causing a crack that splinters me.

I take a step forward.

"Stay where you are," orders Roland, and whether it's his tone or the fact that the cracks hurt so much I can't breathe, I do as he says. Before my eyes, the shelves begin to shift. Ben's red-marked drawer pulls backward with a hush until it's swallowed by the wall. The surrounding drawers rearrange themselves, gliding to fill the gap.

Ben's drawer is gone.

I sink to my knees on the old wood floor.

"Get up," orders Roland.

My body feels sluggish, my lungs heavy, my pulse too slow. I haul myself to my feet, and Roland grabs my arm, forcing me out of the room into an empty hall.

"Who opened the drawer, Miss Bishop?"

I won't rat out Carmen. She only wanted to help.

"I did," I say.

"You don't have a key."

"'Two ways through any lock,'" I answer numbly.

"I warned you to stay away," growls Roland. "I warned you not to draw attention. I warned you what happens to Keepers who lose their post. What were you *thinking?*"

"I wasn't," I say. My throat hurts, as if I've been screaming. "I just had to see him—"

"You woke a History."

"I didn't mean to—"

"He's not a goddamn puppy, Mackenzie, and he's not your brother. That *thing* is not your brother, and you know that."

The cracks are spreading beneath my skin.

"How can you not know that?" Roland continues. "Honestly—"

"I thought he wouldn't slip!"

He stops. *"What?"*

"I thought . . . that maybe . . . he wouldn't slip."

Roland brings his hands down on my shoulders, hard. "Every. History. Slips."

Not Owen, says a voice inside me.

Roland lets go. "Turn in your list."

If there's any wind left in my lungs, that order knocks it out.

"What?"

"Your list."

If she proves herself unfit in any way, she will forfeit the position.

And if she proves unfit, you, Roland, will remove her yourself.

"Roland . . ."

"You can collect it tomorrow morning, when you return for your hearing."

He promised me he wouldn't. I trusted . . . but what have I done with *his* trust? I can see the pain in his eyes. I force one shaking hand into my pocket and pass him the folded paper. He takes it and motions toward the door, but I can't will myself to leave.

"Miss Bishop."

My feet are nailed to the floor.

"Miss Bishop."

This isn't happening. I just wanted to see Ben. I just needed—

"Mackenzie," says Roland. I force myself forward.

I follow him through the maze of stacks. There is no warmth and there is no peace. With every step, every breath, the cracks deepen, spread. Roland leads me through the atrium to the antechamber and the front desk, where Elliot sits diligently.

When Roland turns to look at me, anger has dulled into something sad. Tired.

"Go home," he says. I nod stiffly. He turns and vanishes back into the stacks.

Elliot glances up from his work, a vague curiosity in the arch of his brows.

I can feel myself breaking.

I barely make it through the door and into the Narrows before I shatter.

It *hurts*.

Worse than anything. Worse than noise or touch or knives. I don't know how make it stop. I have to make it stop.

I can't breathe.

I can't——

"Mackenzie?"

I turn to find Owen standing in the hall. His blue eyes hangs on me, the smallest wrinkle between his brows.

"What's wrong?" he asks.

Everything about him is calm, quiet, level. Pain twists into anger. I push him, hard.

"Why haven't you slipped?" I snap.

Owen doesn't fight back, not even reflexively, doesn't try to escape, the slightest clenching of his jaw the only sign of emotion. I want to push him over. I want to make him slip. He has to. Ben did.

"Why, Owen?"

I push him again. He takes a step away.

"What makes you so special? What makes you so different? Ben slipped. He slipped right away, and you've been here for days and you haven't slipped at all and it isn't fair."

I shove him again, and his back hits the wall at the end of the corridor.

"It isn't fair!"

My hands dig into his shirt. The quiet is like static in my head, filling the space. It is not enough to erase the pain. I am still breaking.

"Calm down." Owen wraps his hands around mine, pinning them to his chest. The quiet thickens, pours into my head.

My face feels wet, but I don't remember crying. "It's not fair."

"I'm sorry," he says. "Please calm down."

I want the pain to stop. I need it to stop. I won't be able to claw my way back up. There is all this anger and this guilt and—

And then Owen kisses my shoulder. "I'm so sorry about Ben."

The quiet builds like a wave, drowning anger and pain.

"I'm sorry, Mackenzie."

I stiffen, but as his lips press against my skin, the silence flares in my head, blotting something out. Heat ripples through my body, pricking my senses as the quiet deadens my thoughts. He kisses my throat, my jaw. Each time his lips brush my skin, the heat and silence blossom side by side and spread, drowning a little bit of the pain and anger and guilt, leaving only warmth and want and quiet in their place. His lips brush my cheek, and then he pulls back, his pale eyes leveled cautiously on mine, his mouth barely a breath from mine. When he touches me, there is nothing but touch. There is no thought of wrong and no thought of loss and no thought of anything, because thoughts can't get through the static.

"I'm sorry, M."

M. That drags me under. That one little word he can't possibly understand. M. Not Mackenzie. Not Mac. Not Bishop. Not Keeper.

I want that. I need that. I cannot be the girl who broke the rules and woke her dead brother and ruined everything. . . .

I close the gap. Pull Owen's body flush with mine.

His mouth is soft but strong, and when he deepens the kiss, the quiet spreads, filling every space in my mind, washing over me. Drowning me.

And then his mouth is gone, and his hands let go of mine. Everything comes back, too loud. I pull his body against mine, feel the impossibly careful crush of his mouth as it steals the air from my lungs, steals the thoughts from my head.

Owen steps forward, urging my body against the wall, pushing me with his kisses and the quiet that comes with his touch. I am letting it all wash over me, letting it wash away the questions and doubts, the Histories and the key and the ring and everything else, until I am just M against his lips, his body. M reflected in the pale blue of his eyes until he closes them and kisses me deeper, and then I am nothing.

TWENTY-THREE

I **CANNOT STAY HERE** forever, buried under Owen's touch.
At last I push away, break the surface of the quiet, and before I
lose my will, before I cave, I leave. I can't hunt, so I spend what's left
of the night searching the Coronado, moving numbly from floor to
floor, trying to read the walls for any clues, anything the Archive—
or whoever in it tried to cover things up—might have missed, but
that year is shot full of holes. I run through the time lines, scour the
memories for leads, and find only dull impressions and stretches of
too-flat black. Elling's old apartment is locked, but I read the south
stairs, where Eileen supposedly fell, and even brave the elevators
in search of Lionel's stabbing, only to find the unnatural nothing of
excavated pasts. Whatever happened here, someone went out of
their way to bury it, even from people like me.

A dull ache has formed behind my eyes, and I've lost hope of finding
any useful memory intact, but I keep searching. I have to. Because
every time I stop moving, the thought of losing Ben—really losing
him—catches up, the pain catches up, the thought of kissing Owen—
of using a History for his touch—catches up. So I keep moving.

I start searching for more of Regina's story. I put my ring on,
hoping to dull the headache, and search the old-fashioned way,
thankful for the distraction. I check table drawers and shelves, even
though sixty years have passed, and the chances of finding anything
are slim. I search for hidden compartments in the study, and take
down half the books to check behind them. I remember Owen saying

something about garden cracks. I know paper would never last out here, but I still search the mossy stones by feel in the dark, grateful for the quiet predawn air.

The sun is rising as I look behind the counters and around the old equipment in the coffee shop, careful not to touch the half-painted walls. And just as I'm about to abandon the search, my eyes drift to the sheeting thrown over the rose pattern in the floor to keep it safe. *In garden cracks and under tiles,* Owen said. It's a long shot, but I kneel and pull aside the plastic tarp. The rose beneath is as wide as my arm span, each inlaid marble petal piece the size of my palm. I brush my hand back and forth across the rust-colored pattern. Near the center, I feel the subtle shift of stones beneath my touch. One of the petals is loose.

My heart skips as I get my fingers under the lip of the petal. It lifts. The hiding place is little more than a hole, the walls of which are lined with white cloth. And there, folded and weighted down by a narrow metal bar, is another piece of Regina's story.

The paper is yellowing but intact, protected by the hidden chamber, and I lift it to the morning light.

The red stones shifted and became steps, a great flight of stairs that led the hero up and up. And the hero climbed.

The pieces are out of order. The last fragment spoke of facing gods and monsters at the top of something. This one clearly goes before. But what comes after?

My attention shifts to the small bar that had held the note in place. It's roughly the size of a pencil but half the length, one end tapering just like a graphite point. A groove has been cut from the blunt end down, and it's made of the same metal as the ring that held the first note.

For one horrible, bitter moment, I consider putting the pieces back, leaving them buried. It seems so unfair that Owen should have pieces of Regina when I can have none of Ben.

But as cruel as it is that Ben slipped when Owen didn't, it isn't Owen's fault. He's the History, and I'm the Keeper. He couldn't have known what would happen, and I'm the one who chose to wake my brother.

The sun is up now. The morning of my trial. I slip both the paper and the bar into my pocket and make my way upstairs.

Dad is already up, and I tell him I went running. I don't know if he believes me. He says I look tired, and I admit that I am. I shower numbly and stumble through the early hours, trying not to think of the trial, of being deemed unfit, of losing everything. I help Mom settle on new paint chips and pack up half the oatmeal raisin cookies for Nix before I make a lame excuse to leave. Mom is so distracted by the paint dilemma—*it's still not right, not quite right, has to be right*—that she simply nods. I pause in the doorway, watching her work, listening to Dad on a call in the other room. I try to memorize this *before*, not knowing what *after* will be.

And then I go.

I cut through the Narrows, and the memory of last night sweeps over me with the humid air and the far-off sounds. The memory of quiet. And as panic eats through me, I wish I could disappear again. I can't. But there's something I should do.

I find the alcove, and Owen in it, and press the note and the small iron bar into his hands, staying only long enough to steal a kiss and a moment of quiet. The peace dissolves into fear as I reach the Archive door and step through.

I don't know what I expected—a row of Librarians waiting, ready to strip me of my key and my ring? Someone named Agatha waiting to judge me unfit, to carve my job right out of my life, taking my identity with it? A tribunal? A lynch mob?

I certainly don't expect Lisa to look up from her desk, over her green horn-rimmed glasses, and ask me what I want.

"Is Roland here?" I ask unsteadily.

She goes back to her work. "He said you'd stop by."

I shift my weight. "Is that all he said?"

"Said to send you in." Lisa straightens. "Is everything all right, Miss Bishop?"

The antechamber is quiet, but my heart is slamming in my chest so loudly, I think she'll hear. I swallow and force myself to nod. She hasn't been told. Just then, Elliot rushes in, and I stiffen, thinking he's come to tell her, come to collect me; but when he leans over her, he says only, "Three, four, six, ten through fourteen."

Lisa lets out a tight breath. "All right. Make sure they're blacked out."

I frown. What kind of technical difficulty is this?

Elliot retreats, and Lisa looks at me again, as if she'd forgotten I was there.

"Firsts," she says, meaning first wing, first hall, first room. "Can you show yourself?"

"I think I can handle it."

She nods and throws open several massive ledgers on the desk. I step past her into the atrium. Looking up at the vaulted ceiling of stone and colored glass, I wonder if I'll ever feel at peace here again. I wonder if I'll have the chance.

Something in the distance rumbles, followed shortly by an aftershock of sound. Startled, I scan the stacks and spot Patrick on the far side of the atrium, and when he hears the noise, he vanishes down the nearest wing, pulling the doors closed behind him. I pass Carmen standing by a row of stacks before the first hall. She gives me a small nod.

"Miss Bishop," she says. "What brings you back so soon?"

For a moment, I just stare at her. I feel like my crimes are written on my face, but there's nothing in her voice to suggest she knows. Did Roland really say nothing?

"Just here to talk to Roland," I say at last, managing only a ghost of calm. She waves me on, and I turn down the first wing, then the first hall, and stop at the first door. It's closed, a heavy, glassless thing, and I press my fingertips against it and summon the courage to go in.

When I do, two pairs of eyes meet mine: one gray and quite stern; the other brown and rimmed with black.

Wesley perches on a table in the middle of the room.

"I believe you two know each other," says Roland.

I consider lying, based on the gut sense that Keepers are supposed to work alone, to exist alone. But Wes nods.

"Hey, Mac," he says.

"What's *he* doing here?" I ask.

Roland steps up. "Mr. Ayers will be assisting you in your territorial duties."

I turn to him. "You gave me a babysitter?"

"Hey, now," says Wes, hopping down from the table. "I prefer the term *partner*."

I frown. "But only Crew are partnered."

"I am making an exception," Roland says.

"Come on, Mac," says Wes, "it will be fun."

My mind flicks to Owen, waiting in the dark of the Narrows, but I force the image back. "Roland, what's this about?"

"You've noticed an uptick in your numbers."

I nod. "And ages. Lisa and Patrick both said there was some minor technical difficulty."

Roland crosses his arms. "It's called a disruption."

"A disruption, I take it, is worse than a minor technical difficulty."

"Have you noticed how quiet the Archive is kept? Do you know why that is?"

"Because Histories wake up," says Wesley.

"Yes, they do. When there's too much noise, too much activity, the lighter sleepers begin to stir. The more noise, the more activity, the more Histories. Even deep sleepers wake up."

Which explains the older Histories in my territory.

"A disruption happens when the noise Histories make waking up causes other Histories to wake up, and so on. Like dominoes. More and more and more, until it's contained."

"Or they all fall down," I whisper.

"As soon as it started, we acted, and began blacking out rooms. Lighter sleepers first. It should have been enough. A disruption starts in one place, like a fire, so it has a core. Logic says that if you can douse the hottest part, you can tamp out the rest. But it's not working. Every time we put out a fire, a new one flares up in a perfectly quiet place."

"That doesn't seem natural," says Wes.

Roland shoots me a meaningful glance. *That's because it isn't.*

So, is the disruption a distraction from the altered Histories? Or is it something more? I wish I could ask, but following Roland's lead, I don't want to say too much in front of Wes.

"And the Coronado," Roland continues, "is being hit harder than other territories at the moment. So, Mackenzie, until this *minor technical difficulty* is resolved and your numbers return to normal, Wesley will be assisting you in your territory."

My mind spins. I came in here expecting to lose my job, lose my self, and instead I get a partner.

Roland holds out a folded slip of paper.

"Your list, Miss Bishop."

I take it, but hold his gaze. What about last night? What about Ben? Questions I know better than to ask aloud. So instead I say, "Is there anything else?"

Roland considers me a moment, then draws something from his back pocket. A folded black handkerchief. I take it and frown at the weight. Something is wrapped in the fabric. When I peel back the cloth, my eyes widen.

It's a key.

Not like the simply copper one I wear around my neck, or the thin gold ones the Librarians use, but larger, heavier, colder. A near-black thing with sharp teeth and pricks of rust. Something tugs at me. I've seen this key before. I've felt this key.

Wesley's eyes widen. "Is that a *Crew* key?"

Roland nods. "It belonged to Antony Bishop."

"Why do you have two keys?" I ask.

You look at me like you never thought I'd notice the second cord around your neck. Now you tug it up over your head and hold it out for me, the metal hanging heavy on the end. When I take the key, it is cold and strangely beautiful, with a handle at one end and sharp teeth at the other. I can't imagine a lock in the world those teeth would fit.

"What does it do?" I ask, cradling the metal.

"It's a Crew key," you say. "When a History gets out, you've got to return them, fast. Crew can't waste time searching for doors into the Narrows. So this turns any door into an Archive door."

"Any door?" I ask. "Even the front door? Or the one to my room? Or the one on the shed that's falling down—"

"*Any* door. You just put the key in the lock and turn. Left for the Librarians, right for Returns."

I run a thumb over the metal. "I thought you stopped being Crew."

"I did. Just haven't brought myself to give it back yet."

I hold up the key, sliding it through thin air as if there's a door with a lock I simply can't see. And I'm about to turn it when you catch my wrist. Your noise washes through my head, all winter trees and far-off storms.

"Careful," you say. "Crew keys are dangerous. They're used to rip open the seams between the Outer and the Archive, and let us through. We like to think we can control that kind of power with left turns and right turns, but these keys, they can tear holes in the world. I did it once, by accident. Nearly ate me up."

"How?"

"Crew keys are too strong and too smart. If you hold that piece of rusted metal up, not to a door, just a bit of thin air, and give it a full turn, all the way around, it'll make a tear right in the world, a bad kind of door, one that leads to nowhere."

"If it leads nowhere," I ask, "then what's the harm?"

"A door that leads nowhere and a door that leads *to* nowhere are totally different things, Kenzie. A door that leads *to* nowhere is dangerous. A door to nowhere is a door into nothing," you say, taking the key back and slipping the cord over your head. "A void."

I look down at the Crew key, mesmerized. "Can it do anything else?"

"Sure can."

"Like what?"

You give a tilted smile. "Make it to Crew and you'll find out."

I chew my lip. "Hey, Da?"

"Yes, Kenzie?"

"If Crew keys are so powerful, won't the Archive notice it's gone?"

You sit back and shrug. "Things get misplaced. Things get lost. Nobody's going to miss it."

"Da gave you his key?" I ask. I'd always wondered what happened to it.

"Do I get a Crew key, too?" asks Wes, bouncing slightly.

"You'll have to share," says Roland. "The Archive keeps track of these. It notices when they go missing. The only reason they won't notice this key is gone is because—"

"It stayed lost," I say.

Roland *almost* smiles. "Antony held on to it as long as he could, and then he gave it back to me. I never turned it in, so the Archive still considers the key lost."

"Why are you giving this to me now?" I ask.

Roland rubs his eyes. "The disruption is spreading. Rapidly. As more Histories wake, and more escape, you need to be prepared."

I look down at the key, the weight of the memory pulling at my fingers. "These keys go to and from the Archive, but Da said they did other things. If I'm going to have it and play Crew, I want to know what he meant."

"That key is not a promotion, Miss Bishop. It's to be used only in case of emergency, and even then, only to go to and from the Archive."

"Where else would I go?"

"Oh, oh, like shortcuts?" asks Wes. "My aunt Joan told me about them. There are these doors, only they don't go to the Narrows or the Archive. They're just in the Outer. Like holes punched in space."

Roland gives us both a withering look and sighs. "Shortcuts are used by Crew to move expediently through the Outer. Some let you skip a few blocks, others let you cross an entire city."

Wes nods, but I frown. "Why haven't I ever seen one? Not even with my ring off."

"I'm sure you have and didn't know it. Shortcuts are unnatural—holes in space. They don't look like doors, just a wrongness in the air, so your eyes slide off. Crew learn to look for the places their eyes don't want to go. But it takes time and practice. Neither of which you have. And it takes Crew years to memorize which doors lead where, which is only one of a dozen reasons why you do *not* have permission to use that key on one if you find it. Do you understand?"

I fold the kerchief over the key and nod, sliding it into my pocket. Roland is obviously nervous, and no wonder. If shortcuts barely register as more than thin air, and Da told me what happens when you use a Crew key *on* thin air, then the potential for ripping open a void in the Outer is pretty high.

"Stick together, no playing with the key, no looking for shortcuts." Wes ticks off the rules on his fingers.

We both turn to go.

"Miss Bishop," says Roland. "A word alone."

Wesley leaves, and I linger, waiting for my punishment, my sentence. Roland is silent until the door closes on Wes.

"Miss Bishop," he says, without looking at me, "Mr. Ayers has been made aware of the disruption. He has not been told of its suspected cause. You will keep that, and the rest of our investigation, to yourself."

I nod. "Is that all, Roland?"

"No," he says, his voice going low. "In opening Benjamin's drawer, you broke Archival law, and you broke my trust. Your actions are being overlooked once and only once, but if you ever, *ever* do that again, you will forfeit your position, and I will remove you myself." His gray eyes level on mine. "*That* is all."

I bow my head, eyes trained on the floor so they can't betray the pain I feel. I take a steadying breath, manage a last nod, and leave.

Wesley is waiting for me by the Archive door. Elliot is at the desk, scribbling furiously. He doesn't look up when I come in, even though the sight of two Keepers has to be unusual.

Wes, meanwhile, seems giddy.

"Look," he says cheerfully, holding out his list for me to inspect. There's one name on it, a kid. "That's mine . . ." He flips the paper over to show six names on the other side. "And those are yours. Sharing is caring."

"Wesley, you *were* listening, weren't you? This isn't a game."

"That doesn't mean we won't have fun. And look!" He taps the center of my list, where a name stands out against the sea of black.

Dina Blunt. 33.

I cringe at the prospect of another adult, a Keeper-Killer, the last one still vivid in my mind; but Wesley looks oddly delighted.

"Come, Miss Bishop," he says, holding out his hand. "Let's go hunting."

TWENTY-FOUR

WESLEY AYERS is being too nice.

"So then this wicked-looking six-year-old tries to take me out at the knees . . ."

Too chatty.

". . . but he's two feet shorter so he just ends kicking the crap out of my shins. . . ."

Too peppy.

"I mean, he was six, and wearing soccer cleats—"

Which means . . .

"He told you," I say.

Wesley's brow crinkles, but he manages to keep smiling. "What are you talking about?"

"Roland told you, didn't he? That I lost my brother."

His smile flickers, fades. At last he nods.

"I already knew," he says. "I saw him when your dad touched my shoulder. I saw him when you shoved me in the Narrows. I haven't seen inside your mother's mind, but it's in her face, it's in her step. I didn't mean to look, Mac, but he's right at the surface. He's written all over your family."

I don't know what to say. The two of us stand there in the Narrows, and all the falseness falls away.

"Roland said there'd been an incident. Said he didn't want you to be alone. I don't know what happened. But I want you to know, you're not alone."

My eyes burn, and I clench my jaw and look away.

"Are you holding up?" he asks.

The lie comes to my lips, automatic. I bite it back. "No."

Wes looks down. "You know, I used to think that when you died, you lost everything." He starts down the hall, talking as he goes, so I'm forced to follow. "That's what made me so sad about death, even more than the fact that you couldn't live anymore; it was that you lost all the things you'd spent your life collecting, all the memories and knowledge. But when my aunt Joan taught me about Histories and the Archive, it changed everything." He pauses at a corner. "The Archive means that the past is never gone. Never lost. Knowing that, it's freeing. It gave me permission to always look forward. After all, we have our own Histories to write."

"God, that's cliché."

"I should write greeting cards, I know."

"I'm not sure they have a section for History-based sentimentality."

"It's too bad, really."

I smile, but I still don't want to talk about Ben. "Your aunt Joan. She's the one you inherited from?"

"Great-aunt, technically. The dame with the blue hair . . . also known as Joan Petrarch. And a frightening woman she is."

"She's still alive?"

"Yeah."

"But she passed the job on to you. Does that mean she abdicated?"

"Not exactly." He fidgets, looks down. "The role can only be passed on if the present Keeper is no longer capable. Aunt Joan broke her hip a few years back. Don't get me wrong, she's still pretty damn fierce. Lightning fast with her cane, in fact. I've got the scars to prove it. But after the accident, she passed the job on to me."

"It must be wonderful to be able to talk to her about it. To ask for advice, for help. To hear the stories."

Wesley's smile falls. "It . . . it doesn't work like that."

I feel like an idiot. Of course she *left* the Archive. She would have been altered. Erased.

"After she passed the job on, she forgot." There's a pain in his eyes, a kind I finally recognize. I might not have been able to share in Wes's clownish smile, but I can share in his sense of loneliness. It's bad enough to have people who never knew, but to have one and lose them . . . No wonder Da kept his title till he died.

Wes looks lost, and I wish I knew how to bring him back, but I don't. And then, I don't have to. A History does it for me. A sound reaches us, and just like that, Wesley's smile rekindles. There is a spark in his eyes, a hunger I sometimes see in Histories. I'll bet he patrols the Narrows looking for a fight.

The sound comes again. Gone are the days, apparently, when we actually had to hunt for Histories. There's enough of them here that they find us.

"Well, you've been wanting to hunt here for days," I say. "Think you're ready?"

Wesley gives a bow. "After you."

"Great," I say, cracking my knuckles. "Just keep your hands to yourself so I can focus on my work instead of that horrible rock music coming off you."

He raises a brow. "I sound like a rock band?"

"Don't look so flattered. You sound like a rock band being thrown out of a truck."

His smile widens. "Brilliant. And for what it's worth, you sound like a thunderstorm. And besides, if my soul's impeccable taste in music throws you off, then learn to tune me out."

I'm not about to admit that I can't, that I don't know how, so I just scoff. The sound of the History comes again, a fist-on-door kind of banging, and I pull the key from around my neck and try to calm the sudden jump in pulse as I wrap the leather cord around my wrist a few times.

I hope it's not Owen. The thought surprises me. I can't believe I'd rather face another Hooper than return Owen right now. It can't be Owen, though. He would never make this much noise . . . not unless he's started to slip. Maybe I should have told Wesley about him, but he's part of the investigation, which puts him under the blanket of things I'm not supposed to speak of. Still, if Wes finds Owen, or Owen finds Wes, how will I explain that I need this one History, that I'm protecting him from the Archive, that he's a clue? (And that's all he is, I tell myself as firmly as possible.)

I can't explain that.

I have to hope Owen has the sense to stay as far away from us as possible.

"Relax, Mac," says Wes, reading the tightness in my face. "I'll protect you."

I laugh for good measure. "Yeah, right. You and your spiked hair will save me from the big bad monsters."

Wes retrieves a short cylinder from his jacket. He flicks his wrist, and the cylinder multiplies, becoming a pole.

I laugh. "I forgot about the stick! No wonder the six-year-old kicked you," I say. "You look ready to break open a piñata."

"It's a bō staff."

"It's a stick. And put it away. Most of the Histories are already scared, Wes. You're only going to make it worse."

"You talk about them like they're people."

"You talk about them like they're not. *Put it away.*"

Wesley grumbles but collapses the stick and pockets it. "Your territory," he says, "your rules."

The banging comes again, followed by a small "Hello? Hello?" We round a corner, and stop.

A teenage girl is standing near the end of the hall. She has a halo of reddish hair and nails painted a chipping blue, and she's banging on one of the doors as hard as she can.

Wesley steps toward her, but I stop him with a look. I take a step toward the girl, and she spins. Her eyes are flecked with black.

"Mel," she says. "God, you scared me." She's nervous but not hostile.

"This whole place is scary," I say, trying to match her unease.

"Where have you been?" she snaps.

"Looking for a way out," I say. "And I think I finally found one."

The girl's face floods with relief. "About time," she says. "Lead the way."

"See?" I say, resting against the Returns door once I've led the girl through. "No stick required."

Wesley smiles. "Impressive—"

Someone screams.

One of those horrible asylum sounds. Animal. And close.

We backtrack, reach a T, and turn right, to find ourselves sharing the stretch of hall with a woman. She's gaunt, her head tilted to the left. She's a hair shorter than Wesley, her back is to us, and judging by the sound that just came out of her mouth, which was insane but undeniably adult, I'm willing to bet she's *Dina Blunt. 33.*

"My turn," whispers Wesley.

I slip back into the stem of the T, out of sight, and hear him hit the wall with a sharp clap. I can't see the woman, but I imagine her whipping around to face Wes at the sound.

"Why, Ian?" she whimpers. The voice grows closer. "Why did you make me do it?"

I press myself against the wall and wait.

Something moves in my section of hall, and I turn in time to see a shock of silver-blond hair move in the shadows. I shake my head, hoping Owen can see me, and if he can't, hoping he knows better than to show himself right now.

"I loved you." The words are much, much closer now. "I loved you, and you still made me do it."

Wesley takes a step and slides into view, his eyes flicking to me before leveling on the woman, whose footsteps I can now hear, along with her voice.

"Why didn't you stop me?" she whines. "Why didn't you help me?"

"Let me help you now," says Wesley, mimicking my even tone.

"You made me. You made me, Ian," she says as if she can't hear him, can't hear anything, as if she's trapped in a nightmarish loop. "It's all your fault."

Her voice is high and rising with each word, until the words draw into a cry, then a scream, and then she lunges into view, reaching for him. They both move past me, Wesley stepping back and her stepping forward, pace for pace.

I slip into the hall behind her.

"I can help you," says Wes, but I can tell from the tension around his eyes that he's not used to this level of disorientation. Not used to using words instead of force. "Calm down," he says finally. "Just calm down."

"What's wrong with *her?*" The question doesn't come from Wesley or me, but from a boy behind Wes at the end of the hall, several years younger than either of us.

Wes glances his way for a blink, long enough for Dina Blunt to lunge forward. As she grabs for his arm, I reach for hers. Her balance is off from panic and forward momentum, and I use her strength instead of mine to swing her back, get my hands against her face, and twist it sharply.

The snap of her neck is audible, followed by the thud of her body collapsing to the Narrows floor.

The boy makes a sound between a gasp and a cry. His eyes go wide as he turns and sprints away, skidding around the nearest corner. Wesley doesn't chase him, doesn't even move. He's staring down at Dina Blunt's motionless form. And then up at me.

I can't decide whether the look is solely dumbfounded or admiring as well.

"What happened to the humanitarian approach?"

I shrug. "Sometimes it's not enough."

"You are crazy," he says. "You are a crazy, amazing girl. And you scare the hell out of me."

I smile.

"How did you do that?" asks Wes.

"New trick."

"Where did you learn it?"

"By accident." It's not a total lie. I never meant for Owen to show me.

The History's body shudders on the floor. "It won't last long," I say, taking her arms. Wes takes her legs.

"So this is what the adults are like?" he asks as we carry her to the nearest Returns door. Her eyelids flutter. We walk faster.

"Oh, no," I say when we reach the door. "They get much worse." I turn the key and flood the hall with light.

Wes smiles grimly. "Wonderful."

Dina Blunt begins to whimper as we push her through.

"So," Wesley says as I tug the door shut and the woman's voice dies on the air, "who's next?"

Two hours later, the list is miraculously clear, and I've managed to go, well, one hour and fifty-nine minutes without thinking about Ben's shelf vanishing into the stacks. One hour and fifty-nine minutes without thinking about the rogue Librarian. Or about the string of deaths. The hunting quiets everything, but the moment we stop, the noise comes back.

"All done?" asks Wes, resting against the wall.

I look over the blank slip of paper and fold the list before another name can add itself. "Seems so. Still wish you had my territory?"

He smiles. "Maybe not by myself, but if you came with it? Yeah."

I kick his shoe with mine, and apparently two boots make enough of a buffer that almost none of Wesley's noise gets through. A little flare of feedback—but it's growing on me, as far as sound goes.

We trace our way back through the halls.

"I could seriously go for some Bishop's baked goods right now," he adds. "Think Mrs. Bishop might have something?"

We reach the numbered doors, and I slide the key into I—the one that leads to the third-floor hall—even though it's lazy and potentially public, because I really, really, really need a shower. I turn the key.

"Will oatmeal raisin do?" I ask, opening the door.

"Delightful," he says, holding it open for me. "After you."

It happens so fast.

The History comes out of nowhere.

Blink-and-you-miss-it quick, the way moments play rewinding memory. But this isn't memory, this is now, and there's not enough time. The body is a blur, a flash of reddish-brown hair and a green sweatshirt and lanky teenage limbs, all of which I distinctly remember *returning*. But that doesn't stop sixteen-year-old Jackson Lerner from slamming into Wesley, sending him back hard. I go to shut the door, but Jackson's foot sails through the air and catches me in the chest. Pain explodes across my ribs, and I'm on the ground, gasping for air, as Jackson's fingers catch the door just before it shuts.

And then he's gone.

Through.

Out.

Into the Coronado.

TWENTY-FIVE

FOR ONE TERRIBLE, terrifying moment, I don't know what to do.

A History is out, and all I can think about is forcing air back into my lungs. And then the moment ends, and the next one starts, and Wes and I are somehow on our feet again, rushing through the Narrows door and onto the third floor of the Coronado. The hall is empty.

Wes asks me if I'm okay, and I take a breath and nod, pain rippling through my ribs.

My ring is still off, but I don't need to read the walls to find Jackson, because his green sweatshirt is vanishing through the north stairwell door near my apartment. I sprint after him, and Wes turns and launches down the hall toward the south set of stairs beyond the elevators. Steps echo in the stairwell below, and I plunge down to the second floor as the door swings shut. I'm out in time to see Jackson skid to a stop halfway down the hall, Wesley rushing forward to block the landing to the grand stairs and the lobby and the way *out*.

The History is trapped.

"Jackson, stop," I gasp.

"You lied," he growls. "There is no home." His eyes are wide and going black with panic, and for a moment it's as if I'm back in front of Ben, terrified, and my feet are glued to the ground as Jackson turns and kicks in the nearest apartment door, smashing the wood and charging through.

Wes dashes forward, shocking me into motion, and I run as Jackson vanishes into the apartment.

Beyond the broken door of 2C, the apartment is modern, spare, but very clearly occupied. Jackson is halfway to the window when Wes darts forward and over a low couch. He catches Jackson's arm and spins him back toward the room. Jackson dodges his grasp and cuts to the side down a hall, but I catch up and slam him into the wall, upsetting a large framed poster.

The shower in the bathroom at the end of the hall is going, and someone is singing off-key but loudly as Jackson shoves me away and rears back to kick. I spin as the rubber heel of his shoe lodges in the drywall, and grab his wrist while he's off balance, pulling him toward me, my forearm slamming into his chest and sending him to the floor. When I try to pin him, he catches me with a glancing kick, and pain blossoms across my chest, forcing me to let go.

Wesley is there as Jackson scrambles to his feet and into the living room. Wes swings his arm around Jackson's throat and pulls hard, but Jackson fights like mad and forces him several steps back. A glass coffee table catches Wesley behind the knees, and he loses his balance. The two go down together. The shower cuts off as they crash in a wave of shattered glass. Jackson is up first, a shard jutting from his arm, and he's out the door before I can stop him.

Wesley is on his feet, his cheek and hand bleeding, but we tear into the second-floor hall. Jackson, in his panic, has stormed past the entrance to the landing and toward the elevator. We close in as he rips the glass from his arm with a hiss and forces the grille open. The dial above the cage door says the elevator is sitting on the sixth floor. The lobby is two stories tall. Which means two stories *down*.

"It's over," calls Wesley, stepping toward him.

Jackson stares at the elevator shaft, then back at us.

And then he jumps.

Wes and I groan together and turn, racing for the stairs.

Histories don't bleed. Histories can't die. But they do feel pain. And that jump had to hurt. Hopefully it will at least slow him down.

A scream cuts through the air, but not from the elevator shaft. Someone in 2C lets out a strain of words between a cry and a curse as we hit the landing. Halfway down the main staircase we see Jackson clutching his ribs—serves him right—and making a limping but determined beeline for the front doors of the Coronado.

"Key!" shouts Wes, and I dig the black handkerchief from my pocket.

"Right for Returns," I say as he grabs it, gets a foot up on the dark wood railing and jumps over, dropping the last ten feet and somehow landing upright. I hit the base of the stairs as Wes catches Jackson and slams him against the front doors hard enough to crack the glass. And then I'm there, helping hold the thrashing History against the door as Wes gets the Crew key into the lock and turns hard to the right. The scene beyond the glass is sunlight and streets and passing cars, but when Wes turns the key, the door flies open, ripped from his grip as if by wind, and reveals a world of white beyond. Impossible white, and Jackson Lerner falling through it.

The door slams shut with the same windlike force, shattering the already cracked glass. The Crew key sits in the lock, and through the glassless frame, a bus rambles past. Two people across the street have turned to see what reduced the door to littered shards and wood.

I stagger back. Wesley gives a dazed laugh just before his legs buckle.

I crouch beside him even though the motion sends ripples of pain through my ribs.

"Are you all right?" I ask.

Wes stares up at the broken door. "We did it," he says brightly. "Just like Crew."

Blood is running down his face from the gash along his cheekbone, and he's gazing giddily at the place where the door to Returns formed. I reach out and slide the key from the lock. And then I hear it. Sirens. The people from across the street are coming over now, and the wail of a cop car is getting more and more distinct. We have to get out of here. I can't possibly explain all this.

"Come on," I say, turning toward the elevator. Wes gets shakily to his feet and follows. I hit the call button, cringing at the thought of using this death trap, but I don't exactly want to retrace the path of our destruction right now, especially with Wes covered in blood. He hesitates when I pull open the grille, but climbs in beside me. The doors close, and I punch the button for the third floor and then turn to look at him. He's smiling. I can't believe he's smiling. I shake my head.

"Red looks good on you," I say.

He wipes at his cheek, looks down at his stained hands.

"You know, I think you're right."

Water drips from the ends of my hair onto the couch, where I'm perched, staring down at the Crew key cupped in my hands. I listen to the *shhhhhhh* of the shower running, wishing it could wash away the question that's nagging at me as I turn Da's key over and over in my hands.

How did Roland know?

How did he know that we'd need the key today? Was it a coincidence? Da never believed in coincidence, said chance was just a word for people too lazy to learn the truth. But Da believed in Roland. I believe in Roland. I know Roland. At least, I think I know him. He's the one who first gave me a chance. Who took responsibility for me. Who bent the rules for me. And sometimes broke them.

The water shuts off.

Jackson was returned. I returned him myself. How did he escape a second time in less than a week? He should have been filed in the red stacks. There's no way he would have woken twice. Unless someone woke him and let him out.

The bathroom door opens, and Wesley stands there, his black hair no longer spiked but hanging down into his eyes, the eyeliner washed away. His key rests against his bare chest. His stomach is lean, the muscles faint but visible. Thank god he's wearing pants.

"All done?" I ask, pocketing the Crew key.

"Not quite. I need your help." Wesley retreats into the bathroom. I follow.

An array of first-aid equipment covers the sink. Maybe I should have taken him to the Archive, but the cut on his face isn't so bad— I've had worse—and the last thing I want to do is try to explain to Patrick what happened.

Wesley's cheek is starting to bleed again, and he dabs at it with a washcloth. I fish around in my private medical stash until I find a tube of skin glue.

"Lean down, tall person," I say, trying to touch his face with only the swab and not my fingers. It makes my grip unsteady, and when I slip and paint a dab of the skin glue on his chin, Wes sighs and takes my hand. The noise flares through my head, metal and sharp.

"What are you doing?" I ask. "Let go."

"No," he says, plucking the swab and the skin glue from my grip, tossing both aside and pressing my hand flat against his chest. The noise grows louder. "You've got to figure it out."

I cringe. "Figure what out?" I ask, raising my voice above the clatter.

"How to find quiet. It's not that hard."

"It is for me," I snap. I try to push back, try to block him out, try to put up a wall, but it doesn't work, only makes it worse.

"That's because you're fighting it. You're trying to block out every bit of noise. But people are made of noise, Mac. The world is full of noise. And finding quiet isn't about pushing everything out. It's just about pulling yourself in. That's all."

"Wesley, let go."

"Can you swim?"

The rock-band static pounds in my head, behind my eyes. "What does that have to do with anything?"

"Good swimmers don't fight against the water." He takes my other hand, too. His eyes are bright, flecked with gold even in the dim light. "They move with it. Through it."

"So?"

"So stop fighting. Let the noise go white. Let it be like water. And float."

I hold his gaze.

"Just float," he says.

It goes against every bit of reason in me to stop pushing back, to welcome the noise.

"Trust me," he says.

I let out an unsteady breath, and then I do it. I let go. For a moment, Wesley washes over me, louder than ever, rattling my bones and echoing in my head. But then, little by little, the noise evens, ebbs. It grows *steadier*. It turns to white noise. It is every-where, surrounding me, but for the first time it doesn't feel like it's *in* me. Not in my head. I let out a breath.

And then Wesley's grip is gone, and so is the noise.

I watch him fight back a smile and lose. What comes through isn't smug, or even crooked. It's proud. And I can't help it. I smile a little too. And then the headache hits, and I wince, leaning on the bathroom sink.

"Baby steps," says Wes, beaming. He offers me the tube of skin glue. "Now, if you wouldn't mind fixing me up? I don't want this to scar."

"I won't be able to hide this," he says, examining my work in the mirror.

"Makes you look tough," I say. "Just say you lost a fight."

"How do you know I didn't win?" he asks, meeting my eyes in the glass. "Besides, I can't pull the fight card. It's been used too many times."

His back is to me. His shoulders are narrow but strong. Defined. I feel my skin warm as my gaze tracks between his shoulder blades and down the slope of his back. Halfway down the curve of his spine is a shallow red cut, glittering from the sliver of glass embedded in it.

"Hold still," I say. I bring my fingertips against his lower back. The noise rushes in, but this time I don't push. Instead I wait, let it settle around me, like water. It's still there, but I can think through it, around it. I don't think I'll ever be the touchy-feely type, but maybe with practice I can at least learn to float.

Wes meets my gaze in the mirror, and quirks a brow.

"Practice makes perfect," I say, blushing. My fingers drift up his spine, running over his ribs till I reach the shard. Wesley tenses beneath my touch, which makes me tense too.

"Tweezers," I say, and he hands me a pair.

I pinch the glass, hoping it doesn't go deep.

"Breathe in, Wes," I say. He does, his back expanding beneath my fingers. "Breathe out."

He does, and I tug the glass out, his breath wavering as it slides free. I hold up the fragment for him to see. "Not bad." I put a small bandage over the cut. "You should keep it."

"Oh, yeah," he says, turning to face me. "I think I should wash it off and make a little trophy out of it, 'Courtesy of an escaped History and the coffee table in Two C' etched into the stand."

"Oh, no," I say, depositing the shard in his outstretched hand. "I wouldn't wash it off."

Wes drops it onto the top of a small pile of glass, but keeps his eyes on mine. The crooked smile slides away.

"We make a good team, Mackenzie Bishop."

"We do." We *do*, and that is the thing that tempers the heat beneath my skin, checks the flutter of girlish nerves. This is Wesley. My friend. My partner. Maybe one day my Crew. The fear of losing that keeps me in check.

"Next time," I say, pulling away, "don't hold the door open for me."

I clean off the cluttered sink and leave Wes to finish getting dressed, but he follows me down the hall, still shirtless.

"You see what I get for trying to be a gentleman."

Oh, god—he's flirting.

"No more gentlemanly behavior," I say, reaching my room. "You're clearly not cut out for it."

"Clearly," he says, wrapping an arm loosely around my stomach from behind.

I hiss, less from the noise than the pain. He lets go.

"What is it?" he says, suddenly all business.

"It's nothing," I say, rubbing my ribs.

"Take off your shirt."

"You'll have to try a hell of a lot harder to seduce me, Wesley Ayers."

"*My* shirt's already off," he counters. "I think it's only fair."

I laugh. It hurts.

"And I'm not trying to seduce you, Mackenzie," he says, straightening. "I'm trying to help. Now, let me see."

"I don't want to see," I say. "I'd rather not know." I managed to shower and change without looking at my ribs. Things only hurt more when you can see them.

"That's great. Then you close your eyes and I'll see for you."

Wesley reaches out and slips his fingers around the edge of my shirt. He pauses long enough to make sure I won't physically harm him, then guides my top over my head. I look away, intending to educate myself on the number of pens in the cup on my desk. I can't help but shiver as Wesley's hand slides feather-light over my waist, and the noise of his touch actually distracts me from the pain until his hand drifts up and—

"Ouch." I look down. A bruise is already spreading across my ribs.

"You should really have that looked at, Mac."

"I thought that's what you were doing."

"I meant by a medical professional. We should get you to Patrick, just to be safe."

"No way," I say. Patrick's the last person I want to see right now.

"Mac—"

"I said no." Pain weaves between my ribs when I breathe, but I *can* breathe, so that's a good sign. "I'll live," I say, taking back my shirt.

Wes sags onto my bed as I manage to get the shirt over my head, and I'm tugging it down when there's a knock on my door, and Mom peeks in, holding a plate of oatmeal-raisin cookies.

"Mackenz— Oh."

She takes in the scene before her, Wesley shirtless and stretched out on my bed, me pulling my shirt on as quickly as possible so she won't see my bruises. I do my best to look embarrassed, which isn't hard.

"Hello, Wesley. I didn't know you were here."

Which is a a bald-faced lie, of course, because my mother loves me, but she doesn't show up with a tray of cookies and a pitcher and her sweetest smile unless I've got company. When did she get home?

"We went for a run together," I say quickly. "Wes is trying to help me get back in shape."

Wesley makes several vague stretching motions that make it abundantly clear he's not a runner. I'll kill him.

"Mhm," says Mom. "Well, I'll just . . . put these . . . over here."

She sets the tray on an unpacked box without taking her eyes off us.

"Thanks, Mom."

"Thanks, Mrs. Bishop," says Wesley. I glance over and find him eyeing the cookies with a wolfish smile. He's almost as good a liar as I am. It scares me.

"Oh, and Mac," adds Mom, swiping one of the cookies for herself.

"Yeah?"

"Door open, please," she chirps, tapping the wooden door frame as she leaves.

"How long have we been running together?" asks Wes.

"A few days." I throw a cookie at his head.

"Good to know." He catches and devours the cookie in a single move, then reaches over and lifts Ben's bear from the bedside table. The plastic glasses are no longer perched on its nose but folded on the table, where I dropped them last night before I went to find my brother. My chest tightens. *Gone gone gone* thuds in my head like a pulse.

"Was this his?" Wes asks, blind pity written across his face. And I know it's not his fault—he doesn't understand, he can't—but I can't stand that look.

"Ben hated that bear," I say. Still, Wesley sets it gently, reverently, back on the table.

I sink onto the bed. Something digs into my hip, and I pull the Crew key out of my pocket.

"That was close today," says Wes.

"But we did it," I say.

"We did." Halfway to a smile, his mouth falls. I feel it too.

Wes reaches for his Archive paper as I reach for mine, and we both unfold the lists at the same time to find the same message scrawled across the paper.

Keepers Bishop and Ayers:
Report to the Archive.
NOW.

TWENTY-SIX

I KNOW THIS ROOM.
The cold marble floors and the walls lined with ledgers and the long table sitting in the middle of the chamber: it's the room where I became a Keeper. There are people seated behind that table now, just as there were then, but the faces—most of them, at least—have changed. And even as we gather, I can hear the distant sounds of the disruption spreading.

As Wesley and I stand waiting, my first thought is that I avoided one tribunal only to end up in another. This morning's would have been deserved. This afternoon's makes no sense.

Patrick sits behind the table, glowering, and I wonder how long he's been making that face, waiting for us to walk in. It is, for a moment, absurdly funny, so much so that I'm worried I'll laugh. Then I take in the rest of the scene, and the urge dies.

Lisa sits beside Patrick, her two-toned eyes unreadable.

Carmen is beside Lisa, clutching her notepad to her chest.

Roland heads the table, arms folded.

Two more people—the transfer, Elliot, and the woman with the braid, Beth—stand behind those seated. The expressions in the room range from contempt to curiosity.

I try to catch Roland's eye, but he's not watching me. He's watching them. And it clicks: Wesley and I are not the only ones on trial.

Roland thinks it's one of them who has been altering Histories. Is this his way of rounding up suspects? I scan their faces. Could one of these people be wreaking so much havoc? Why? I scour my memories of them, searching for one that lights up, any moment that makes one of them seem guilty. But Roland is like family; Lisa is sometimes stern but well-meaning; Carmen has confided in me, helped me, and kept my secrets. And little as I like Patrick, he's a stickler for rules. But the two people standing behind them . . . I've never spoken to the woman with the braid, Beth, and I know nothing about Elliot other than the fact that he transferred in just before the trouble started. If I could spend some time with them, maybe I could tell—

A shoe knocks against mine, and a tiny flare of metal and drums cuts through my thoughts. I steal a glance at Wesley, whose forehead is crinkling with concern.

"I still can't believe you told my mother we were going on a date," I say under my breath.

"I told her we were going out. I couldn't exactly be more specific, could I?" Wesley hisses back.

"That's what lying's for."

"I try to keep lies to a minimum. Omissions are much less karmically damaging."

Someone coughs, and I turn to find two more people sidling into the chamber, both in black. The woman is tall, with a ponytail of blue-black hair, and the man is made of caramel—gold skin and gold hair and a lazy smile. I've never seen them before, but there is something lovely and frightening and cold about them, and then I see the marks carved on their skin, just above their wrists. Three lines. They're Crew.

"Miss Bishop," says Patrick, and my attention snaps back to the table. "This is not your first infraction."

I frown. "What infraction have I committed?"

"You let a History escape into the Outer," he says, taking off his glasses and tossing them to the table.

"We also caught him," says Wesley.

"Mr. Ayers, your record has been, before today, impeccable. Perhaps you should hold your tongue."

"But he's right," I say. "What matters is that we caught the History."

"He shouldn't have gotten into the Coronado in the first place," warns Lisa.

"He shouldn't have gotten into the Narrows at all," I answer. "I returned Jackson Lerner this week. So tell me how he managed to wake, find his way back into my territory, and avoid my list? A product of the disruption?"

Roland shoots me a look, but Patrick's eyes flick down to his desk. "Jackson Lerner was a filing error."

I bite back a laugh and he gives me a warning glare, as does Lisa. Carmen avoids eye contact and chews the side of her lip. She's the one who took Jackson from me. She was supposed to return him.

"It was my . . ." she says softly, but Patrick doesn't give her the chance.

"Miss Bishop, this was a filing error precipitated by your incorrect delivery of the History in question. Is it not true you returned Jackson Lerner to the Archive's antechamber, as opposed to the Returns room?"

"I didn't have a choice."

"Jackson Lerner's presence in the Narrows is not the most pressing issue," says Lisa. "The fact that he was allowed into the Outer . . ." *Allowed*, she says, like we just stepped aside. *Allowed*, because we were still alive when he got through. "The fact that two Keepers were patrolling the same territory and yet neither—"

"Who authorized that, anyway?" Patrick cuts in.

"I did," says Roland.

"Why not just give them a Crew key and a promotion while you're at it?" snaps Patrick.

Da's Crew key weighs a thousand pounds in my boot.

"The status of Miss Bishop's territory necessitated immediate aid," says Roland, meeting Patrick's gaze. "Mr. Ayers's territory has yet to experience any increase. Whereas the Coronado and surrounding areas are, for *some* reason, suffering the greatest damage during this disruption. The decision was well within my jurisdiction. Or have you forgotten, Patrick, that I am the highest-ranking official not only in this branch but in this state, and in this region, and, as such, your director?"

Roland? The highest ranking? With his red Chucks and his lifestyle magazines?

"How long have Miss Bishop and Mr. Ayers been paired?" asks Lisa.

Roland draws a watch from his pocket, a grim smile on his lips. "About three hours."

The man in the corner laughs. The woman elbows him.

"Miss Bishop," says Patrick, "are you aware that once a History reaches the Outer, it ceases to be the Keeper's task, and becomes that of the Crew?" On the last word, he gestures to the two people in the corner. "Imagine the level of confusion, then, when the Crew arrives to dispatch the History, and finds it gone."

"We did find some broken glass," offers the man.

"Some police, too," adds the woman.

"And a lady in a robe going off about vandals—"

"But no History."

"Why is that?" asks Patrick, turning his attention to Wesley.

"When Lerner escaped, we went after him," says Wes. "Tracked him through the hotel, caught him before he exited the building, and returned him."

"You acted out of line."

"We did our job."

"No," snaps Patrick, "you did the Crew's job. You jeopardized human lives and your own in the process."

"It was dangerous for you two to pursue the History once it reached the Outer," amends Carmen. "You could have been killed. You're both remarkable Keepers, but you're not Crew."

"Yet," says Roland. "But they certainly demonstrated their potential."

"You cannot be encouraging this," says Patrick.

"I sanctioned their partnership. I should hope I wouldn't do that without believing them capable." Roland stands. "And to be frank, I can't see how reprimanding Keepers for returning Histories is a good use of our time given the current . . . circumstances. And given those circumstances, I believe Mr. Ayers should be allowed to continue assisting Miss Bishop, so long as his own territory does not suffer for it."

"That is not how the Archive functions—"

"Then for now the Archive must learn to be a little more flexible," says Roland. "But," he adds, "if any evidence presents itself that Mr. Ayers is unable to keep his own numbers down, the partnership will be dissolved."

"Granted," says Lisa.

"Very well," says Carmen.

"Fine," says Patrick.

Neither Elliot nor Beth have said a single thing, but now each gives a quiet affirmation.

"Dismissed," says Roland. Lisa stands first and crosses to the doors, but when she opens them, another wave of noise—like metal shelves hitting stone floors—reaches us. She draws her key from her pocket—thin and gleaming gold, like the one Roland drove into Ben's chest—and hurries toward the sound. Carmen, Elliot, and Beth follow. The Crew is already gone, and Wesley and I make our own way out; but Roland and Patrick stay behind.

As I approach the door, I hear Patrick say something to Roland that makes my blood run cold. "Since you are the *director*," he mutters, "it's my duty to inform you that I've asked for an assessment of Miss Bishop."

He says it loud enough for me to hear, but I won't give him the satisfaction of looking back. He's just trying to rattle me.

"You will not bring Agatha into this, Patrick," says Roland, more quietly, and when Patrick answers, it's nothing more than a whisper.

I pick up my pace and force my eyes forward as I follow Wesley out. The numbers of Librarians in the atrium seems to have doubled in the last day. Halfway to the desk, we pass Carmen giving orders to a few unfamiliar faces, listing the wings, halls, rooms to be blacked out. When they peel away, I tell Wes to go on ahead, and stop to ask Carmen something.

"What does that mean, 'blacking out' rooms?"

She hesitates.

"Carmen, I already know what a disruption is. So what does this mean?"

She bites her lip. "It's a last resort, Miss Bishop. If there's too much noise, too many Histories waking, blacking out a room is the fastest way to kill the disturbance, but . . ."

"What is it?"

"It kills the content, too," she says, looking around nervously.

"Blacking out a room blacks out everything inside. It's an irreversible process. It turns the space into a crypt. The more rooms we have to black out, the more content we lose. I've seen disruptions before, but never like this. Almost a fifth of the branch has already been lost." She leans in. "At this rate, we could lose everything."

My stomach drops. Ben is in this branch. Da is in this branch.

"What about the red stacks?" I press. "What about Special Collections?"

"Restricted stacks and Archive members are vaulted. Those shelves are more secure, so they're holding for now, but—"

Just then, three more Librarians rush toward her, and Carmen turns away to speak with them. I think she's forgotten me altogether, but as I turn to go, she glances my way and says only, "Be safe."

"You look sick," says Wes once we're back in the Narrows.

I feel sick. Ben and Da are both in a branch that is crumbling, a branch that someone is trying to topple. And it's my fault. I started the search. I dug up the past. I pushed for answers. Tipped the dominoes . . .

"Talk to me, Mac."

I look at Wesley. I don't like lying to him. It's different lying to Mom and Dad and Lyndsey. Those are big, blanket lies—easy, all-or-nothing lies. But with Wes, I have to sift out what I can say from what I can't, and by *can't* I mean *won't*, because I *could*. I *could* tell him. I tell myself I *would* tell him, if Roland hadn't warned me not to. I *would* tell him everything. Even about Owen. I tell myself I would. I wonder if it's true.

"I've got a bad feeling," I say. "That's all."

"Oh, I don't see why you would. It's not like they just put us on trial, or our branch is falling down, or your territory is out of control in a seriously suspicious way." He sobers. "Frankly, Mac, I'd be worried if you had a *good* feeling about any of this." He glances back at the Archive door. "What's going on?"

I shrug. "No idea."

"Then let's find out."

"Wesley, in case you haven't noticed, I can't afford to get in any more trouble right now."

"I have to admit, I never pegged you as such a delinquent."

"What can I say? I'm the best of the worst. Now, let the Librarians do their job, and we'll do ours. *If* you can handle another day of it."

He smiles, but it seems thinner. "It'll take more than an overflowing Narrows, an escaped History, a glass table, and a tribunal to get rid of me. Pick you up at nine?"

"Nine it is."

Wes veers off into the Narrows toward his own home. I watch him go, then squeeze my eyes shut. What a mess, I think, just before a kiss lands like a drop of water on the slope of my neck.

I shiver, spin, and slam the body into the nearest wall. The quiet floods in where my hand meets his throat. Owen raises a brow.

"Hello, M."

"You should know better," I say, "than to sneak up on someone." I slowly release my hold on him.

Owen's hands drift up to touch mine, then past them to my wrists. In one fluid motion, I'm the one against the wall, my hands pinned loosely overhead. The thrill of warmth washes over my skin, while the quiet courses under it, through my head.

"If I remember correctly," he says, "that's exactly how I saved you."

I bite my lip as he leans in to kiss my shoulder, my throat—heat and silence thrumming through me, both welcome.

"I didn't need saving," I whisper. He smiles against my skin, his body pressing flush with mine. I wince.

"What's wrong?" he asks, lips hovering beneath my jaw.

"Long day," I say, swallowing.

He pulls back a fraction, but doesn't stop brushing me with kisses, leaving a trail of them up my cheek to my ear as his fingers tangle through mine above my head, tighten. The quiet gets stronger, blotting out thoughts. I want to escape into it. I want to vanish into it.

"Who was the boy?" he whispers.

"He's a friend."

"Ah," Owen says slowly.

"No, not 'ah,'" I say defensively. "Just a friend."

Willingly, necessarily just a friend. With Wesley, there is too much to lose. But with Owen, there is no future to be lost by giving in. No future at all. Only escape. Doubt whispers through the quiet. Why does he care? Is it jealousy that flickers across his face? Curiosity? Or something else? It is so easy for me to read people and so hard for me to read him. Is this how people are supposed to look at each other? Seeing only faces, and none of the things behind?

He can read me well enough to know that I don't want to talk about Wesley, because he lets it drop, wraps me in silence and kisses, draws me into the dark of the alcove where we sat before, and guides me to the wall. His hands brush over my skin too gingerly. I pull his body to mine despite the ache in my ribs. I kiss him, relishing the way the quiet deepens when his body is pressed to mine, the way I can blot thoughts out simply by pulling him closer, kissing him harder. What beautiful control.

"M," he moans against my neck. I feel myself blush. In all the strangeness, there's something about the way he looks at me, the way he touches me, that feels so incredibly . . . normal. Boy-and-girl and smiles-and-sideways-glances and whispers-and-butterflies normal. And I want that so, so badly. I can feel the scratch of letters in my pocket, now constant. I leave the list where it is.

A faint smile tugs at the corner of Owen's mouth as it hovers above mine. We are close enough to share breath, the quiet dizzying but not quite strong enough. Not yet. Thoughts keep trickling through my head, warnings and doubts, and I want to silence them. I want to disappear.

As I run my fingers through his hair and pull his face to mine, I wonder if Owen is escaping too. If he can disappear into my touch, forget what he is and what he's lost.

I am blotting out pieces of my life. I am blotting out everything but this. But him. I exhale as he brushes against me, my body beginning to uncurl, to loosen at his fingertips. I am letting him wash over me, drown every part of me that I don't need in order to kiss or to listen or to smile or to want. *This* is what I want. This is my drug. The pain, both skin-deep and deeper, is finally gone. Everything is gone but the quiet.

And the quiet is wonderful.

"Why do you smoke, Da?"

 "We all do things we shouldn't, things that harm us."

 "*I* don't."

 "You're still young. You will."

 "But I don't understand. Why hurt yourself?"

 "It won't make sense to you."

"Try me."

You frown. "To escape."

"Explain."

"I smoke to escape from myself."

"Which part?"

"Every part. It's bad for me and I know it and I still do it, and in order for me to do it and enjoy it, I have to *not* think about it. I can think about it before and after, but while I'm doing it, I stop thinking. I stop being. I am not your Da, and I am not Antony Bishop. I am no one. I am nothing. Just smoke and peace. If I think about what I'm doing, then I think about it being wrong and I can't enjoy it, so I stop thinking. Does it make sense now?"

"No. Not at all."

"I had a dream last night. . . ." says Owen, rolling the iron ring from Regina's note over his knuckles. "Well, I don't know if it was night or day."

We're sitting on the floor. I'm leaning against him, and he has one arm draped over my shoulder, our fingers loosely intertwined. The quiet in my head is like a sheet, a buffer. It is water, but instead of floating, like Wes taught me, I am drowning in it. This is a thing like peace but deeper. Smoother.

"I didn't know Histories could dream," I say, wincing when it comes out a little harsh, making Histories into an *it* instead of a *him* or *you*.

"Of course," he says. "Why do you think they—we—wake up? I imagine it's because of dreams. Because they're so vivid, or so urgent, that we cannot sleep."

"What did you dream about?"

He navigates the iron ring to his palm, folds his fingers over it.

"The sun," he says. "I know it seems impossible, to dream of light in a place as dark as this. But I did."

He rests his chin on my hair. "I was standing on the roof," he says. "And the world below was water, glittering in the sun. I couldn't leave, there was no way off, so I stood and waited. So much time seemed to pass—whole days, weeks—but it never got dark, and I kept waiting for something—someone—to come." The fingers of his free hand trace patterns on my arm. "And then you came."

"What happened then?" I ask.

He doesn't speak.

"Owen?" I press, craning to look at him.

Sadness flickers like a current through his eyes. "I woke up."

He pockets the iron ring and produces the iron bar and the second piece of the story, the one I handed him before the trial.

"Where did you find this?" he asks.

"Under a marble rose," I say. "Your sister picked some clever hiding places."

"The Even Rose," he says softly. "That was the name of the café back then. And Regina was always clever."

"Owen, I've looked everywhere, and I still haven't found the ending. Where could it be?"

"It's a large building. Larger than it looks. But the pieces of the story seem to fit where they've been hidden. The Even Rose fragment spoke of climbing out of stones. The fragment from the roof spoke of reaching the top, battling the monsters. The ending will fit its place, too. The hero will win the battle—he always does—and then . . ."

"He'll go home," I finish quietly. "You said it was a journey. A quest. Isn't the point of a quest is to get somewhere? To get home?"

He kisses my hair. "You're right." He twirls the trinket piece. "But where is home?"

Could it be 3F? The Clarkes lived there once. Could the ending to Regina's story be hidden in their home? In mine?

"I don't know, M," he whispers. "Maybe Regina won this last game."

"No," I say. "She hasn't won yet."

And neither has the rogue Librarian. Owen's quiet calms my panic and clears my head. The more I think about it, the more I realize that there's no way this disruption is just a distraction from the dark secrets of the Coronado's past. It's something more. There was no need to shatter the peace of the Archive after erasing evidence in both the Archive and the Outer. No, I'm missing something; I'm not seeing the whole picture.

I disentangle myself from Owen and turn to face him, forfeiting the quiet to ask a question I should have asked long ago. "Did you know a man named Marcus Elling?"

A small crease forms between Owen's eyes. "He lived on our floor. He was quiet but always kind to us. Whatever happened to him?"

I frown. "You don't know?"

Owen's face is blank. "Should I?"

"What about Eileen Herring? Or Lionel Pratt?"

"The names sound familiar. They lived in the building, right?"

"Owen, they all died. A few months after Regina." He just stares at me, confused. My heart sinks. If he can't remember anything about the murders, about his own death on the roof . . . I thought I was protecting him from the Archive, but what if I'm too late?

What if someone's already taken the memories I need? "What *do* you remember?"

"I . . . I didn't want to leave. Right after Regina died, my parents packed up everything and ran away, and I couldn't do it. If there was any part of her left in the Coronado, I couldn't leave her. That's the last thing I can remember. But that was days after she died. Maybe a week."

"Owen, you died five *months* after your sister."

"That's not possible."

"I'm sorry, but it's true. And I've got to find out what happened between her death and yours." I drag myself to my feet, pain rippling through my ribs. It's late, it's been a hell of a day, and I have to meet Wesley in the morning.

Owen stands too, and pulls me in for a last, quiet kiss. He leans his forehead against mine, and the whole world hushes. "What can I do to help?"

Keep touching me, I want to say, because the quiet soothes the panic building in my chest. I close my eyes, relish the moment of nothing-ness, and then pull away. "Try to remember the last five months of your life," I say as I go.

"The day's almost over, isn't it?" he asks as I reach the corner.

"Yeah," I call back. "Almost."

TWENTY-SEVEN

WESLEY IS LATE.

He was supposed to pick me up at nine. I woke at dawn and spent the hour before Mom and Dad got up scouring the apartment for loose boards and any other hiding places where Regina could have hidden a scrap of story. I dragged the boxes from my closet, pulled half the drawers from the kitchen, tested every wooden plank for give, and found absolutely nothing.

Then I put on a show for my parents, doing stretches as I told them how Wes was on his way, how we were planning to hit Rhyne Park today (I found a map in the study, and the splotch of green labeled RHYNE seemed to be within walking distance). I mentioned that we'd grab lunch on the way back, and shooed my parents to their respective work with promises that I'd stay hydrated, wear sunscreen.

And then I waited for Wes, just like we'd agreed.

But nine a.m. came and went without him.

Now my eyes flick to the tub of oatmeal raisin cookies on the counter, and I think of Nix and the questions I could be asking him. About Owen and the missing months.

I give my partner another ten minutes, then twenty.

When the clock hits nine thirty, I grab the tub and head for the stairs. I can't afford to sit still.

But halfway down the hall, something stops me—that gut sense Da was always talking about, the one that warns when something is off. It's the painting of the sea. It's crooked again. I reach out and straighten the frame, and that's when I hear a familiar rattling sound, like something is sliding loose inside, and everything in me grinds to a halt.

I was born up north, by the sea, said Owen.

My heart pounds as I carefully lift the painting from the wall and turn it over. There's a backing, like a second canvas, one corner loose, and when I tip the painting in my hands, something falls free and tumbles to the old checkered carpet with a whispered thud. I return the painting to the wall and kneel, retrieving a piece of paper folded around a chip of metal.

I unfold the paper with shaking hands, and read. . . .

He fought the men and he slayed the monsters and he bested the gods, and at last the hero, having conquered all, earned the thing that he wanted most. To go home.

The end of Regina's story.

I read it twice more, then look closer at the bit of dark metal it was wrapped around. It's the thickness of a nickel and about as large, if a nickel were hammered into a roughly rectangular shape. The two sides opposite each other are regular and straight, but the other two are off. The top side has a notch cut out, as if someone ran a knife across the stone just below the edge. The notch is on both sides. The bottom side of the square has been filed till it is sharp enough to cut with, the metal tapering to a point.

There's something familiar about it, and even though I can't place it, a small sense of victory flutters through me as I pocket the metal and the paper scrap and head upstairs.

On the seventh floor I knock, wait, and listen to the sound of the wheelchair rolling across the wood. Nix maneuvers the door with even less grace than the first time. When he's got it open, his face lights up.

"Miss Mackenzie."

I smile. "How did you know it was me?"

"You or Betty," he says. "And she wears perfume thick as a coat." I laugh. "Told her to stop bathing in it."

"I brought the cookies," I say. "Sorry it took so long."

He pivots the wheelchair and lets me guide him back to the table.

"As you can see," he says as he waves a hand at the apartment, "I've been so busy, I've hardly noticed."

It looks untouched, like a painting of the last visit, down to the cigarette ash and the scarf around his neck. I'm relieved to see he didn't set the thing on fire.

"Betty hasn't been in to clean up," he says.

"Nix . . ." I'm afraid to ask. "Is Betty still around?"

He laughs hoarsely. "She's no dead wife, if that's what you think, and I'm too old for imaginary friends." A breath of relief escapes. "Comes 'round to check on me," he explains. "Dead wife's sister's daughter's friend, or something. I forget. She tells me my mind is going, but really I just don't care enough to remember." He points to the table. "You left your book here." And sure enough, the *Inferno* is sitting where I left it. "Don't worry. Not like I peeked."

I consider leaving it again. Maybe he won't notice. "Sorry about that," I say. "Summer reading."

"What do schools do that for?" he grumbles. "What's the point of summer if they give you homework?"

"Exactly!" I set him up at the table and put the Tupperware in his lap.

He rattles it. "Too many cookies here for just me. You better help."

I take one and sit down across from Nix. "I wanted to ask you—"

"If it's about those deaths," he cuts in, "I've been thinking about 'em." He picks at the raisins in his cookie. "Ever since you asked. I'd almost forgotten. Scary, how easy it is to forget bad things."

"Did the police think the deaths were connected?" I ask.

Nix shifts in his seat. "They weren't certain. I mean, it was suspicious, to be sure. But like I said, you can connect the dots or you can leave them be. And that's what they did, left 'em random, scattered."

"What happened to the brother, Owen? You said he stayed here."

"You want to know about that boy, you know who you should ask? That antiques collector."

I frown. "Ms. Angelli?" I remember the not-so-subtle gesture of her door shutting in my face. "Because she has a thing for history?"

Nix takes a bite of cookie. "Well, that too. But mostly because she lives in Owen Clarke's old place."

"No," I say slowly, "I do. Three F."

Nix shakes his head. "You live in the Clarke *family's* old place. But they moved out right after the murder. And that boy, Owen, he couldn't go, but he couldn't stay either, not there where his sister was . . . Well, he moved into a vacant apartment. And that Angelli woman lives there now. I wouldn't have known it if she hadn't come up to see me, a few years back when she moved in, curious about the history of the building. You want to know more about Owen, you should talk to her."

"Thanks for the tip," I say, already on my feet.

"Thanks for the cookies."

Just then the front door opens and a middle-aged woman appears on the mat. Nix sniffs the air once.

"Ah, Betty."

"Lucian Nix, I know you're not eating sugar."

271

Betty makes a beeline for Nix, and in the scramble of cookies and curses, I duck out and head downstairs. Names are still scratching on the list in my pocket, but they'll have to wait just a little longer.

When I reach the fourth floor, I run through the spectrum of lies I could use to get Angelli to let me in. I've only passed her once since she shut the door in my face, and earned little more than a curt nod.

But when I reach her door and press my ear to the wood, I hear only silence.

I knock and hold my breath and hope. Still silence.

I test the door, but it's locked. I search my pockets for a card or a hairpin, or anything I can use to jimmy the lock, silently thanking Da for the afternoon he spent teaching me to do that.

But maybe I won't need to. I step back to examine the door. Ms. Angelli is a bit on the scattered side. I'm willing to bet that she's a touch forgetful, and with the amount of clutter in her apartment, the odds of misplacing a key are high. The door frame is narrow but wide enough to form a shallow shelf on top, a lip. I stretch onto my toes and brush my fingertips along the sill of the door. They sweep against something metal, and sure enough, a key tumbles to the checkered carpet.

People are so beautifully predictable. I take up the key and slide it into the lock, holding my breath as I turn it and the door pops open, leading into the living room. Across the threshold, my eyes widen. I'd nearly forgotten how much stuff was here, covering every surface, the beautiful and the gaudy and the old. It's piled on shelves and tables and even on the floor, forcing me to weave between towers of clutter and into the room. I don't see how Ms. Angelli can walk through without upsetting anything.

The layout of 4D is the same as 3F, with the open kitchen and the hallway off the living room leading to the bedrooms. I slowly make my way toward them, checking each room to make sure I'm alone. Every room is empty of people and full of things, and I don't know if it's the clutter or the fact that I've broken in, but I can't shake the feeling that I'm being watched. It trails me through the apartment, and when a small crash comes from the direction of living room, I spin, expecting to see Ms. Angelli.

But no one's there.

And that's when I remember. The cat.

Back in the living room, a few books have been toppled, but there's no sign of Angelli's cat Jezzie. My skin crawls. I try to convince myself that if I stay out of her way, she'll stay out of mine. I shift the stack of books, a stone bust, and the edge of the carpet out of the way, clearing a space so I can read.

I take a deep breath, slide off my ring, and kneel on the exposed floorboards. But the moment I bring my hands to the wood, before I've even reached for the past, the whole room begins to hum against my fingers. Shudders. Rattles. And it takes me a moment to realize that I'm not feeling the weight of the memory in the floor alone, that there are so many antiques in this room, so many things with so many memories, that the lines between the objects are blurring. The hum of the floor touches the hum of things sitting on the floor, and so on, until the whole room sings, and it hurts. A pins-and-needles numb that climbs my arms and winds across my bruised ribs.

It's too much to read. There is too much *stuff* in here, and it fills my head the way human noise does. I haven't even started reaching past the hum to whatever memories are beyond it; I can hardly think through the noise. Pain flickers behind my eyes, and I realize I'm pushing back against the hum, so I try to remember Wesley's lessons.

Let the noise go white, he said. I crouch in the middle of Angelli's apartment with my eyes squeezed shut and my hands glued to the floor, waiting for the noise to run together around me, for it to even out. And it does, little by little, until I can finally think, and then focus, and reach.

I catch hold of the memory, and time spirals back, and with it the clutter shifts, changes, then lessens, piece after piece vanishing from the room until I can see most of the floor, the walls. People slide through the space, earlier tenants—some of the memories dull and faded, others bright—an older man, a middle-aged woman, a family with young twins. The room clears, morphs, until finally it is Owen's space.

I can tell even before I see his blond head flicker through the room, moving backward because I'm still rewinding time. At first I'm filled with relief that there *is* a memory to read, that it hasn't been blacked out along with so much of that year. And the memory suddenly sharpens, and I swear I see—

Pain shoots through my head as I slam the memory's retreat to a stop, and let it slide forward.

In the room with Owen, there is a girl.

I only catch a glimpse before he blocks my view. She's sitting in a bay window, and he's kneeling in front of her, his hands up on either side of her face, his forehead pressed to hers. The Owen I know is calm to a fault, composed, and sometimes, though I wouldn't tell him, ghostly. But this Owen is alive, full of restless energy woven through his shoulders and the way he's subtly rocking on his heels as he speaks. The words themselves are nothing more than a murmur, but I can tell they are low and urgent; and as suddenly as he knelt, he's up, hands falling from the girl's face as he turns away. . . . And then I'm not looking at him anymore, because I'm looking at *her*.

She's sitting with her knees drawn up just the way they were the night she was killed, blond hair spilling over them, and even though she's looking down, I know exactly who she is.

Regina Clarke.

But that's not possible.

Regina died before Owen ever moved into this apartment.

And then, as if she knows what I'm thinking, she looks up, past me, and she is Regina and not Regina all at once, a twisted version. Her face is tight with panic and her eyes are too dark and getting darker, the color smudging into—

A screaming sound tears through my head, high and long and horrible, and my vision plunges into color, then black, then color as something shoves up against my bare arm. I jerk back, out of the memories and away from the floor, but the stone bust catches my heel and sends me backward to the carpet, hard. Pain cuts across my ribs as I land, and my vision clears enough to take in the *thing* that attacked me. Jezzie's small black form bobs toward me, and I scoot back, but—

A high-pitched howl grates against my bones as another cat, fat and white with an encrusted collar, wraps its tail around my elbow. I wrench free and—

A third cat brushes my leg, and the world explodes into keening and red and light and pain, metal dragging beneath my skin. Finally I tear free and scramble backward out into the hall, and force the door shut.

My back hits the opposite wall, and I slide to the floor, my eyes watering from the headache that's as sudden and brutal as the cats' touch. I need quiet, true quiet, and I reach into my pocket to fetch my ring, but my fingers meet with nothing.

No.

I look at the door to 4D. My ring must still be in there. I curse not so softly and put my forehead against my knees, trying to think through the pain and piece together what I'd seen before the onslaught of cats.

Regina's eyes. They were going dark. They were smudging into black, like she was *slipping*. But only Histories slip. And only a History could be sitting in her brother's apartment *after* she died, and that means it wasn't Regina, in the way that the body in Ben's drawer wasn't Ben, and that means she got *out*. But how? And how did Owen find her?

"Mackenzie?"

I glance up to see Wes coming down the hall.

He quickens his step. "What's wrong?"

I return my forehead to my knees. "I will give you twenty dollars if you go in there and get my ring."

Wesley's boots come to a stop somewhere to the right of my leg. "What's your ring doing in Ms. Angelli's place?"

"Please, Wes, just go get it for me."

"Did you break in—"

"*Wesley.*" My head snaps up. "Please." And I must look worse than I feel, because he nods and goes inside. He reappears a few moments later and drops the ring to the carpet, at my feet. I pick it up and slide it on.

Wesley kneels down in front of me. "You want to tell me what happened?"

I sigh. "I was attacked."

"By a *History?*"

"No . . . by Ms. Angelli's cats."

The corner of his mouth twitches.

"It's not funny," I growl, and close my eyes. "I'm never going to live this down, am I."

"Never. And damn, way to give a guy a scare, Mac."

"You scare too easily."

"You haven't seen yourself." He fetches a compact from one of the many pockets of his pants, and flicks it open so I can see the ribbon of blood running from my nose down over my chin. I wipe it away with my sleeve.

"Okay, that's terrifying. Put it away," I say. "So the cats won that round."

I lick my lips, taste blood. I push myself to my feet. The hall sways slightly. Wesley reaches for my arm, but I wave him off and head for the stairs. He follows.

"What were you doing in there?" he asks.

The headache makes it hard to focus on the nuances of lying. So I don't.

"I was curious," I say as we descend the stairs.

"You had to be pretty damn curious to break into Angelli's apartment."

We reach the third floor. "My inquisitive nature has always been a weakness." I can't stop seeing Regina's eyes. How did she get out? She wasn't a Keeper-Killer, wasn't a monster. She wasn't even a punk, like Jackson. She was a fifteen-year-old girl. The murder could have been enough to unsettle her mind, even cause her to wake, but she never should have made it through the Narrows.

I step out of the stairwell, but when I turn to face Wes, he's frowning at me.

"Don't look at me like that with those big brown eyes."

"They're not just brown," he says. "They're hazel. Can't you see the flecks of gold?"

"Good god, how much time do you spend looking at yourself in the mirror each day?"

"Not enough, Mac. Not enough." But the laughter is gone from his voice. "You're clever, trying to distract me with my own good looks, but it won't work. What's going on?"

I sigh. And then I *really* look at Wesley. The cut on his cheek is healing, but there's a fresh bruise blossoming against his jaw. He's guarding his left arm in a way that makes me think he took a hit, and he looks utterly exhausted.

"Where were you this morning?" I ask. "I waited."

"I got held up."

"Your list?"

"The names weren't even *on* my list. When I got into the Narrows . . . I didn't have enough hands. I didn't have enough time. I barely got through in one piece. Your territory's bad, but mine is suddenly impassable."

"Then you shouldn't have come." I turn and walk down the hall.

"I'm your partner," he says, trailing me. "And apparently that's the problem. You were there at the trial, Mac. You heard the caveat. We could only be partners as long as my territory stayed clear. Someone *did* this. And I've been trying to understand all morning why a member of the Archive wouldn't want us working together. All I can think is that I'm missing something." Halfway down the hall he catches my arm, and I force myself not to pull back as the noise floods through me. "*Am* I missing something?"

I don't know how to answer. I don't have a truth or a lie that will fix anything. I've already put him in danger just by having him near, already painted a target on his back. He'd be safer if he just stayed away. If I could keep him away from this mess. Away from me.

"Wesley . . ." Everything else is falling apart. I don't need this to crumble, too.

"Do you trust me?" His question is so sudden and honest that I'm caught off guard.

"Yeah. I do."

"Then talk to me. Whatever's going on, let me help. You're not alone, Mackenzie. Our whole lives are about lying, keeping secrets. I just want you to know that you don't have to keep them from me."

And that breaks my heart. Because I know he means every word. And because I can't confide in him. *I won't.* I won't tell him about the murders or the altered Histories or the rogue Librarian or Regina or Owen. And it's not some noble endeavor to keep him out of harm's way—there is no such thing right now. The truth is I'm scared.

"Thank you," I say, and it has all the terrible awkwardness of someone responding to a heartfelt *I love you* with an *I know.* So I add, "We're a team, Wes."

I hate myself as I watch his shoulders slacken. His hand drops, leaving a quiet that's even heavier than noise. He looks tired, his eyes ringed dark even beyond the makeup.

"You're right," he says hollowly. "We are. Which is why I'm giving you one last chance to tell me exactly what's going on. And don't bother lying. Right before you lie, you test out the words and your jaw shifts a fraction. You've been doing it a lot. So just *don't.*"

And that's when I realize how tired I am, of lies and omissions and half-truths. I put Wes in danger, but he's still here—and if he's willing to brave this chaos with me, then he deserves to know what I know. And I'm about to speak, about to tell him that, tell him everything, when he brings his hand to the back of my neck, pulls me forward, and kisses me.

The noise floods in. I don't push back, don't block it out, and for one moment, all I can think is that he tastes like summer rain.

His lips linger on mine, urgent and warm.

Lasting.

And then he pulls away, breath ragged.

His hand falls from my skin, and I understand.

He's not wearing his ring.

He didn't just kiss me.

He *read* me.

Wesley's face is bright with pain, and I don't know what he saw or what he felt, but whatever he read in me, it's enough to make him to turn and storm out.

TWENTY-EIGHT

WESLEY SLAMS the stairwell door, and I turn and punch the wall, hard enough to dent the faded yellow paper, pain rolling up my hand. My reflection stares at me from the mirror on the opposite wall, and it looks . . . lost. It's finally showing in my eyes. Da's eyes. I hold my gaze and search for some of him in me, search for the part that knows how to lie and smile and live and be. And I don't see any of it.

What a mess. Truths are messy and lies are messy, and I don't care what Da said, it's impossible to cut a person into pielike pieces, neat and tidy.

I shove off the wall, the anger coiling into something hard, stubborn, restless. I've got to find Owen. I turn for the Narrows door, pulling the key from around my neck and the list from my pocket. My stomach sinks when I unfold it. The scratch of letters has been near constant, but I didn't expect the paper to be *covered* with names. My feet slow, and for a moment I think it's too many, that I shouldn't go alone. But then I think of Wesley, and speed up. I don't need his help. I was a Keeper before he even knew what Keepers were. I slide off my ring and step into the Narrows.

There is so much noise.

Footsteps and crying and murmurs and pounding. Fear runs through me but doesn't fade, so I hold on to it, use it to keep me sharp. The movement feels good, the pulse in my ears its own white noise, blotting out everything but instinct and habit and muscle memory as I cross through the Narrows in search of Owen.

I can't seem to cover more than a hall without trouble, and I dispatch two feisty teens. But by the time the door to the Returns room shuts, more names flash up to fill their spots. A bead of sweat runs down my neck. The metal of the knife is warm against my calf, but I leave it there. I don't need it. I fight my way toward Owen's alcove.

And then Keeper-Killers begin to blossom across my list.

Two more Histories.

Two more fights.

I brace myself against the Returns door, breathless, and look at the paper.

Four more names.

"Damn it." I slam my fist against the door, still out of air. Fatigue is starting to creep in, the high of the hunt brought down by the fact that the list is matching me one for one, and sometimes two or three for one. It's not possible to dent the list, let alone clear it. If it's this bad here, what's happening in the Archive?

"Mackenzie?"

I spin to find Owen. He wraps his arms around me, and there's a moment of relief and quiet, but neither is thick enough to block out the hurt I saw in Wesley's eyes, or the pain or guilt or anger at him, myself, everything.

"It's falling apart," I say into his shoulder.

"I know," Owen answers, laying a kiss on my cheek, then one on my temple before resting his forehead there. "I know."

Quiet blossoms and fades, and I think of him holding Regina's face, pressing his forehead to hers, the low static of his voice as he spoke to her. But what was she doing there? How did he find her?

Did he even know what she was? Is that why they carved it out of his memory?

But it doesn't add up. The walls of the Coronado and the minds of the Histories were altered by different people, but in both cases the excavations were meticulous, and the time missing from the walls seems to nearly match the time missing from the people's minds. But Angelli's place was left unaltered, which means they missed a spot, or it didn't need to be erased. So why would it be gone from Owen's mind? On top of that, the other altered Histories had *hours* erased, a day or two at most. Why would Owen be missing *months*?

It doesn't make sense. Unless he's lying.

As soon as I think it, the horrible gut feeling that I'm right hits in a wave, like it's been waiting. Building.

"What's the last thing you remember?" I ask.

"I already told you . . ."

I pull free. "No, you told me what you felt. That you didn't want to leave Regina there. But what's the last thing you *saw*? The very last moment of your life?"

He hesitates.

In the distance, someone cries.

In the distance, someone screams.

In the distance, feet are stomping and hands are pounding, and it is all getting closer.

"I don't remember. . . ." he starts.

"This is important."

"You don't believe me?"

"I want to."

"Then do," he says softly.

"Do you want to know the end of your story, Owen?" I say, the gut sense twisting inside me. "I'll tell you what I've pieced together, and maybe it will jog your memory. Your sister was murdered. Your parents left, and you didn't. Instead you moved into another apartment, and then Regina came back, only it wasn't Regina, Owen. It was her History. You knew she wasn't normal, didn't you? But you couldn't help her. So you jumped off the roof."

For one long moment, Owen just looks at me.

And then he says in a calm, quiet voice, "I didn't want to jump."

I feel ill. "So you do remember."

"I thought I could help Regina. I really did. But she kept slipping. I never wanted to jump, but they gave me no choice."

"Who?"

"The Crew who came to take her back. And arrest me."

Crew? How would he know that word unless . . .

"You were part of it. The Archive."

I want him to deny it, but he doesn't.

"She didn't belong there," he says.

"Did you let her out?"

"She belonged with me. She belonged home. And speaking of home," he says, "I think you have something of mine."

My hand twitches toward the last piece of the story in my pocket. I catch myself, too late.

"I'm not a monster, Mackenzie." He takes a step toward me as he says it, hand drifting toward mine, but I step away. His eyes narrow, and his hand drops back to his side. "Tell me you wouldn't have done it," he says. "Tell me you wouldn't have taken Ben home."

Behind my eyes I see Ben, moments after he woke, already slipping, and me, kneeling before him, telling him it would be okay, promising to take him home. But I wouldn't have. I wouldn't have gone this far. Because the moment he pushed me away, I saw the truth in the spreading black of his eyes. It wasn't my brother. It wasn't Ben.

"No," I say. "You're wrong. I wouldn't have gone that far."

I take another step back, toward a bend in the hall. Owen is blocking the way to the numbered doors, but if I can get to the Archive . . .

"Mackenzie," he says, reaching out again, "please don't—"

"What about those other people?" I ask, retreating. "Marcus and Eileen and Lionel? What happened to *them?*"

"I didn't have a choice," he says, following. "I tried to keep Regina in the room, but she was upset—"

"She was slipping," I say.

"I tried so hard to help her, but I couldn't always be there. Those people saw her. They would have ruined everything."

"So you *murdered* them?"

He smiles grimly. "What do you think the Archive would have done?"

"Not this, Owen."

"Don't be naive," he snaps, anger flashing through his eyes like light.

The bend in the hall is only a few steps behind me, and I break into a run as he says, "I wouldn't go that way," and I don't grasp why until I round the corner and come face-to-face with a vicious-looking History. Beyond him there are a dozen more. Standing, staring, black-eyed.

"I told them they had to wait," he says as I retreat into his stretch of hall, "and I would let them out. But they must be losing patience. So am I." He extends his hand. "The ending, please."

He says it softly, but I can see his stance shifting, the series of minute changes in his shoulders and knees and in his hands. I brace myself.

"I don't have it," I lie.

Owen lets out a low, disappointed sigh.

And then the moment collapses. In a blink, he closes the gap between us, and I crouch, free the knife from my leg, and bring it up to his chest as his hand catches my wrist and slams it into the wall hard enough to crack the bones. He catches my free hand, and before I can get my boot up, he forces me against the wall, his body flush with mine. My ribs ache beneath his weight. The quiet pushes in, too heavy.

"Miss Bishop," he says, tightening his grip on my hands. "Keepers should know better than to carry weapons." Something crunches inside my wrist, and I gasp as my grip gives way, the knife tumbling toward the floor. Owen lets go of me, and I lunge to the side, but he catches the falling knife with one hand and my arm with the other, and rolls me back into his arms, bringing the blade up beneath my chin. "I'd stay still, if I were you. I haven't held my knife in sixty years. I might be a little rusty."

His free hand runs over my stomach and down the front of my jeans, sliding into the pocket. His fingers find the note and the metal square, and he sighs with relief as he pulls both free. He kisses the back of my hair, the knife still against my throat, and holds the two things up so I can see. "I was beginning to worry that the painting wasn't there anymore. I didn't expect to be gone so long."

"You hid the story."

"I did, but it's not the *story* I was trying to hide."

The knife vanishes from my throat and he shoves me forward. I spin and find him putting away the note, and lining up the metal pieces in his palm. A ring, a bar, a square.

"Want to see a magic trick?" he asks, gesturing to the pieces.

He palms the square and holds up the ring and the bar. He slides the tapered point of the bar into the small hole drilled into the ring and twists the two pieces together. He produces the square and slides the notched edge of it along the groove in the bar.

And then he holds it up for me to see, and my blood runs cold. It's not as ornate as the one Roland gave me, but there's no mistaking what it is.

The ring, the bar, the square.

The handle, the stem, the teeth.

It's a Crew key.

"I'm not impressed," I say, cradling my wrist. When I flex my fingers, pain sears through my hand. But my key hangs around my good wrist, and if I can find a Returns door . . . I scan the hall, but the nearest white chalk circle is several yards behind Owen.

"You should be," he says. "But if it's credit you want, I'm happy to give it. I couldn't have done it without you."

"I don't believe that," I say.

"I couldn't risk it myself. What if the Crew found me before I found the pieces? What if the pieces weren't where they should be? No, this"—he holds up the key—"this was all you. You delivered the key that makes doors between worlds, the key that will help me tear the Archive down, one branch at a time."

Anger ripples through me. I wonder if I can break his neck before he stabs me. I chance a step forward. He doesn't move.

"I won't let that happen, Owen." I have to get the key back before he starts throwing open doors. And then, as if he can read me from here, the key vanishes into his pocket.

"You don't have to stand in my way," he says.

"Yes I do. That is exactly my job, Owen. To stop the Histories, however *deranged* they are, from getting out."

"I just wanted my sister back," he says, still spinning his knife. "They made it worse than it had to be."

"It sounds like you made it pretty bad yourself." I steal another step toward him.

"You don't know anything about it, little Keeper," he growls. Good. He's getting mad, and angry people make mistakes. "The Archive takes *everything* and gives nothing back. I just wanted one thing—"

The sound of a scuffle echoes down the hall, a shout, a scream, and Owen's attention wavers for an instant. I attack, shifting my weight forward. The toe of my boot catches the bottom of his knife midspin and sends it up into the ceilingless dark of the Narrows. My next kick knocks him backward as the knife falls and clatters to the floor several feet behind me. Owen hits the ground, too, and rolls over into a crouch, somehow straightening in time to dodge another blow. He catches my leg, pulls me forward, and brings his arm to my chest, slamming me to the floor. Pain burns across my injured ribs.

"It's too late," he says as I try to force air back into my lungs. "I will tear the Archive down."

"The Archive didn't kill Regina," I gasp, rolling up onto my hands and knees. "Robert did."

His eyes darken. "I know. And I made him pay for that."

My stomach turns. I should have known.

He got away. They let him get away. I let him get away. I was her big brother. . . .

Owen took everything I felt and mimicked it, twisted it, used it. Used *me*.

I spring to my feet, lunging for him, but he's too fast, and I barely touch him before his hand wraps around my throat and he slams me back into the door. I can't breathe. My vision blurs as I claw at his arm. He doesn't even flinch.

"I didn't want to do this," he says.

And then his free hand drifts to the leather cord around my wrist. My key. He pulls sharply, snapping the cord, and drives the key into the door behind me.

He turns it, and there's click before the door swings open behind me, showering us both in crisp white light. And then he leans in close enough to rest his cheek on mine as he whispers in my ear.

"Do you know what happens to a living person in the Returns room?"

I open my mouth, but no words come out.

"Neither do I," he says, just before he pushes me back, and through, and slams the door.

TWENTY-NINE

THE WEEK before you die, I can see it coming.

I see the good-bye in your eyes. The too-long looks at everything, as if by staring you can make memories strong enough to last you through.

But it's not the same. And those lingering looks scare me.

I am not ready.

I am not ready.

I am not ready.

"I can't do this without you, Da."

"You can. And you have to."

"What if I mess up?"

"Oh, you will. You'll mess up, you'll make mistakes, you'll break things. Some you'll be able to piece together, and others you'll lose. That's all a given. But there's only one thing you have to do for me."

"What's that?"

"Stay alive long enough to mess up again."

The moment the Returns door closes, there is no door, and the white is so bright and shadowless that it makes the room look like infinite space: no floor, no walls, no ceiling. Nothing but dizzying white. I know I have to focus, have to find the place where the door was and get out and find Owen—and I can do that, the rational Keeper part of me reasons, if I can just breathe and make my way to the wall.

I take a step, and that's when the white on every side explodes into color and sound and life.

My life.

Mom and Dad on the porch swing of our first house, her legs draped across his lap and his book propped against her legs, and then the new blue house with Mom too big to fit through the door, and Ben climbing the stairs like they were mountain rocks, and Ben drawing on walls and floors and any-thing but paper, and Ben turning the space under the bed into a tree house because he was scared of heights, and Lyndsey hiding there with him even though she barely fit, and Lyndsey on the roof and Da in the summer house teaching me to pick a lock, to take a punch, to lie, to read to be strong, and hospital chairs and too-bright smiles and fighting and lying and bleeding and breaking into pieces, and moving and boxes and Wesley and Owen, and it all pours out of me and onto every surface, taking something vital with it, something like blood or oxygen because my body and mind are shutting down more and more with every frame extracted from my head.

And then the images begin to fold inward as the white recovers the room square by square by square, blotting out my life like screens being switched off. I sway on my feet. The white spreads, devouring, and I feel my legs buckle beneath me. The images blink out one by one by one, and my heartbeat skips.

No.

The air and the light are thinning.

I squeeze my eyes shut and focus on the fact that gravity tells me I'm on the floor. Focus on the fact that I have to get up. I can hear the voices now. I can make out Mom's voice chirping about the coffee shop; Dad's telling me it will be an adventure; Wesley's saying he's not going anywhere; Ben's asking me to come see; and Owen's telling me it's over.

Owen. Anger flares strong enough to help me focus, even as the voices weaken. Eyes still shut, I beg my body to stand. It doesn't, so I focus on crawling, on making my way to the wall I know exists somewhere in front of me. The room is becoming too quiet, and my mind is becoming too slow, but I keep crawling forward on my hands and knees—the pain in my wrist a reminder that I am still alive—until my fingers skim the base of the wall.

My heart skips again, falters.

My skin is going pins-and-needles numb as I manage to reach into my boot and pull Da's Crew key out. I use the wall to get myself up, brace myself when my body sways, and run my hands over the surface until I catch the invisible lip of a door frame.

The scenes have all gone quiet now except for one with Da.

I can't make out the words, and I can't tell anymore if my eyes are open or closed, and it's terrifying, so I focus on the smooth Louisiana lilt in Da's voice as he talks, and I bring my hands back and forth, back and forth, until my fingers graze the keyhole.

I get the key into the lock and turn hard to the left as Da's voice stops. Everything goes black a moment before the lock clicks and the door opens. I stumble through, gasping for air, every muscle shaking.

I'm back in the Narrows. Crew keys aren't even supposed to lead here. Then again, I'm pretty sure Crew keys aren't supposed to be used from *within* a Returns room. As I force my body to its feet, my pulse pounds in my ears. I'm thankful to still have a pulse. A scrap of paper is crumpled on the floor. My list. I lift it, expecting names, but there are no names at all, only an order.

Get out of the Narrows. Stay out of the Narrows. It's too late. —R

I look around.

The Narrows are empty and painfully quiet, and when I round the corner I see that my cluster of numbered doors have all been flung open. The rooms beyond are cast in shadow, but I can hear shouting in the lobby and the coffee shop—orders, the cold, composed kind given by members of the Archive, not Histories or residents. Only the third floor is quiet. Something in me twists, whispers *wrong wrong wrong*, and I shut the other two doors and step out into the hall.

The first thing I see is the red streaking across the faded yellow wallpaper.

Blood.

I drop to my knees and say a prayer even as I touch the floor and reach. The memory hums into my bones and numbs my hands as I roll it back. The scene is right at the top, and it skips away too fast, a blur of black-spiked hair and metal and red. Everything in me tightens. I slam the memories to a stop, and play them forward.

Anger washes over me as I watch Owen step out from the Narrows door and pull a pen and slip of paper from his pocket. It's the same size as the one with my list. Archive paper. There's a muffled sound down the hall, like knocking, as Owen leans the page against the mirror and writes one word. *Out.*

Moments later, a hand writes back. *Good.*

Owen smiles and pockets the slip.

The knocking stops, and I see Wesley standing by my door. He turns, his fist slipping back to his side; and judging by the way he's looking at Owen, he saw quite enough when he read my skin.

293

Owen only smiles. And then he says something. The words are nothing more than a hush, a murmur, but Wesley's face changes. His lips move, and Owen's shoulders shrug, and then the knife appears in his hand. He slips his finger into the hilt's hole, twirls the blade casually.

Wesley's hand curls into a fist, and he swings at Owen, who smiles, dodges fluidly, and follows upward with his knife. Wesley leans back just in time, but Owen spins the blade in his fingers at the top of its arc and swings down. This time Wesley isn't fast enough. He gasps and staggers back, gripping his shoulder. Owen strikes again, and Wes avoids the blade but not Owen's free hand, now a fist, as it comes down across his temple. One knee buckles to the floor, and before Wes can get up, Owen slams him back into the wall. Wes's shoulder leaves a blossom of red against one of the hall's ghosted doors, and the left side of his face is stained with blood, a gash on his forehead spilling down like a mask over his left eye. He collapses to the floor, and Owen vanishes into the stairwell.

Wesley staggers to his feet and follows.

And so do I.

I spring up from the floor, the past vanishing into present as I race down the hall and up the stairs. I'm close. I can hear the footsteps floors above. I vault up past the sixth floor—more blood on the steps. Above me, I hear the roof door slam shut, and the sound is still echoing as I reach it and stumble through into the garden of stone demons.

And there they are.

Wesley catches Owen once across the jaw. Owen's face flicks sideways, and the smile sharpens before Wes throws another fist, and Owen catches his hand, pulls him forward, and plunges the knife into his stomach.

THIRTY

A SCREAM RISES in my throat as Owen pulls the knife free and Wesley collapses to the concrete.

"I'm impressed, Miss Bishop," Owen says, turning toward me. The sun is sinking, the gargoyles multiplied by shadows.

Wesley coughs, tries to move, can't.

"Hang in there, Wes," I say. "Please. I'm sorry. Please." I step forward, and Owen holds the knife over Wes in warning.

"I tried to miss the vital organs," he says. "But I told you, I'm rusty."

He extends one foot toward the ledge of the roof as he looks down, the blood-soaked knife hanging lazily from his fingers.

"It's a long way down, Owen. And there are plenty of Crew at the bottom."

"And they're going to have their hands full with the Histories," he says. "Which is why I'm up here."

He pulls the Crew key from his pocket and reaches out, slides it through the air as if there were . . . a door. My eyes slip off it several times before I can find the edges.

A *shortcut*.

The teeth vanish into the door.

"Is that why you were on the roof last time? To get away?"

"If they'd caught me alive," he says, still gripping the key, "they would have erased my life."

I have to get him away from that door before he goes through.

"I can't believe you're running away," I say, making the disgust in my voice clear.

And sure enough, his hand slips from the key. It hangs in the air as his foot slides from the ledge. "How did you get out?" he asks.

"It's a secret." I pivot and step back, the weight of my Crew key heavy in my coat. I have an idea. "There's something I don't get. So what if you were Crew—you're still a History." I take another step. "You should have slipped."

He pulls the key out of the air and pockets it as he steps over Wesley's body toward me.

"There's a reason Histories slip," he says. "It's not anger, or even fear. It's confusion. Everything is foreign. Everything is frightening. It's why Regina slipped. It's why Ben slipped."

"Don't talk to me about my brother." I take another step back, and nearly stumble on the base of a statue. "You knew what would happen."

Owen steps over a broken statue limb without looking down. "Confusion tips the scale. And that's why all members of the Archive are kept in the Special Collections. Because *our* Histories don't slip. Because we open our eyes and know where we are. We're not simple and scared and easily stopped."

I slip through a gap between the statues, and Owen falls out of sight. Moments later he reappears, following me through the maze of gargoyles. Good. That means he's away from his shortcut. Away from Wes.

"But other Histories aren't like us, Owen. They *do* slip."

"Don't you get it? They slip because they're lost, confused. Regina slipped. Ben slipped. But if we had been allowed to tell them about the Archive when they were still alive, maybe they would have made it through."

"You don't know that," I say, vanishing just long enough to pull the Crew key from my pocket, guard it against my wrist.

"The Archive owed us a chance. They take everything. We deserve something back. But no, it would be against the rules. Do you know why the Archive has so many rules, Miss Bishop? It's because they're afraid of us. Terrified. They make us strong, strong enough to lie and con and fight and hunt and kill, strong enough to rise up, to break free. All they have are their secrets and their rules."

I hesitate. He's right. I've seen it, the Archive's fear, in their strictures and their threats. But that doesn't mean what he's *doing* is right.

"Without the rules," I force myself to say, "there would be chaos." I step back, feel the front of a gargoyle come up against my shoulders. I slip sideways, never taking my eyes off Owen. "That's what you want, isn't it? Chaos?"

"I want freedom," he says, stalking me. "The Archive is a prison, and not only for the dead. And that's why I'm going to tear it down, shelf by shelf and branch by branch."

"You know I won't let you."

He steps forward, knife hanging loosely at his side. He smiles. "You wanted this to happen."

"No, I didn't."

He shrugs. "It doesn't matter. That's how the Archive will see it. And they will carve you up and throw you away. You're nothing to them. Stop running, Miss Bishop. There's nowhere to go."

I know he's right. I'm counting on it. I'm standing in a ring of winged statues, their faces crumbling with age, their bodies set too close. Owen looks at me as if I'm a mouse he's cornered, his eyes bright despite the dusk.

"I'll stand trial for my mistakes, Owen, but not for yours. You are a monster."

"And you aren't? The Archive makes us monsters. And then it breaks the ones who get too strong, and buries the ones who know too much."

I dart sideways as his hand flies forward. I pretend to notice too late, pretend to be too slow. He catches my elbow and forces me back against a demon, his arms caging me. And then he smiles, pulls me toward him just enough to rest the tip of the bloodstained knife between my shoulder blades.

"I wouldn't be so quick to pass judgment. You and I are not so different."

"You twisted it so I would think so. You conned my trust, made me think we were the same, but I am *nothing* like you, Owen."

He presses his forehead against mine. The quiet slides through me, and I hate it.

"Just because you can't read me," he whispers, "doesn't mean I can't read you. I've seen inside you. I've seen your darkness and your dreams and your fears, and the only difference between us is that I know the true extent of the Archive and its crimes, and you are only just learning."

"If you're talking about my inability to quit, I already know."

"You know *nothing*," Owen hisses, forcing my body against his. I wrap my empty hand around his back for balance, and bring the one with the key up behind him.

"But I could show you," he says, softening. "It doesn't have to end like this."

"You used me."

"So did they," he says. "But I'm giving you the one thing they never have, and never will. A choice."

I slide the key through the empty air behind his back and begin to turn. Da said it had to make a full circle, but halfway through the turn, the air *resists* and coalesces around the metal like a lock forming. A strange sense bleeds up the key into my fingers as the door takes shape out of nothing, barely visible and yet there, a shadow hovering in the air behind Owen. I look into his eyes, hold their focus. They are so cold and empty and cruel. No butterflies, no shoulders-to-shoulders, knees-to-knees, no sideways smiles. It makes this easier.

"I'd never help you, Owen."

"Well, I'll help you," he says. "I'll kill you before they do."

I hold fast to the key, but let my other arm fall away from his back. "Don't you see, Owen?"

"See what?"

"The day's over," I say, turning the key the rest of the way.

His eyes widen with surprise as he hears the click behind him, but it's too late. The moment the key finishes the full turn, the door opens backward with explosive force, not onto the dark halls of the Narrows or the white expanse of the Archive, but a cavernous black, a void, like space without stars. A nothing. A nowhere. Just like Da warned. But Da didn't convey the crushing force, the pull, like air being sucked out of an open plane door. It rips Owen and the knife backward, the void at once swallowing him and wrenching me forward to follow; but I cling to the broken arms of a gargoyle with all that's left of my strength. The violent wind within the doorway twists and, having devoured the History, reverses, slamming the door shut in my face.

It leaves nothing. No door, nothing but the key Roland lent me, which hangs in the air, still jammed in the invisible lock, its cord swaying from the force.

My knees buckle.

Then someone lets out a shuddering cough.

Wesley.

I pull the key free and run, weaving through the gargoyles and back to the edge of the roof where Wesley is lying, curled, red spreading out beneath him. I drop to the ground beside him.

"Wes. Wes, please, come on."

His jaw is clenched, his palm pressed against his stomach. I'm still not wearing my ring, and as I take his arm and try to wrap it around my shoulders, he gasps, and it's *pain fear worry anger pacing the hall not home where is she where is she I shouldn't have left and something tight like panic* before I can focus on getting him to his feet.

"I'm sorry," I whisper, dragging him up, his fear and pain washing over me, his thoughts running into mine. "I need you to stand. I'm sorry."

Tears escape down his cheeks, dark from the eyeliner. His breath is ragged as I lead him, too slowly, to the roof door. He leaves a trail of red.

"Mac," he says between gritted teeth.

"Shhh. It's okay. It's going to be okay." And it's such a bad lie, because how can it possibly be okay when he's losing this much blood? We'll never make it down the stairs. He won't last long enough for an ambulance. He needs medical attention. He needs Patrick. We reach the roof door, and I get the Crew key into the lock.

"I'll kick your ass if you die on me, Wes," I say, pulling him close as I turn the key left and drag him through into the Archive.

THIRTY-ONE

THE DAY BEFORE YOU DIE, I ask if you're afraid.

"Everything ends," you say.

"But are you scared?" I ask.

You are so thin. Not brittle bone so much as barbed wire, your skin like paper over the top.

"When I first learned about the Archive, Kenzie," you say, smoke leaking out of the corner of your mouth, "every time I touched something, someone, I thought, That's going to be recorded. My life is going to be a record of every moment. It can be broken down like that. I relished the logic of it, the certainty. We are nothing but recorded moments. That's the way I thought."

You put the cigarette out on Mom's freshly painted porch rail.

"Then I met my first Histories, face-to-face, and they weren't books, and they weren't lists, and they weren't files. I didn't want to accept it, but the fact is, they were people. Copies of people. Because the only way to truly record a person is not in words, not in still frames, but in bone and skin and memory."

You use the cigarette to draw those same three lines in ash.

"I don't know whether that should terrify or comfort me, that everything is backed up like that. That somewhere my History is compiling itself."

You flick the cigarette butt into Dad's bushes but don't brush away the ash on the rail.

"Like I said, Kenzie. Everything ends. I'm not afraid to die," you say with a wan smile. "I just hope I'm smart enough to stay dead."

The first thing I notice is the noise.

In a place where quiet is mandatory, there is a deafening clatter, a banging and scraping and slamming and crashing loud enough to wake the dead. And clearly it *is* waking them. The doors behind the desk have been flung back to reveal the chaos beyond, the vast peace shattered by toppled stacks, people rushing, breaking off in teams down halls, shouting orders, and all of them too far away. Da is in there. Ben is in there. Wes is dying in my arms, and there is no one at the desk. How can there be no one at the desk?

"Help!" I shout, and the word is swallowed by the sound of the Archive crumbling around me. "Someone!" Wesley's knees buckle beside me, and I slide to the ground under his weight. "Come on, Wes, *please*." I shake him. He doesn't respond.

"Help!" I shout again as I feel for a pulse, and this time I hear footsteps and look up to see Carmen striding through the doors. She closes them behind her.

"Miss Bishop?"

"Carmen, I'm so glad to see you."

She frowns, looks down at Wesley's body. "What are you doing here?"

"Please, I need you to—"

"Where's Owen?"

Shock hits, and the whole world slows. And stops.

It was Carmen all along.

The Archive knife in Jackson's hands.

Hooper's name showing up late on my list.

Jackson escaping a second time.

The disruption spreading through the stacks.

Altering Marcus Elling and Eileen Herring and Lionel Pratt.

Flooding Wesley's territory after the trial.

Writing back to Owen the moment he got out.

It was all her.

Beneath my hands, Wesley gasps and coughs blood.

"Carmen," I say, as calmly as I can, "I don't know how you know Owen, but right now we have to get Wesley help. I can't let him—"

Carmen doesn't move. "Tell me what you did with Owen."

"He's going to die!"

"Then you'd better tell me quickly."

"Owen is nowhere," I snap.

"What?"

"You'll never find him," I say. "He's gone."

"No one's ever *gone*," she says. "Look at Regina."

"You're the one who woke her."

Carmen's brow knits. "You really should be more sympathetic. After all, you woke Ben."

"Because you both manipulated me. And you betrayed the Archive. You covered up Owen's murders. You altered *Histories*. Why? Would you do that for him?"

Carmen holds up the back of her hand to show the three lines of the Archive carved into her skin. Crew marks. "We were together, once upon a time. Before I got promoted. You're not Crew. You've never had a partner. If you had, you'd understand. I'd do anything for him. And I did."

"Wes is the closest thing I have to a partner," I say, running my fingers over his jacket until I find the collapsed bō staff. "And you're *killing* him."

I drag myself to my feet, vision blurring as I stand. With a flick of my wrist, the staff expands. It gives me something to hold on to.

"You can't hurt me, Miss Bishop," Carmen says with a withering look. "You think I'm here by choice? You think anyone would give up a *life* in the Outer for this place? They wouldn't. They don't."

And for the first time I notice the scratches on her arms, the cut on her cheek. Each mark is little more than a thin, bloodless line.

"You're dead."

"Histories are *records* of the dead," she says. "But yes, we're all Histories here." She comes toward me, blocking my path to the doors and the rest of the Archive. "Appalling, isn't it? Think about it: Patrick, Lisa—even your Roland. No one told you."

I ignore my lurching stomach. "When did you die?"

"Right after Regina. Owen was so broken without his sister, and so angry at the Archive. I just wanted to see him smile again. I thought Regina would help. In the end, he made such a mess, I couldn't save him." And then her green eyes widen. "But I knew I could bring him back."

"Then why did you wait so long?"

She closes in. "You think I wanted to? You think I didn't miss him every day? I had to transfer branches, had to wait for them to forget, to lose track of me, and then"—her eyes narrow—"I had to wait for a Keeper to take over the Coronado. Someone young, impressionable. Someone Owen could use."

Use. The word crawls over my skin.

The crashing of the Archive mounts behind her, and she glances back. "Amazing how easy it is to make a little noise."

In that moment, when she looks away, I make a run for the doors. I push as hard as I can before her hand grabs my arm and she wrenches me backward to the stone floor. The doors open, chaos and noise flooding in, but before I can get up, Carmen is straddling me, holding the staff across my throat.

"Where. Is. Owen?" she asks.

A few feet away, Wesley groans. I can't reach him.

"Please," I gasp.

"Don't worry," says Carmen. "It'll be over soon, and then he'll come back. The Archive doesn't let you go. You serve until you die, and when you do, they wake you on your shelf and they give you a choice, a one-time offer. Either you get up and work, or they close the drawer on you forever. Not much of a choice, is it?" She presses down on the staff. "Can't you see why Owen hates this place so much?"

Over her shoulder and through the doors I can see people. I get my fingers between the pole and my throat, and shout for help before Carmen cuts me off.

"*Tell me what you've done with Owen,*" she orders.

People are coming through the doors, past the desk, but Carmen doesn't see, because all of her fear and anger and attention is focused on me.

"I sent him home," I say. And then I manage to get my foot between us and kick, and Carmen stumbles back into Patrick and Roland.

"What the hell?" growls Patrick as they wrestle her arms behind her back.

"He'll come back," she shrieks as they force her to her knees. "He would never leave me here——" Her eyes go wide as the life goes out of them. The Librarians let go, and she crumples to the floor with the sickening sound of dead weight. Patrick's key, gleaming and gold, is clutched in his grip.

I cough, gasping for breath as the room fills with sound—not just the chaos of the Archive pouring in through the doors, but with people shouting.

"Patrick! Hurry!"

I turn to see Lisa and two other Librarians kneeling over Wesley. He's not moving. I can't look at his body, so I look through the doors at the Archive, at the people hurrying about, barricading doors, making so much noise.

I hear Patrick ask, "Is there a pulse?"

My hands won't stop shaking.

"It's slowing. You have to hurry."

I feel like I should be breaking down, but there's nothing left of me to break.

"He's lost so much blood."

"Get him up, quickly."

A Librarian I've never met takes me by the elbow, guides me to the front desk and a chair. I slip into it. She has a deep scratch on her collar. There's no blood. I close my eyes. I know I'm hurt but I can't feel it anymore.

"Miss Bishop." I blink and find Roland kneeling beside my chair.

"Who are all those people?" I ask, focusing on crumbling world beyond the antechamber.

"They work for the Archive. Some are Librarians. Some are higher up. They're trying to contain the disruption."

Another deafening crash.

"Mackenzie . . ." Roland grips the arm of the chair. There's blood on his hands. Wesley's. "You have to tell me what happened."

I do. I tell him everything. And when I'm done, he says, "You should go home."

I look at the slick of red on the floor. Behind my eyes I see Wes collapsing on the roof, see him storming away, see him sitting on the floor outside Angelli's, teaching me to float, hunting with me, reading to me, draped over a wrought iron chair, showing me the gardens, leaning in the hall in the middle of the night with his crooked smile.

"I can't lose Wes," I whisper.

"Patrick will do everything he can."

I look back at Wes's body. It's gone. Carmen's body is gone. Patrick is gone. I look down at my hands. Dried blood is flaking from my palms. I blink, focus on Roland. His red Chucks and his gray eyes and that accent I could never place.

"Is it true?" I ask.

"Is what true?" asks Roland.

"That all Librarians . . . that you're dead?"

Roland's face sinks.

"How long have you been . . ." I trail off. What word do I even want? *Dead?* We're trained to think of a History as something other, something less than a person, but how could Roland ever be less?

He smiles sadly. "I was about to retire."

"You mean, go back to being dead." He nods. I shudder. "There's an empty shelf here with your name and dates?"

"There is. And it was beginning to sound nice. But then I got called in to this meeting. An induction ceremony. Some crazy old man and his granddaughter." He stands, guides me up beside him. "And I don't regret it. Now, go home."

Roland walks me toward the Archive door. A man I don't know comes over and begins to speak to him in hushed, hurried tones.

He tells him that the Archive is hemorrhaging, but more staff have been called in from other branches. Sections are still being sealed off to stem the flow. Almost half of the standard stacks had to be sealed. Red stacks and Special Collections were spared.

Roland asks and confirms that Ben and Da are safe.

The Crew appears, the cocky smiles from the trial replaced by grim, tired frowns. They report that the Coronado has been contained. No casualties. Two Histories made it out, but both are being pursued.

I ask about Wesley.

They tell me I'll be summoned when they know.

They tell me to go home.

I ask again about Wesley.

They tell me again to go home.

THIRTY-TWO

THE DAY YOU DIE, you tell me I have a gift.
The day you die, you tell me I am a natural.
The day you die, you tell me I am strong enough.
The day you die, you tell me it will be okay.
None of that is true.

In the years and months and days before, you teach me everything I know. But the day you die, you don't say anything.

You flick away your cigarette, put your hollow cheek against my hair and keep it there until I began to think you've gone to sleep. Then you straighten and look me in the eye, and I know in that moment that you are going to be gone when I wake up.

There is a note on my desk the next morning, pinned beneath your key. But the note is blank, save for the mark of the Archive. Mom is in the kitchen, crying. Dad, for once, is home from the school and sitting by her. As I press my ear to my bedroom door, trying to hear over my pulse, I wish that you had said something. It would have been nice, to have words to cling to, like all those other times.

I lie awake for years and re-imagine that good-bye, rewrite that note, and instead of the heavy quiet, or the three lines, you tell me exactly what I need to hear, what I need to know, in order to survive this.

• • •

Every night I have the same bad dream.

I'm on the roof, trapped in the circle of gargoyles, their claws and arms and broken wings holding me in a cage of stone. Then the air in front of me shivers, ripples, and the void door takes shape, spreading across the sky like blood until it's there, solid and dark. It has a handle, and the handle turns, and the door opens, and Owen Chris Clarke stands there with his haunted eyes and his wicked knife. He steps down to the concrete roof, and the stone demons tighten their grip as he comes toward me.

"I will set you free," he says just before he buries the knife in my chest, and I wake up.

Every night I have that dream, and every night I end up on the roof, checking the air in the circle of demons for signs of a door. There is almost no mark of the void I made; nothing but the faintest ripple, like a crack in the world; and when I close my eyes and press my hands against the space, they always go straight through.

Every night I have that dream, and every day I check my list for signs of a summons. Both sides of the paper are blank, and have been since the incident, and by the third day I'm so scared that the list is broken that I dig out a pen and write a note, not caring who finds it.

Please update.

I watch the words dissolve into the page.

No one answers.

I ask again. And again. And again. And every time I'm met with silence and blank space. Panic chews through my battered body. As my bruises lighten, my fear gets worse. I should have heard by now. I should have heard.

On the third morning, Dad asks about Wes, and my throat closes up. I can barely make it through a feeble lie. And so when, at the end of the third day, a summons finally writes itself across my paper . . .

Please report to the Archive. —A

I drop everything and go.

I tug my ring off and pull the Crew key from my pocket—Owen took my Keeper key with him into the void—and slide it into the lock on my bedroom door. A deep breath, a turn to the left, and I step through into the Archive.

The branch is still recovering, most of the doors still closed; but the chaos has subsided, the noise diminished to a dull, steady din, like a cooling engine. I'm not even over the threshold when I open my mouth to ask about Wes. But then I look up, and the question catches in my throat.

Roland and Patrick are standing behind the desk, and in front of it is a woman in an ivory coat. She is tall and slim, with red hair and creamy skin and a pleasant face. A sharp gold key hangs on a black ribbon around her throat, and she's wearing a pair of black fitted gloves. There is something calm about her that clashes with the lingering noise of the damaged Archive.

The woman takes a fluid step forward.

"Miss Bishop," she says with a warm smile, "my name is Agatha."

THIRTY-THREE

A GATHA, THE ASSESSOR.
Agatha, the one who decides if a Keeper is fit to serve, or if they should be dismissed. Erased. Her expression is utterly unreadable, but the stern look on Patrick's face is clear, as is the fear in Roland's eyes. I suddenly feel like the room is filled with broken glass and I'm supposed to walk across it.

"Thank you for coming," she says. "I know you've been through a lot recently, but we need to talk—"

"Agatha," says Roland. There is a pleading in his tone. "I really think we should leave this—"

"Your parental sense is admirable." Agatha gives a small, coaxing smile. "But if Mackenzie doesn't mind . . ."

"I don't mind at all," I say, mustering a calm I don't feel.

"Lovely," says Agatha, turning her attention to Roland and Patrick. "You're both excused. Surely you've got your hands full right now."

Patrick leaves without looking at me. Roland hesitates, and I beg him with a look for news of Wes, but it goes unanswered as he retreats into the Archive and closes the doors behind him.

"You've had quite an exciting few days," says Agatha. "Sit."

I do. She sits down behind the desk.

"Before we begin, I believe you have a key you shouldn't have. Please place it on the desk."

I stiffen. There's only one way out of the Archive—the door at my back—and it requires a key. I force myself to take Da's old Crew key from my pocket and set it on the desk between us. It takes all my strength to withdraw my hand and leave the key there.

Agatha folds her hands and nods approvingly.

"You don't know anything about me, Miss Bishop," she says, which isn't true. "But I know about you. It's my job. I know about you, and about Owen, and about Carmen. And I know you've discovered a lot about the Archive. Most of which we'd rather you'd learned in due course. You must have questions."

Of course I have questions. I have nothing but questions. And it feels like a trap to ask, but I have to know.

"A friend of mine was wounded by one of the Histories involved in the recent attacks. Do you know what happened to him?"

Agatha offers an indulgent smile. "Wesley Ayers is alive."

These are the four greatest words I've ever heard.

"It was close," she adds. "He's still recovering. But your loyalty is touching."

I try to soothe my frayed nerves. "I've heard it's an important quality in Crew."

"Loyal and ambitious," she notes. "Anything else you want to ask?"

The gold key glints on its black ribbon, and I hesitate.

"For instance," she prompts cheerfully, "I imagine you're wondering why we keep the origin of the Librarians a secret. Why we keep so many things a secret."

Agatha has a dangerous ease about her. She's the kind of person you *want* to like you. I don't trust it at all, but I nod.

"The Archive must be staffed," she says. "There must always be Keepers in the Narrows. There must always be Crew in the Outer. And there must always be Librarians in the Archive. It is a choice,

Mackenzie, do know that. It's simply a matter of when the choice is given."

"You wait until they're dead," I say, straining to keep the contempt from my voice. "Wake them on their shelves when they can't say no."

"*Won't*, Mackenzie, is a very different thing from *can't*." She sits forward in her chair. "I'll be honest with you. I think you deserve a bit of honesty. Keepers worry about being Keepers, and rest assured that they'll learn about being Crew if and when the time comes. Crew worry about being Crew, and rest assured that they'll learn about being Librarians if and when the time comes. We've found that the easiest way to keep people focused is to give them one thing to focus on. The question is, given the influx of distraction, will you be able to continue focusing?"

She's asking me, but I know my fate doesn't lie in my decision. It lies in hers. I'm a loose thread. Owen is gone. Carmen is gone. But I'm here. And even after everything, or maybe because of every-thing, I need to remember. I don't want to be erased. I don't want to have the Archive cut out of my life. I don't want to die. My hands start shaking, so I hold them beneath the edge of the table.

"Mackenzie?" nudges Agatha.

There's only one thing I can do, and I'm not sure I can pull it off, but I don't have a choice. I smile. "My mother says there's nothing that a hot shower can't fix."

Agatha laughs a soft, perfect laugh. "I can see why Roland fights for you."

She stands, circles the desk, one hand brushing its surface.

"The Archive is a machine," she says. "A machine whose purpose is to protect the past. To protect knowledge."

"Knowledge is power," I say. "That's the saying, right?"

"Yes. But power in the wrong hands, in too many hands, leads to danger and dissent. You've seen the damage caused by two."

I resist the urge to look away. "My grandfather used to say that every strong storm starts with a breeze."

She crosses behind me, and I curl my fingers around the seat of the chair, pain screaming through my wounded wrist.

"He sounds like a very wise man," she says. One hand comes to rest on the back of the chair.

"He was," I say.

And then I close my eyes because I know this is it. I picture the gold key plunging through the chair, the metal burying itself in my back. I wonder if it will hurt, having my life hollowed out. I swallow hard and wait. But nothing happens.

"Miss Bishop," says Agatha, "secrets are an unpleasant necessity, but they have a place and a purpose here. They protect us. And they protect those we care about." The threat is subtle but clear.

"Knowledge is power," she finishes, and I open my eyes to find her rounding the chair, "but ignorance can be a blessing."

"I agree," I say, and then I find her gaze and hold it. "But once you know, you can't go back. Not really. You can carve out someone's memories, but they won't be who they were before. They'll just be full of holes. Given the choice, I'd rather learn to live with what I know."

The room around us settles into silence until, at last, Agatha smiles. "Let's hope you're making the right choice." She pulls something from the pocket of her ivory coat and places it in my palm, closing my fingers over it with her gloved hand.

"Let's hope I am, too," she says, her hand over mine. When she pulls away, I look down to find a Keeper's key nestled there, lighter than the one Da gave me, and too new, but still a handle and a stem and teeth and, most of all, the freedom to go home.

"Is that all?" I ask quietly.

Agatha lets the question hang. At last she nods and says, "For now."

THIRTY-FOUR

BISHOP'S IS PACKED with people.

It's only been two days since my meeting with Agatha, and the coffee shop is nowhere near finished—half the equipment hasn't even been delivered—but after the less-than-successful *Welcome!* muffins, Mom insisted on throwing a soft opening for the residents, complete with free coffee and baked goods.

She beams and serves and chats, and even though she's operating at her suspiciously bright full-wattage, she does seem happy. Dad talks coffee with three or four men, leads them behind the counter to see the new grinding machine Mom broke down and got for him. A trio of kids, Jill among them, sits on the patio, dangling their legs in the sun and sipping iced drinks, sharing a muffin between them. A little girl at a corner table doodles on a paper mat with blue crayons. Mom only ordered blue. Ben's favorite. Ms. Angelli admires the red stone rose set in the floor. And, miracle of miracles, Nix's chair is pulled up to a table on the patio, my copy of the *Inferno* in his lap as he flicks ash onto a low edge when Betty looks away. The place is brimming.

And all the while, I cling to the four words—*Wesley Ayers is alive*—because I still haven't seen him. The Archive is still closed and my list is still blank, and all I have are those four words and Agatha's warning buzzing around in my head.

"Mackenzie Bishop!"

Lyndsey launches herself at me, throws her arms around my neck, and I stagger back, wincing. Beneath my long sleeves and my apron, I am a web of bruises and bandages. I could hide most of the damage from my parents, but not the wrist. I claimed it was a bad fall on one of my runs. It wasn't one of my strongest lies, but I am so tired of lying. Lyndsey is still hugging me. With my ring on, she sounds like rain and harmony and too-loud laughter, but the noise is worth it, and I don't pull back or push away.

"You came," I say, smiling. It feels good to smile.

"Duh. Nice apron, by the way," she says, gesturing to the massive *B* on its front. "Mom and Dad are around here somewhere. And good job, Mrs. Bishop, this place is full!"

"Free caffeine and sugar, a recipe for making friends," I say, watching my mother flit between tables.

"You'll have to give me a proper tour later— Hey, is that Guyliner?"

She cocks her head toward the patio doors, and everything stops.

His eyes are tired, his skin a touch too pale, but he's there with his spiked hair and his black-rimmed eyes and his hands buried in his pockets. And then, as if he can feel my eyes on him, Wes finds my gaze across the room, and beams.

"It is," I say, my chest tightening.

But rather than cross the crowded café, Wes nods once in the direction of the lobby and walks out.

"Well, go on, then," says Lynds, pushing me with a giggle. "I'll serve myself." She leans across the counter, swipes a cookie.

I pull off the apron, tossing it to Lyndsey as I trail Wes through the lobby—where more people are milling about with coffee— down the hall and past the study and out into the garden. When we reach the world of moss and vine, he stops and turns, and I throw

318

my arms around him, relishing the drums and the bass and the metal rock as they wash over me, blotting out the pain and guilt and fear and blood of the last time we touched. We both wince but hold on. I listen to the sound of him, as strange and steady as a heartbeat, and then I must have tightened my grip, because he gasps and says, "Gently, there," and braces himself against the back of a bench, one palm gingerly against his stomach. "I swear, you're just looking for excuses to get your hands on me."

"You caught me," I say, closing my eyes when they start to burn. "I'm so sorry," I say into his shirt.

He laughs, then hisses in pain. "Hey, don't be. I know you can't help yourself."

I laugh tightly. "I'm not talking about the hug, Wes."

"Then what are you apologizing for?"

I pull back and look him in the eyes. "For everything that happened." His brow creases, and my heart sinks.

"Wes," I say slowly, "you do remember, don't you?"

He looks at me, confused. "I remember making a date to hunt with you. Nine sharp." He eases himself onto the stone bench. "But to be honest, I don't remember anything about the next day. I don't remember being stabbed. Patrick said that's normal. Because of trauma."

Everything aches as I sink down onto the bench beside him. "Yeah . . ."

"What *should* I remember, Mac?"

I sit and stare at the stones that make up the garden floor.

Knowledge is power, but ignorance can be a blessing.

Maybe Agatha is right. I think of that moment in the stacks when Roland told me about altering, when he warned me what happened to those who failed and were dismissed. That moment when I hated him for telling me, when I wished I could go back. But there is no going back.

So can't we just go forward?

I don't want to hurt Wes anymore. I don't want to cause him pain, make him relive the betrayal. And after Agatha's unfriendly meeting, I have no desire to disobey the Archive. But what sets me over the edge is the fact that there, in my mind, louder than all those other thoughts, is this:

I don't want to confess.

I don't want to confess because *I* don't want to remember. But Wesley doesn't have that choice, and the only reason he's missing that time is because of me.

The truth is a messy thing, but I tell it.

We sit in the garden as the day stretches out, and I tell him everything. The easy and the hard. He listens, and frowns, and doesn't interrupt, except to punctuate with a small "Oh" or "Wow" or "What?"

And after all of it, when he finally speaks, the only thing he says is, "Why couldn't you come to me?"

I'm about to tell him about Roland's orders, but that's only a partial truth, so I start again.

"I was running away."

"From what?"

"I don't know. The Archive. That life. This. Ben. Me."

"What's so wrong with you?" he asks. "I quite like you." And then, a moment later, he adds, "I just can't believe I lost to a skinny blond guy with a knife."

I laugh. Pain ripples through me, but it's worth it. "It was a very big knife," I say.

Silence settles over us. Wes is the one to break it.

"Hey," he says.

"Hey."

"Are you going to be okay?"

I close my eyes. "I don't know, Wes. Everything hurts. I don't know how to make it stop. It hurts when I breathe. It hurts when I think. I feel like I'm drowning, and it's my fault, and I don't know how to be okay. I don't know if I *can* be okay. I don't know if I should be *allowed* to be okay."

Wesley knocks his shoulder against mine.

"We're a team, Mac," he says. "We'll get through this."

"Which part?" I ask.

He smiles. "All of it."

And I smile back, because I want him to be right.

ACKNOWLEDGMENTS

TO MY FATHER, for liking this book more than the first one. And for wanting to tell everyone. And to my mother, for elbowing my father every time he did. To Mel, for always knowing what to say. And to the rest of my family, who smiled and nodded even when they weren't sure what I was doing.

To my agent, Holly, for putting up with the often pathetic—but undeniably cute—animal pictures I use to explain my emotional state, and for believing in me and in this book.

To my editor, Abby, for building this world brick by brick beside me, then helping me tear it down and build it again out of stronger stone. And to Laura, for every bit of mortar added. It is a joy and an adventure.

To my freakishly talented cover designer, Tyler, and to my entire publishing family at Disney-Hyperion, for making me feel like I am home.

To my friends, who bolstered me with bribes and threats and promises, and followed through. Specifically, to Beth Revis, for her stern looks and gold stars when I needed them most. To Rachel Hawkins, for brightening every day with a laugh or a photo of Jon Snow. To Carrie Ryan, for mountain walks and long talks and for being an incredible person. To Stephanie Perkins, for shining so brightly when I needed a light. To Ruta Sepetys, for believing in me, often more than I believe in myself. To Myra McEntire, for dragging me back from the cliffs of insanity. To Tiffany Schmidt, for reading, and for loving Wesley so much. To Laura Whitaker, for the tea and good talks. To Patricia and Danielle, for the kindness and the care. And to the Black Mountain crew, who helped me meet my deadline and then thrust a flask and a jar of Nutella into my hands immediately afterward.

To my Liverpool housemates, for always wanting to help, whether it was making tea or creating quiet spaces so I could work. And to my New York housemates, for not giving me weird looks when they find me talking to myself, or rocking in corners, or when I burst into nervous laughter.

To the online community, for its constant love and support.

To the readers, who make every bad day good and every good day better.

And to Neil Gaiman, for the hug.